Evilution

By Shaun Jeffrey

The Invisible College Press, LLC

Arlington VA

Publisher's Note:
This is a work of fiction. Names, characters, places, and incidents are either the product of the author's imagination or are used fictitiously, and any resemblance to actual persons living or dead, events, evil government conspiracies, or locales is entirely coincidental.

ISBN: 1-931468-13-3

Cover Design by Kirk Heydt
First Printing

The Invisible College Press, LLC
P.O. Box 209
Woodbridge VA 22194-0209
http://www.invispress.com

Please send question and comments to:
editor@invispress.com

Chapter 1

The letter was delivered as innocuously as any other, its arrival announced by the sprung letterbox which snapped shut like a mantrap with a resounding metallic crack – Chase Black always imagined the postman and paperboy wincing whenever they had to deliver something to the house with the snapping letterbox.

Picking the letter up with the rest of the morning post, she walked through to the dining room and dropped the letters on the table. Opening the curtains, she took in the bleak suburban view and yawned, stretching her arms to try and shrug off the last vestiges of sleep.

Since being made redundant, life had become monotonous, a mundane carousel of television and comfort food. She rarely got out of bed before noon; rarely went to bed before 3 a.m., existing in the hours of the insomniac. She had only risen early this morning because sleep eluded her. She wondered where her life had gone wrong?

To kill the silence, she switched on the radio - just catching the end of a Limp Bizkit track – and turned her attention to the highlight of her day: the morning mail. Most of the letters were bills, which she threw aside. She knew she would have to pay them, especially as some of them were red letters, but she liked to leave it to the last minute, as though in a final act of defiance. Recognising her own handwriting, she knew that one of the letters was a reply to a job she had applied for and she opened it with an excited flutter in her stomach. Perhaps this would be the one!

But the anticipation soon turned to a sickly feeling - the position had already been filled and she silently cursed the company for wasting her time by advertising a non-existent job. They hadn't even given her a chance. How many jobs had she applied for now? One hundred? Two hundred?

However many it was, she had only received a handful of replies, and out of the handful she had only secured three interviews. All unsuccessful.

The last letter caught her attention as it was in a crisp white envelope with elegant Gothic handwriting. Curious, her chocolate coloured eyes sparkled as she examined the envelope, turning it this way and that, delaying the moment of opening to prolong the anticipation. Even though she was twenty-five years old, she still got the same feeling on Christmas morning. Now she only hoped the letter wasn't junk mail in pretty packaging, a postal Trojan horse designed to entice.

Who could it be from? Feeling a tingle of excitement, she slid her long nail along the gummed flap and tore it open, quickly pulling out a single sheet of paper that sliced through her finger like a razor.

"*Shit...*" She winced, leaving a smear of blood on the paper. Putting her finger in her mouth she sucked at the wound, tasting the coppery tang of her own vital fluid as she read the letter:

Dear Ms Black,

It is with great pleasure that I am writing to inform you that your entry into the Dream House competition has been selected as the winning entry. A representative of Storm will call on you on Saturday, 27th of July at 9.00 a.m. to drive you to view your prize, High Top Cottage, a picturesque period house of great charm and character, overlooking the village of Paradise in Staffordshire. The viewing will necessitate staying over, so can you please keep this in mind when thinking what to bring in the way of clothes and toiletries.

Yours sincerely,

Nigel Moon

Chase read the letter again - several times.

What competition?

She'd entered a few in the past, but she was sure none of them were for a house.

It must be a joke, but she failed to find it funny.

The heading on the paper read: Storm Enterprises, P.O. Box 666, London. There was no telephone number.

She suddenly wondered if it had been delivered to the wrong house? Wasn't it illegal to open someone else's mail? She checked the name and address on the envelope. But no, thankfully it was addressed to her, so she hadn't broken the law. She frowned. Having never won anything in her life, not even a pound on a scratch card, she didn't think she was going to start now, especially with something like a house!

Making a cup of tea and some toast, she sat and contemplated the letter, absently wiping crumbs from the corner of her thin lips. Staring out of the window at the depressing urban street of terraced houses, she wished she really had won a house.

Running a hand through her unruly short brown hair failed to stop it looking as if a madman had struck during the night. Her pretty features had a pixie-like quality that could be mistaken for impishness, and she had a wicked sense of humour, but she failed to find anything funny about the letter.

A couple of the buildings over the road had been boarded up after being burnt by teenage arsonists; vandals daubed others with graffiti, marking their territory like dogs. The area had not always been like this, but it had slowly deteriorated and her house was now way beyond negative equity - you couldn't give it away. At one time the houses would have been the first rungs on the homeowners ladder; now they were the impoverished dwellings of those resigned to a life of unemployment and drudgery. The only people who lived here were forced to by monetary circumstances or by the council.

When the sun went down, it just got worse. Gangs of teenagers gathered on corners and in doorways, the night their domain as they smoked cigarettes and swigged bottles of beer, the smashed bottles sparkling like diamonds on the floor; broken dreams.

***

Roberta's Wine Bar was virtually deserted; its chrome fittings and neon lights made it look like the set from a science fiction movie. "Of course I don't believe it, Jane. I've never won anything in my life, never mind bloody High Top Cottage." Chase let the name linger on the tip of her tongue, savouring it before complementing the taste with a mouthful of wine. If only it was true. "You didn't really think I'd fall for your joke, did you?" Reclining in her seat, she smiled, waiting for Jane to burst out laughing.

Jane brushed a strand of long black hair from her face. Her Caribbean roots gave her a sultry, exotic appearance that Chase envied. At six feet tall, Jane also had five inches on Chase, and as Chase knew, size does matter! Where Jane looked like an Amazonian warrior, Chase felt like one of the seven dwarfs. It wasn't that she was unattractive. Far from it. It was just that she felt she looked plain when Jane was with her. Men always noticed Jane, which would be fine if she wasn't gay. When they found out, they would either try harder in the misguided belief that they could *convert* her, or they scurried off, tails between their legs. Either way, Chase was ignored as they assumed she was Jane's partner.

"Not guilty, sugar," Jane said in her Caribbean lilt. She took a sip of wine, her purple latex top stretching over her ample charms like a bizarre second skin.

Although Chase didn't want to believe her, she did. The one thing Jane couldn't do very convincingly was lie. But if it wasn't Jane, then who was it?

Gazing out of the window, she absently noticed a man leaning in the doorway of the house over the road. He was

8

staring at the wine bar; Chase felt he was staring right at her and the hairs on her neck prickled. A lorry trundled past, and when it had gone, so had the man.

Up until now she had assumed the letter was a joke. But after talking to Jane, she was beginning to wonder, and perhaps even secretly hope that it was real. But she still couldn't bring herself to get excited. Things like this didn't happen to Chase Black.

But what if...?

Then it would be her first bit of good luck in ages. First, Mat had dumped her after six years, with no explanation bar a hastily scribbled note pushed through her letterbox (she hoped it had bitten him), announcing he was going away 'to sort his head out,' and it would be better, in the circumstances, to stop seeing each other. She had noticed he had gone moody and taciturn before disappearing, and their lovemaking, when it occurred, had become more urgent, but she had just put it down to stress. Although they had never officially moved in together, Mat stayed at her house whenever he wasn't working away, so bar the piece of paper they were as good as married (she often practised his surname in her head to see if it felt right: Chase Underwood, and she did think it had a certain ring to it). But then on top of Mat disappearing she had lost her job as an administrative assistant in a car manufacturing company that was 'down sizing' to revive a flagging share price. But didn't luck, good or bad, always come in three's? So where was piece of bad luck number three? Could she really dare to hope that her luck was changing?

"So where is it again, this house?" Jane asked.

"Paradise. It says it's somewhere in Staffordshire."

"Somewhere?"

"Well, I looked for it on a map but I couldn't find it. The place doesn't seem to exist."

"Just because it's not on a map, it doesn't mean it doesn't exist. Perhaps it's too small to put on. Let me have another look at that letter."

Chase passed her the letter, absently noticing the dried

bloodstain that looked disturbingly like the silhouette of a devil.

"It's a bit obscure isn't it?" Jane turned the piece of paper over, as though looking for more writing. "You'd have thought they would have put a phone number on so you could ring to confirm."

Chase had already considered this. "The post mark's too smudged to read, so I can't even tell where it was posted from. I even rang directory enquiries, but they couldn't help me unless I said what town I wanted. So I said London because of the address, but there was no listing. I also tried the Internet which just directed me to a porn site!"

"Strange." Jane frowned, shook her head and handed the letter back.

"No you would have liked it, lots of flesh." Chase laughed.

Jane raised her eyebrows in feigned disgust.

Chase didn't want to think about it anymore. Her head was spinning, but a funny feeling danced in the pit of her stomach. She didn't know whether it was excitement or apprehension.

Unlike Jane's daring manner of dress, Chase was wearing a smart blue, knee length skirt and a white blouse, allowing her to blend in with the few office workers drowning another day in an alcoholic haze. She envied them the luxury of receiving a wage, but not the tedium of a nine to five.

The thought of Mat came uninvited and unwanted into her mind. Tears bristled in her eyes. Wiping them away, she took a sip of wine.

"Are you okay?" Jane asked.

"Yes, just smoke in my eyes."

Jane frowned, "No one's smoking. What is it? Is it Mat?"

Chase nodded, instantly regretting the action as the room started to spin.

"That bastard. He isn't worth spitting on, never mind crying over. It's his loss. He won't get a honey like you again. Now if you batted for the other side..."

Chase laughed. "Then you would be my first choice, but I

doubt Gina would like it."

"What she don't see, sugar."

"Now you know you don't mean that."

"Just don't ever try me."

Chase wagged her finger in mock admonishment. "Easy tiger, I don't want Gina scratching my eyes out, so don't even think about it."

"Oh, I think about it all right!"

"You're terrible. I don't know how Gina ever trusts you."

Jane laughed. "I'm going to have to go to the toilet, and I may be some time." She winked salaciously.

"Get out of here." She watched Jane walk away, as did most of the men in the room, and turned her thoughts back to Mat. She still couldn't believe he had left her in such a cowardly way. It was just not like him. They had been able to talk about anything. She would have known if there was a problem. He was her soul mate, or at least she'd thought he was. In the last year he had performed more disappearing acts than Houdini.

At first she had thought he might have another girlfriend; that he was leading a double life, flitting between two partners, but she knew that was just silly. He wouldn't do that to her. Would he? There were times when she did wonder. Especially when he once called her by another girl's name. It had only been a slip of the tongue, and Mat couldn't even remember doing it, but she had definitely heard him. He didn't offer any explanation for the disappearances - he said that he couldn't remember where he'd been. When she questioned him further, he got angry. She had never seen him like that before and when he started smashing plates, he had scared her more than she would like to admit, and she had run out of the house. When she returned, it was as if nothing had happened. The incident was never mentioned again. Another time he assaulted a man in a bar who accidentally knocked into him. That just wasn't like Mat. He was a pacifist.

But this time he had been gone for nearly four months! She had tried to find him, unconcerned that she might not

11

like what she found, but not even his friends or family knew where he was. Or so they said - she had her doubts, especially as his mother never seemed to like her, always staring down her nose, as though Chase wasn't good enough for her son.

She had even considered reporting him as missing, but shrugged it off as a stupid idea. He was an adult, and free to do as he pleased. More tears bristled in her eyes and she wiped them away before Jane came back and admonished her again.

It was at times like this that she wished her parents hadn't emigrated to the other side of the world.

As she waited for Jane, she read the letter again.

It *had* to be a joke.

Didn't it?

Outside, the night smothered the world beneath its huge raven wing.

As a car drove past, its headlights momentarily illuminated the doorway of the building opposite.

The man was back.

And he was still staring at the wine bar.

Chapter 2

Chase woke on Saturday morning with a splitting headache. She didn't know what time she had finally gone to bed as Jane had stopped over and they had made a night of it, but it must have been about 4 a.m. She glanced bleary eyed at the digital alarm clock: 6.30, and pressed her palms to her temples, trying to stem the pain. Why had she drunk so much?

Getting out of bed, the room began to spin and she felt a ship-bobbing surge of queasiness in her stomach. Her mouth began to salivate with what she knew was the first sign she was going to be sick. Lurching to the bathroom, she was met by the site of Jane hunched over the toilet, retching. The sound and smell caused Chase to follow suit into the sink. Her throat felt like it was burning and her nose stung with acrid bile. Blowing her nose, she looked down at Jane who smiled weakly back before her head disappeared back into the toilet.

"What a night," Jane said before throwing up again.

As though it was contagious, Chase followed suit until there was nothing left in her stomach to bring up. She washed her mouth out with water and brushed her teeth to take the vile taste away. It was not the first time she had been sick lately, and she wondered if it was more to do with a bug, than the excessive alcohol.

"Remind me never to invite you round again." Chase shook her head and sighed. Jane had been her best friend since they were at school, but she was a terrible influence.

Walking down stairs to the kitchen, she grimaced when she saw the empty wine bottles and she quickly drank several glasses of water and swallowed a couple of headache tablets before popping some bread in the toaster. If she hadn't needed to be sick, she would still be in bed, but now she was up it hardly seemed worth trying to go back to sleep, especially as the room kept spinning like a carousel.

When the toast was done, she buttered it, smeared on a thin layer of honey and sat at the table, head in hands, still feeling too ill to eat. It took her half an hour to nibble the toast, but only five seconds to bring it back up. Luckily, there was no dirty washing in the sink and she swilled the mess away.

Jane didn't even come down to attempt breakfast and it was 8.45 before she walked into the kitchen, her blue night-dress leaving little to the imagination and her olive skin unable to disguise her washed out complexion. "You look like shit," she groaned.

"And you think you don't!"

"What time is it?" Jane yawned and walked to the sink. Turning on the tap she splashed water over her face.

"Almost nine o'clock. I really, really regret asking you to stop over."

Before Jane could reply, there was a knock at the door that made Chase wince.

She walked slowly to answer it, her head pounding with every step. In the hallway, she caught sight of herself in the mirror on the wall. Her usually bright eyes were bloodshot and her hair looked as though a combine harvester had ploughed through it. She felt as bad as she looked. Turning the latch, she opened the door and blinked as bright sunlight stung her eyes, making them water and momentarily blurring the figure standing before her.

"Miss Black. My name's Drake. I'm here to collect you."

Chase rubbed her eyes, focusing on the heavy set man stood before her. He was dressed in a chauffeur's uniform and a peaked cap shadowed his eyes. Ten o'clock shadow etched his angular jaw and a harelip marred his mouth, giving him a perpetual sneer. He looked vaguely familiar.

"Collect me?" She frowned. What was he on about? Again she regretted drinking too much. Suddenly conscious of the fact she was wearing a nightshirt that hardly covered

14

her bottom, she closed the door a fraction and peered around the edge, only too aware that she was naked beneath the thin material and that her nipples had risen in the cold.

"Yes, I'm here to take you to High Top Cottage."

Chase opened her mouth to speak and then closed it again. In her drunken stupor she had forgotten all about the letter and the supposed prize. "What sort of a joke is this? Can't you see that I'm not laughing?"

Drake scowled. "Joke!"

"Come on, you can stop pretending."

"Miss Black, nobody's pretending. Now are you ready?"

She tried to think clearly but her head was throbbing. "You mean I've really won a house?"

Drake nodded.

"Come on, you're just winding me up. I haven't *really* won a house?"

He nodded again, impatient.

Chase didn't know what to do. It had to be a joke, but he seemed so sincere. "Well... I'm bringing a friend," she blurted, momentarily unsettled by Drake's demeanour as he leant forward, striking a threatening pose. "Is that a problem?" she squeaked, taking a step back.

Drake straightened himself up. "I was told you would be coming alone. I don't have any instructions concerning you bringing a companion. Wait here while I make a call."

Chase stood on the step and watched Drake walk down the path to a black limousine parked at the end of the drive. She shook her head. What the hell was going on?

Drake took out a mobile telephone and punched a number, animatedly talking into the receiver and glancing back at Chase. The vehicle and driver looked out of place in the rundown area and Chase noticed a gang of kids checking out the car, most probably with an eye to stealing it.

"What is it?"

Chase jumped as Jane grabbed her shoulders. "Don't creep up on me like that, you'll give me a bloody heart attack." She clutched her chest.

"What's that doing here?" Jane pointed at the limousine.

"It's for me!" She still couldn't believe it.

Obviously Jane couldn't either. "For you?"

"Yes, he says he's here to take me to see the house I've won."

"The house?" As if suddenly remembering the letter, Jane grinned. "You're joking, right?"

"I'm not, but someone is." She hesitated. "Oh I don't know. It's freaking me out."

"Well it won't hurt to go with him, will it?"

"Won't hurt! He could be anyone. And I wouldn't go anywhere without you, but he said something about not having instructions for me to bring a friend... You will come, won't you?"

"Are you joking, of course I'll come. It's the weekend, so I don't have to work."

Chase sighed with relief.

"But if it's your prize, you can bring who you goddamn like."

Drake walked back toward the house and Jane put her hands on her hips, puffing out her chest as though steeling herself for an argument.

"Sorry about that, Miss Black. You can bring whomever you like. I just had to check." He shrugged.

"Damn right she can bring whom she likes," Jane mumbled, relaxing her stance a little.

"Thanks. I understand. We'll be ready in a minute." Chase grabbed Jane's arm and steered her away. She was only too aware that Jane's bosom was on display beneath the almost diaphanous nightdress, and that Drake's eyes kept wandering.

"Where are your bags?" Drake called after them.

"Bags?"

"You're expected to stay at the house. Didn't the letter explain? Don't worry, the house is fully furnished."

Chase looked at Jane and raised her eyebrows in surprise. "Are you okay with that?"

"I haven't got to get up to go to work tomorrow, and you certainly haven't." She turned to Drake. "Are they laying on

16

free food and drink?"

"Refreshments will be available."

"Well that's all we need to know."

Chase sighed. A party was the last thing she needed at the moment. She didn't know whether the queasy feeling in her stomach was still caused by the drink or by the uneasy sensation that settled over her like a dark cloud.

***

Sitting in the spacious rear of the limousine, Chase felt like a rock star. The vehicle had more mod cons than her house! There was a television and DVD player, a games machine, and the all important drink cabinet that Jane helped herself to, the hangover dismissed in favour of free alcohol. Drake had put up a screen between them, making it appear they were cocooned within the back of the vehicle. The illusion of seclusion was made more apparent because no one could see through the blackened windows.

Chase lay down on the roomy seat, her hands over her face.

"Get some of this down you, girl," Jane said, pouring herself another glass of wine. "This will have you feeling fine in no time. Hair of the dog."

Chase peeked out from behind her fingers. "Hair? I think you're drinking the whole damn mutt. The way I'm feeling, it wouldn't stay down."

While Chase tried to recover, Jane rang her girlfriend, Gina on her mobile phone. Chase got the impression that Gina was not too happy about Jane going away with another girl, and if she was in her place, she supposed she would feel the same.

It was another half an hour before Chase finally sat up. Taking a bottle of mineral water from the drink cabinet she gulped it back, hoping it would stay down long enough to quench her thirst.

"You don't get to travel in one of these every day," Jane said, stretching out on the seat opposite. "I wish Gina could see this. Damn what we could do together in a car like this. I'm horny just thinking about it."

"Don't you ever think about anything else?" Chase asked, shaking her head in mock disgust.

"Sex is a beautiful thing. P'raps you aren't doing it right." She winked and licked her lips.

Chase laughed. "You're incorrigible, and I don't just mean your mind." While Chase had opted for denim jeans and jacket, Jane had squeezed into a tight red dress.

"If I knew what it meant, I might agree with you."

"Do you know where we are?"

"Haven't got a clue!"

"That wouldn't be the first time." Ignoring Jane's indignant scowl, she leant forward and knocked on the window that shut them off from the driver.

The partition slid silently down. "How long before we get there?" She could see Drake's steely eyes watching her in the rear-view mirror and a shiver ran down her spine. He was too brooding and quiet for her liking: there was something dangerous about him.

"We will be at the airfield in another ten minutes."

"*Airfield*?" Chase and Jane said in unison.

"Yes, due to the weather, we can only reach Paradise by helicopter."

"The weather?" Chase frowned.

"There's been a band of low lying fog surrounding the village. It's too thick to drive through."

"But we can fly through it?"

"Not through it, over it. Don't worry, just settle back and enjoy the trip."

The partition slid back up before Chase could ask any further questions. "Helicopter! I feel sick enough now, never mind flying." She collapsed back in her seat, her mind a whirl of confusion. If it was a joke, it was a damn expensive one and she couldn't see anyone going to this much trouble to wind her up. That only left one option: that it was real, and that she really had won a cottage. Her stomach lurched in sickly anticipation.

18

"I've always wanted to fly in a helicopter. Gina will be green with envy. This is the life."

"Well I'm a little green around the gills myself, but it isn't through envy." Leaning forward, she motioned for Jane to come closer. "Don't you think he's a little weird," she whispered, glancing at the front of the car.

"All men are a little weird, sugar. Now you're beginning to see what I mean. There's hope for you yet."

"Don't you ever stop? I'm being serious."

"That's what I'm afraid of. You've got to learn to relax. He may be a bit funny, but that's men for you, always thinking they're superior. Take it from me, men are full of shit. Don't sweat it."

But Chase couldn't relax. Something didn't feel right.

"So do you really think I've won a house?"

Jane shrugged. "I don't know. But if you haven't, I wish someone would play tricks like this on me."

Chase sat back, deep in thought.

Eventually the car came to a stop at the entrance to a small airfield. Barbed wire topped the high fences surrounding the area and two armed guards were on gate duty. Chase saw one of the guards try to peer through the rear window before the other guard waved them through.

Beyond the runway she could see large, empty hangers, but as they turned toward the hanger furthest away, she saw the sleek, black helicopter with its blackened windows. The limousine came to a smooth stop forty feet away from the helicopter and Chase heard Drake exit the car before the rear door opened. As she stepped out onto the tarmac, a cold gust of wind ruffled her short hair and even though dressed for the weather, she shivered. Jane stepped out behind her, glass of wine still in hand as though she travelled like this all the time. She was lapping it up and Chase wished she could too, but she was still too nervous and wary to relax and enjoy it. Something wasn't right. She was almost convinced there must be a mistake.

"If you make your way to the helicopter, I'll bring your bags," Drake said, taking his cap off and throwing it in the car before taking their luggage out of the boot of the limousine.

Looking around, Chase tried to spot a sign advertising where they were, but she couldn't see anything. There didn't appear to be anything with writing on. What looked like a signpost had been painted over with black paint. The acrid smell of diesel filled the air, making her stomach curdle again. Walking arm in arm with Jane toward the helicopter, she expected someone to jump out and shout 'surprise!'

"Boys and their toys," Jane mumbled, slurring her words slightly under the influence of fresh alcohol.

The helicopter door was open and Chase stepped into the spacious rear. A pilot and co-pilot sat at the controls wearing helmets with dark visors that hid their faces. Neither of them acknowledged Chase or Jane. Moments later, they fired up the engines and the rotors started to rotate.

"All settled?" Drake asked above the roar of the engines as he entered the helicopter and secured the door.

Chase nodded, feeling her stomach lurch as the helicopter left the ground. She felt quite disorientated as the nose dipped down, the ground starting to blur beneath them as they increased speed. The ride was like an uncomfortable roller coaster as they pitched and yawed across the countryside. Even Jane remained quiet, looking queasy.

With no idea how long they would be in the air, she tried to sleep, and although the motion of the helicopter was too violent she still kept her eyes closed so she didn't have to look at Drake.

It seemed as though they had been in the air for hours before Drake said, "Almost there."

Chase opened her eyes and stared in awe at the carpet of fog obscuring the land. She could see that they were in a valley, the hills in the distance trapping the fog in a natural bottleneck. As they skimmed over the fog, an occasional tree was just visible like a strange island in a seething white sea. In the distance she could make out a hill rising from the fog like a lighthouse in a storm. The closer they got, the more she could make out. Houses became discernible, dotted across the hillside. The buildings were interspersed by trees, tall Poplars, Noble firs and Scots pine that looked like bonsai trees in an oriental setting. Most of the houses appeared old, late sixteenth, early seventeenth century, which made Chase wonder what had come first, the houses or the trees? She didn't realise her mouth was open until Drake spoke.

"Beautiful, isn't it!"

"Beautiful, it's..." Chase was lost for words. "Paradise."

"And you've won one of those!" Jane squealed and shook her head. "Damn, why don't I enter competitions?"

Chase didn't say anything, too afraid that if she did, the illusion would fade and she would wake up.

The helicopter descended into a field, causing an impromptu crop circle.

"Mind your heads when we exit. Keep low and run for the lane over there." As he opened the door, Drake pointed out a lane that snaked into the village.

Chase and Jane did as they were told and ran from beneath the rotors to stand marvelling at the village. From a lower perspective it looked even more beautiful. Many of the houses were black and white beamed structures, half hidden by the majestic trees that stood guard like proud soldiers. Chase hardly noticed the helicopter engine noise increase as it took off, banking to return the way it had come. She was too awe-struck. As the noise and draft receded, the smell of fresh pine invaded the air. Chase inhaled deeply and closed her eyes, savouring the moment and the fresh smell. She no longer felt sick; too awed to feel ill.

"Follow me," Drake barked, striding off along the lane, a holdall slung over his shoulder and Chase's suitcase and Jane's overnight bag in each hand making his muscles bulge.

The fir trees lining the lane were gnarled and old. Sunlight danced through the needle foliage, stabbing the ground with flickering hypodermic shadows.

Chase saw movement from the corner of her eye and she caught sight of the grey bushy tail of a squirrel racing around the trunk of a tree. Turning to face back the way they had come, she found it surreal to see a wall of fog not two hundred feet away. It felt as though Paradise was cocooned from the outside world by a protective barrier, keeping civilisation and all of its problems away.

Feeling the need to share her good news (or secretly gloat), she took out her mobile phone.

As though he had eyes in the back of his head, Drake turned around, his steely eyes narrowed into suspicious slits. "Mobile's don't work here."

Although she didn't want to believe him, she disappointedly saw that he was right, and that there was no reception available to make a call.

She put her phone away.

Watching Drake stride off, she was suddenly struck by his resemblance to the man she had seen lurking in the doorway opposite the wine bar the other night and an uneasy feeling settled over her.

Apart from Jane, no one knew where she was.

Come to that, she didn't even know where she was herself.

Chapter 3

"Go on, Ratty, I dare you."

Peter Rathbone, otherwise known as Ratty, stopped picking at his fingernails with the Swiss Army penknife and looked at the undulating wall of fog; he bit his lower lip.

"Not scared are you?"

"Course not. Why, are you?" He turned to look at Isabelle Adams who was sitting on the stile, swinging her legs and smoking a cigarette. Her shoulder length, blond hair hid her features until she lifted her head, revealing her clear complexion and bright blue eyes. Her pert nose wrinkled as she shook her head, disagreeing with his accusation.

Tendrils of fog swirled around his feet, making them feel unnaturally cold in what was otherwise a bright summer day. Almost sixteen, Ratty was six months older than Izzy, but she had the annoying knack of making him feel like a baby. Although he really liked her, she was always teasing him, especially in front of the rest of the gang who now stood around watching and sniggering. And now here was his chance to prove he wasn't a coward, but he couldn't. The fog was too intimidating and he'd heard too many horror stories about it. Snapping the penknife shut, he dropped it in his pocket.

"Come on Ratty, we haven't got all day. The school holidays will be over by the time you actually do it," Spotty Smitty said, spitting out the blade of grass he had been chewing.

"Fuck you, Smitty."

"Not scared of the bogey man are you?" Zak asked, breaking off from kissing Julie Rogers long enough to draw breath.

The sudden roar of a low flying helicopter made them all jump as it appeared to materialise out of nowhere, black and sleek. They all watched it disappear over the horizon.

"Ratty's scared of the bogey man." Izzy jumped down from the stile and flicked the butt of her cigarette into the fog.

"There ain't no bogey man." Why did she have to keep teasing him? "Then what about all them stories?" Smitty said. "You know, them people who disappeared after going into the fog. They say the whole village has disappeared. Everyone's dead."

"There ain't no bogey man," Ratty repeated. "Besides, they turned up. No one's disappeared. My granddad lives in Paradise and the police say everyone's fine." He hoped he sounded more convincing than he felt.

"No. My old man says they've gone for good. 'Won't find 'em now' he says, 'bogey man's 'ad 'em'."

"Then your old man's as daft as you, Smitty."

"Say that again and I'll fuckin' twat yer."

"Daft as a brush."

"That's it, yer in fer a kickin'."

Smitty advanced with his fists raised and a scowl on his face. Ratty took a step back, then another. The last thing he wanted to do was to start fighting. Running a hand through his crew cut, he shook his head. With his tall, skinny frame, he was made more for running than fighting.

"This is stupid."

"So now you're calling me stupid, are you?"

As Ratty stumbled back into the fog, Smitty became less distinct, his shape beginning to blur. Starting to panic, Ratty suddenly tripped over his own feet and slipped; although he tried to keep his balance, he fell into the cold, dewy grass, the wind momentarily knocked out of him. As he regained his feet, he was alarmed to see that the fog was so dense he couldn't even see his hands in front of his face.

"Hey, you lot, where are you?" Ratty's voice wavered slightly. "Come on, where are you. I can't see anything in here." The fog seemed to muffle his cries. "Come on, don't mess around. This isn't funny." He couldn't believe the fog was so damn thick. He could have only stumbled a few feet

24

into it.

No one replied, or if they did, he didn't hear them.

Stumbling around, arms outstretched to feel his way through the white void he looked like a lurching zombie. He couldn't believe that he was completely disorientated. Understandably, the fog had been a local talking point since it first appeared. What couldn't be understood was why it hadn't dissipated. It just hung around like a huge blanket and there had been no contact with anyone from the village since it descended. The fog was too thick to safely navigate on foot or by car, although some people had tried following the only road into the village, but they were turned back at a roadblock. A report was released saying everyone in the village was fine and they preferred to stay where they were as they were being looked after and supplies were being regularly flown in. When Ratty's father had asked if he could go in on one of the helicopters to visit his own father, the request had been turned down 'due to safety issues', whatever they were.

Ratty remembered his father got very angry about being refused. He had never seen him so angry. Even Ratty's mother hadn't been able to calm him down, which was why they gave him a tranquilliser injection, 'for his own good'. Ratty's father had been docile ever since. No one had been able to offer any explanation about where the fog had come from, or when it would disappear. And for such an unusual occurrence, there had been little or no news coverage about it.

Stumbling around, Ratty thought this was how it must be to go blind. As if in response to the thought, his foot snagged on something he couldn't see and he fell face first into the wet grass.

"Come on, a joke's a joke. Where are you?" As he regained his feet, tears stung his eyes and he wiped his face on his sleeve. His jeans were now soaking wet.

A faint sound caught his attention and he tensed, listening. Whatever it was made a wet, slithering sound, as though something was being dragged through the grass. He had a vision of a giant slug slithering toward him and he shivered. He could feel his heart beating fast. His blood froze and he could feel his temples pounding in time with his fear as the noise drew nearer.

They say the whole village has disappeared. Everyone's dead...

Bogey man's 'ad 'em'.

What the hell was it?

Knowing that he was most likely panicking over nothing didn't help. In the fog he was in a nether world where he had lost the sense of sight and where he had to rely on his other senses, straining his ears to detect where the noise originated.

A shape flashed before his eyes, lunging toward him in a swirl of mist before it grabbed his shoulders. Ratty screamed. He almost wet himself.

"Ratty, is that you?"

"Izzy. Izzy. It's you, I thought..."

"Thought what? What are you screaming for?"

"I wasn't screaming." He hoped she couldn't see him blush. "I've been shouting for ages! Why didn't anyone answer?"

"We heard you shouting, but the rest of them thought that it would be funny not to answer. And as no one else would come in to find you, well, here I am. It was partly my fault you're here anyway, I suppose."

Ratty let out a relieved sigh. "So come on then, lead the way."

"Lead the way where?"

"Out of the fog."

"I don't know the way."

"You mean you're lost too!"

"Well, Sherlock, nothing gets past you does it!"

"So why did you come to find me?"

"Because I'm stupid like that."

Ratty grabbed Izzy's warm hand and squeezed it. "Thanks."

"Yeh, whatever, come on."

26

They began to walk, stumbling through the fog in what they hoped was the right direction.

***

"Here's your house," Drake said, dropping the suitcases and taking a key out of his pocket to unlock the door.

Chase looked at the house in wide-eyed wonder. "This... this is mine!" She could hardly believe it. The house was near the top of the hill, reached by a winding lane with the unsavoury name of Slaughter Hill that snaked past cottage gardens and picturesque houses. Some of the houses leaned slightly, their walls bowed as though tired and sagging. If anything, this accentuated their beauty, giving them charm and character. The house she was looking at was small with tiny windows like canvases, displaying captured reflections of the trees and the blue sky like miniature oil paintings. One side of the house was covered by red and purple Clematis. Sat on the apex, the chimney smoked away like a contented old man, puffing on a pipe. Black wooden beams made up the framework of the house, the walls a faded white. The roof sagged slightly in the middle, as though a giant had sat down to rest, bowing the walls out beneath his weight and the front door was covered by a rickety old porch that had flowers winding up its frame.

The sloping garden was a wash of colour with Red Hot Pokers, blue Lobelia, yellow and pink Lupin, Daylilies of all colours, Viola, Buddleja, the list went on. A giant Scots Pine shaded some of the garden, the tiered branches reaching down to caress the eaves of the house. Beyond the garden, more trees stood proud and strong, lining the lane and hiding some of the houses below.

Chase felt tears fill her eyes.

"Are you okay?" Jane asked.

"Look at it, Jane. Just look. Have you ever seen anywhere this beautiful?"

Jane shook her head. "It beats looking out on terraced houses, that's for sure."

Chase looked back down the hill, the fog visible on the horizon like a mantle, beautiful and surreal as it reflected the sun.

Shaking slightly, she brushed past Drake and entered the house, breathing in the aroma of wood smoke and fresh flowers. A small hallway stretched before her and she stepped through a door on her left into a lounge, tastefully decorated in blue pastel shades. The furniture was practical, but sparse, consisting of a settee, a chair, and a bureau. The main feature was the fireplace where a coal fire blazed away. She assumed that although it wasn't cold, they had lit the fire to make it feel more homely. It worked. She imagined toasting bread or marshmallows over the coals. Walking to the window, she looked out over the front garden and down the hill.

"Jane, can you believe this. Tell me I'm not dreaming."

Shaking her head, Jane said, "You're not dreaming sugar. Or if you are, then I am too."

Still unable to believe that the house was hers, she walked back into the hall and continued down to the kitchen where there was an old fashioned range to cook on. The fridge freezer and washing machine were out of site in a small utility room. There was a dining room adjacent to the kitchen and this opened out onto the back garden, which was as colourful as the one out front. More trees led to the top of the hill, a couple of them looking as though they had been struck by lightning, their trunks split salaciously. Upstairs, there were two bedrooms and a bathroom. There was a double bed and a wardrobe in each room. The front bedroom also had a period dressing table, the mirror of which reflected the light from outside to brighten the room even more. All of the windows were open and a cool breeze aired the rooms, filling them with the smell of pine.

"Come on, the competition sponsors want to meet you," Drake shouted from the hallway, bringing Chase out of her reverie. "So get a move on."

"Yes, yes of course they do." Even Drakes surly attitude couldn't wipe the grin off her face as they left the house. She couldn't believe her good fortune. Walking arm in arm with Jane, even she seemed lost for words.

Walking back down the lane they strolled toward a small church on the edge of the fog, the adjoining hall losing its solidity as the fog encroached leaving only half of it visible.

The sound of voices could be heard from inside the hall and as Drake opened one of the double doors, the voices went quiet. Stepping through the door, Chase felt a little apprehensive. Although there were only seven people gathered, she didn't like being the object of such close scrutiny and she crossed her arms in front of her chest, as though to establish a barrier. Jane's manner of dress didn't help as people couldn't help but stare.

There were a few tables set out with food and another table with drinks. It wasn't much of a spread, a few sandwiches, pork pie, sausage rolls and a quiche was all she could see. Turning away, she noticed a stocky man in the corner of the room. He had long, unkempt hair and close-set eyes in a greasy face, but it was the knife in his hand that alarmed her. He was dragging the point of the knife across the wall, gouging out thick veins of plaster. Why didn't someone stop him? Couldn't they see what he was doing?

"Ah, Miss Black, it's a pleasure to finally meet you."

Chase turned to see a smartly dressed, middle-aged man walking toward her with his hand outstretched. He had a neatly clipped greying beard that softened the shape of his face and was only a bit shorter than the hair on his head. His blue eyes were cold, in sharp contrast with the warm smile he wore.

Shaking his hand, Chase was surprised by how cold his skin was. A chill ran through her.

"My name is Nigel Moon," he said. "And this must be your companion." He brusquely shook Jane's hand without enquiring her name and turned back to Chase.

"How did you know I was Miss Black?" Chase asked, realising Moon had greeted her by name before being formally introduced.

"I just presumed as you had entered the hall first that you

must be our esteemed and, might I say, extremely attractive winner."

Rather than being flattered by Moon's comment, Chase found herself feeling angry he could be so personal, especially as the assembled crowd were listening so intently. She felt in some imperceptive way that the comment was meant to make her feel uneasy; off guard.

"I am the managing director of Storm, the competition organisers. I believe you have already viewed your prize? I hope it's to your liking?"

"Yes, it's fantastic," Chase gushed.

"Well I hope you will be very happy living here."

"Hold on a minute," Jane said, placing a protective hand on Chase's shoulder. "What do you mean, living here?"

"Pardon?"

"You know, who said she's going to live in the house?"

Moon's smile dropped imperceptibly. "Who wouldn't want to live here?"

"Chase." Jane placed her hands on her hips, assuming her verbal fighting stance.

"Jane, I'm sure Mr. Moon didn't mean it quite so literally." Chase was eager to defuse the situation. She was also embarrassed that Jane was talking about her as though she wasn't here; as though she couldn't speak for herself.

"On the contrary, Miss Black. It was in the competition rules that the winner undertakes to move into the house. *Immediately*, for at least twelve months. Otherwise they would forfeit the prize."

"Bullshit," Jane said.

Moon reached into his jacket pocket and pulled out a sheet of paper. "Of course you can re-read the rules if you like. It was a condition of entry that the winner had to be ready to move. Didn't you read the rules, Miss Black?" He frowned.

Chase felt like Moon was trying to belittle her with his patronising tone, and that he was boxing her into a corner. She suddenly felt hot and claustrophobic. "Yes, I read the rules." But no matter how hard she tried, she couldn't even

30

remember entering the competition, never mind reading the rules. "If you could just let Jane see them?" What she really wanted was to read them herself without appearing too foolish. Hopefully they would spark a memory.

"Of course. I know you may be a bit overwhelmed by it all. We *will* understand if you don't wish to accept the prize. Take your time." Moon handed Jane the sheet of paper, which she snatched out of his hand.

"I think we'll just go outside to discuss the matter." Chase headed for the door, dragging Jane after her. She felt too embarrassed to ask Moon for more details about the competition, afraid if she did, they might realise she wasn't the winner after all.

She felt the small group watch her walk out; when the door shut, the voices started up again.

"What's the story?" Jane asked. "You can't seriously want to live here?"

"Let me see that sheet of paper, Jane." Begrudgingly, Jane handed it over and they both read it together.

"Well, it seems Mr. Moon is right. It does say I have to move into the house, or forfeit it! Well, twelve months isn't that long. It'll just be like a long holiday."

"Well that's it then, sugar, we'll get our bags and quit the sticks. You aren't staying here on your own for twelve months."

"Hold it, Jane. Perhaps I don't want to leave."

Jane frowned. "You can't be serious."

"What have I got to go back for? No job, no man, and you know where I live. This could be just what I'm after, a fresh start."

"I think this fresh air's fuzzed your brain. This is no place for you."

"No, I think this is *just* the place for me. I need something like this to sort myself out."

"What you *need* is your friends. No, I can't let you do it."

"You can't let me do it!" Chase felt her anger rising. "Just who do you think you are?"

"I'm your friend."

"If that's true, then you'll see it's what I want. Didn't you see that house. It's lovely. More than lovely, it's beautiful. I could never afford something like that, not in a place like this, but now it's mine."

Jane closed her eyes and looked away. "You're my home girl. What would I do without you?" She quickly wiped her eyes with the back of her hand.

Chase hugged her. "I'll still be your home girl, just in a different home."

"Are you really sure?"

"Yes."

Jane sighed and shook her head, conceding defeat.

Chase smiled. "That's why I love you."

"I know, now let's do the deed before I say something else."

They walked back into the hall and the chattering stopped once more. Chase could see Moon and Drake were apart from everyone else, skulking in the corner, deep in heated conversation. They stopped talking when they realised Chase and Jane had re-entered the hall.

"Mr. Moon," Chase said, walking toward him, "when do I get the keys to my new house?"

Moon's smile returned. "I take it you will be accepting the prize then. Congratulations, Miss Black. Everyone," Moon clapped his hands together, "if I could have your attention, I would like to introduce you to Chase Black, the newest resident of Paradise. I hope you all make her feel at home." Two people clapped; one of them was the man with the knife. "Now if you would like to sign a few documents accepting the conditions of the prize, then the house is yours. We can also arrange the sale of your own property, which would give you some capital while you resettle yourself. Of course, we can also arrange to have your belongings collected and delivered to your new house."

Chase didn't really like the thought of strangers going through her property. "I would like to do my own packing," she said, too caught up in the whirlwind of events to think clearly. As far as selling her house went, she doubted they could even give it away. Then there was the problem of work. What could she do out here? Perhaps Jane was right; perhaps she hadn't thought this through properly. She bit her fingernail, deliberating.

"Now if you can just sign this for me." Moon held out a document and a pen.

"Well, I'll need to read it first."

"No need for that, Miss Black. I can assure you everything is all right. It's only full of the usual legal mumbo jumbo, nothing to concern yourself over."

"If she wants to read the document, then let her."

Moon pensively eyed Jane. "Drake, why don't you take this young lady and show her where the refreshments are."

"I'll go when I'm ready." As Drake grabbed her elbow to steer her away, Jane shrugged him off.

"Miss Black will join you in a moment. Don't worry, I'm not going to bite her." Moon gave a hollow laugh.

"It's okay, Jane. I know what I'm doing." Even though she knew Jane was only trying to look out for her, Chase was embarrassed. Jane was making it seem as though she couldn't think for herself. "Honestly, go on. Get me a drink ready, I'll be over in a moment."

Jane bit her top lip. "Just you be careful girl." She eventually turned away, obviously unsure whether she should leave her friend.

Chase watched Jane and Drake walk toward a small bar at the far end of the room before turning back to Moon and accepting the document and pen. She quickly scanned through the long text, noticing words like: relinquish, binding, waive, terms and prize. She tried reading it, but it went beyond her comprehension.

"If you would just like to sign at the bottom, where it says signature," Moon said, visibly agitated.

Chase didn't know what to do. She felt as though she was being rushed, as though everything was happening too quickly. She saw Moon watching her, impatient, and she thought about her house in the city and before she knew what she was doing, she signed on the dotted line and Moon snatched the document and pen back from her.

"Welcome to Paradise, Miss Black. I hope you will be very happy here."

"Yes, I'm sure I will," she said without conviction, her head spinning and her nausea returning.

"Well, here are the keys to your new house. And now if you'll excuse me, I've got some business to attend to. Drake will be available if there are any problems. There's food and drink available for you, and please, enjoy yourself." Without another word, Moon walked away and left the building.

Chase watched him go before looking at the keys in her hand. She couldn't believe the house was really hers. She felt like jumping up and down and screaming with joy, but she thought better of it - she didn't want the locals to think she was mad. Hurriedly, she crossed the room, jangling the keys in front of Jane who shook her head.

"So you've done it then! Well, I hope it makes you happy, I really do." She passed Chase a glass of wine. "Here's to the future."

"Cheers." Chase clinked glasses, a toast. "By the way, where's Drake gone?"

"I don't know, he just made some excuse and wandered off."

Chase looked around the hall and spotted Drake lurking near the man with the knife.

Turning away, she smiled at a pleasant looking old lady with grey hair tied up in a bun. The lady barely nodded in response as she continued to converse with a short, grey haired old man, stealing furtive glances when she thought Chase wasn't looking.

"Well this is fun." Jane shook her head.

Chase ignored the sarcasm, too concerned by the sly glances she was attracting. She felt as though everyone was talking about her.

She noticed Drake ushering the man with the knife out of the room, and she relaxed slightly. Knives made her nervous. As she stared at the gashes he had made on the wall, she noticed there was an order to them, the semblance of a word:

hell. She shivered.

Outside the window, the fog obscured the view, and for a moment, Chase thought she saw a ghostly face at the glass, peering in, the features pained and forlorn, the eyes dark and foreboding. Thinking it was a reflection, she looked around the room for the source, but couldn't find it. When she turned back to the window, the image had gone. It had been so fleeting she didn't know whether it had been real or imagined; the pallor had been that of the fog, and could have been just that, a will-o'-the-wisp in the ethereal ocean that eddied and flowed at the shores of Paradise.

Chapter 4

Ratty and Izzy had been wandering around for what seemed like hours. Neither of them had a clue where they were, and the fog wouldn't dissipate enough to allow them to pick out any landmarks.

Ratty shivered. His feet were soaking wet, and he felt generally uncomfortable and miserable. If he wasn't lost in it, he wouldn't have believed fog could be so dense. At his side, Izzy was an indistinct blur, but he was glad he was not alone as he had the distinct feeling they were being followed. He couldn't quite explain why he had the feeling, but it persisted, raising the hairs on his neck like a conjuror.

But he couldn't think of anyone he would rather have with him than Izzy. She had only recently broken up with Nigel 'the Neanderthal' Jones, and whenever Ratty had seen them together, a pang of jealousy had pierced him. He didn't like Nigel, didn't like the way he grabbed Izzy's bottom, didn't like the way he shoved his tongue in her mouth, and he definitely didn't like the way he bragged about copping a feel of her pert breasts in the cinema. Ratty was glad they had broken up, because if Nigel had bragged about getting any further than a quick grope, he was sure he would have punched his lights out.

Using their free hands to feel their way through the fog in case they walked into something or fell into a ditch, they shuffled along at a snails pace. As they had been concentrating so much on just staying upright and not walking into things, they hadn't said much to each other. At first they had shouted for help, but they had eventually stopped when their throats began to hurt.

"Izzy, can you feel that?" Ratty thought it strange speaking to someone he could hardly see.

"Feel what?"

"It feels like tarmac. A road." It surprised Ratty how different tarmac felt underfoot after traipsing through sodden fields; it was like reaching a semblance of civilisation.

"Where, I can't feel anything."

"Step this way, toward me. There, can you feel it?"

"Yes, we must be on a farm track or the lane into the village."

"Well, if we follow it, it must lead somewhere."

"That's true, Sherlock and at least we won't get any wetter."

"Well what are we waiting for?" Ratty said, sounding slightly more cheerful.

Izzy grunted a reply that sounded more like a condemnation, but she followed anyway.

They shuffled along for about half an hour when Ratty heard what sounded like the faint murmur of voices. "Can you hear that?" he asked.

"Shush, let me listen."

"We're saved."

"Shut up."

"Well we are!" He wished she wouldn't be so brusque with him.

"Look, just keep quiet for a minute. If we're caught in here, you know we'll be in trouble. They haven't posted those signs warning people to stay away for nothing."

"You're being stupid, they could help us get out. Perhaps they're even looking for us."

"Do you want your parents to know where you've been?"

Ratty didn't answer. His mother had repeatedly warned him about going anywhere near the fog. She'd said it was a bad omen - look what had happened to his father.

"Come on, over here, off the road," Izzy said, dragging Ratty behind her.

They had hardly taken two steps when they fell into a rancid, water-filled ditch.

"Bloody hell..."

Izzy covered Ratty's mouth with her hand before he could finish.

"Shush."

Ratty pulled her hand away from his mouth, his face set in a petulant grimace. Why did he let her boss him around so much? He had to be more assertive, show her she couldn't always tell him what to do.

"I thought I heard something?" a man's brusque, disembodied voice said.

"Probably your imagination," another man replied. Their voices were faint, muffled.

Ratty shuddered and peered into the fog.

He heard the voices again, drawing closer, louder.

"Remind me later to check on the generator. Damn things been wheezing like a whore," the brusque voice said.

"Since when do you know what a whore sounds like? You're too ugly to even pay for it."

"Fuck you, Davis. I'm God's gift, the ladies just don't realise."

"Even the fuckin' tide wouldn't take you out." The men laughed.

The footsteps were getting louder, drawing closer. Ratty felt his mouth go dry, but he couldn't swallow. Knowing that he was trespassing made him tremble; fear squeezed his heart with bony fingers and his penis shrank.

"There, look, movement," the brusque speaker said.

"Got it."

Ratty held his breath. Had they been seen?

He heard a metallic click; the sudden retort of a rifle made his heart stop and he flinched. A dark, indistinct shape flew out of the fog toward him, twisting and somersaulting like a grotesque Catherine wheel emitting dark sparks. Ratty almost squealed; he wanted to run, but Izzy held him back as the indistinct shape flopped beside them, landing with a wet splash in the ditch.

Looking down, Ratty saw it was a fox, it's tongue lolling from a bloodied maw and a small hole punched in the side of its skull where the bullet had entered. He felt slightly sick.

"It was only a fox," one of the voices said. "Come on, let's head back to base."

Ratty peeked above the edge of the ditch. Even though it was difficult to see, he could just make out two figures wearing white fatigues that blended into the mist like chameleons, ghosts in the fog. Luckily they were facing each other, their features masked by a device that resembled binoculars.

He quickly ducked back down before they spotted him.

When he was sure the men had moved out of earshot, he said, "Did you see them?" He turned to look at Izzy, but she was staring open-mouthed at the dead fox.

"Izzy, are you OK?"

"They shot it!"

Ratty hesitated, then put his arm around her shoulder. "It's okay."

"It's not okay." She shrugged his arm away. "What if they had seen us, they might have shot us, too."

Ratty didn't think they would, but he couldn't be sure. "Well, I think they might have been using some sort of thermal imaging device, like on the computer game, Metal Gear Solid. As we're lying in water, it might have cooled us down slightly so we didn't register." He wasn't really sure what was going on, but he wanted to make it sound as though he was to mask his own fear.

"And why would they do that? What were they looking for?" The fear was evident in her voice.

"I don't have a clue."

"Clueless as well as stupid."

Trying to keep the disappointment and hurt out of his voice, Ratty said, "Come on, we'd better get out of here before we freeze to death." He helped Izzy out of the ditch. "I just hope they don't have scent detectors, because we stink."

"That's not funny, Ratty. This isn't a computer game. There's something strange going on here. I think we're in real trouble." She shrugged his helping hand away.

I know, Ratty thought, not just shaking from the cold as they clambered back onto the tarmac road and began walking.

***

Chase wandered from room to room, getting the feel of her new house. Now she was alone with Jane, she felt more at ease. The villagers hadn't been openly hostile or ignorant, but she had felt uneasy in their presence, especially the man with the knife. She had spoken to a couple of people and they had welcomed her to the village, but their words seemed hollow, lacking real emotion. After a couple of drinks she had excused herself and returned to the house. Jane had pocketed a couple of bottles of wine and a few nibbles, which they consumed in the back garden, enjoying the last rays of the sun as it set behind the hill.

"So what do you think of the locals?" Chase asked as they moved back into the house, the glowing embers of the coal fire offering residual warmth from the pervasive cold that had descended with the night.

"Chilled, but not in a cool sense."

"What do you mean?" Settling herself in the armchair, she tucked her feet underneath her, a glass of wine cupped in her hands.

"They just seem, I don't know, remote, as though they're not running on all cylinders. They sure ain't party animals."

Chase looked into the embers, watching sparks drift up the chimney like phoenixes. "Did you see that man with the knife?"

"Yeah, he was freaky, with a capital F."

Chase nodded. "I don't know why someone didn't stop him."

"Would you?"

Chase shook her head.

"Well, there you go then." She took a sip of her drink before putting the glass down. "As it's getting late, I think I'll text Gina rather than ringing her."

"You just don't want her to know you're drunk, although having received some of your text messages, it's hard to decipher them even when you're sober."

40

Unclipping her mobile phone from her belt, Jane said, "I'm not drunk. I'm pleasantly merry." Looking at the phone, she frowned. "There's still no damn signal available!"

Chase shrugged. She had forgotten about Drake's earlier announcement. "Perhaps it's just atmospherics because of the fog."

"Either that or we've come too far from civilisation."

She hadn't told Jane about her suspicions that Drake had been lurking around outside the wine bar. The more she thought about it, the more stupid it sounded, and she knew Jane would laugh at her.

After a couple more glasses of wine, they decided to retire to bed. Chase took the largest bedroom at the front of the house. Walking across the room to close the curtains, she noticed the moon cast a silvery glare on the sea of fog, giving it a strange luminescence. The effect was hypnotic; strange and unearthly like a vast exhaled breath from the sandman, circling the village in tides of slumber.

Pulling the curtains across, she broke the spell and turned back toward the room. For the first time, she noticed bright oblong areas on the walls where pictures had hung. Absently, she wondered who the previous owner of the house had been, and where they were now? How could anyone leave such a lovely house? The thoughts were dispelled as she heard Jane snoring softly across the hall and she smiled. Perhaps her luck was now on the up.

***

It had gone dark far too quickly for Ratty and Izzy. The mantle of fog around them took on an even more eerie aspect at night. Even though it was hard to see anything in daylight, at least the hazy illumination gave a sense of security; but at night, all sense of reality departed with the sun. Noises took on an unfamiliar resonance; the call of an owl was a wailing banshee, branches creaked with primordial timbre and the wind cast sibilant spells.

41

Izzy had gone unusually quiet after the episode with the fox; she jumped at the slightest sound. Ratty couldn't blame her; he felt scared himself in case they ran into the armed men. He didn't have a clue who the men were, but they seemed to have the advantage of being able to navigate and see in the fog. Knowing they possessed this superiority made Ratty feel naked, vulnerable and helpless.

He supposed they could be hunters, shooting for sport, but hunting what?

The fogs pervasiveness only helped to heighten Ratty's misery. His clothes were soaking wet. So were Izzy's. Her hair was plastered to her face, but she looked beautiful to Ratty no matter how dishevelled she was. Even though she teased him, Ratty felt there was an unspoken attraction between them. He was now of an age where friends of the opposite sex began to lose their familiarity; they became creatures of mystery.

"What's that?" Izzy asked, peering through the darkness.

Ratty narrowed his eyes, straining to pierce the gloom. He could just make out a luminous shape looming out of the fog. "I'm not sure," he whispered, too afraid to raise his voice in case the hunters were near by.

They crept closer to the luminous structure, watching it slowly acquire the shape and form of a white painted farmhouse. As the first floor was above the fog, the walls absorbed the moonlight, giving the ground floor an eerie lustre like a spectral lighthouse. As they got closer, Ratty saw the windows were broken, leaving fangs of glass in the beading. As the front door was hanging off its hinges, he guessed it was uninhabited and they squeezed past into the living room. The fog stayed outside, but Ratty pulled the door shut anyway.

"At least it's dry in here." Ratty wiped his face on his sleeve and stifled a yawn.

It was too dark to make out very much but he could see the building had been gutted; even the fireplace had been ripped out. He tried a light switch, but nothing happened. With Izzy following silently at his side, they walked carefully through the living room, floorboards creaking into life. Every sound made his heart lurch as he panicked that it would alert someone to their presence. What if someone was hiding upstairs, waiting to pounce on them? He knew it was stupid, that there wasn't anyone here, but he couldn't shake the notion. The men had scared him more than he realised.

Through a door at the far end of the room they found themselves in a hallway; light flooded down the stairs and putting his fears aside, Ratty ascended, drawn to the light like a moth to a flame.

It was surprising how bright the moon was after the time they had spent in the dark. From a first floor window, they could see they were above the fog, which glowed around them like a magical sea.

"We should be all right here," Ratty said, walking into a bedroom, the ceiling of which was partially collapsed and lying in a heap of plaster and wooden slats on the floor.

"All right for what?" Izzy asked, scowling.

"Just, you know, all right. At least we should be able to dry off."

"And then what?"

Ratty shrugged. He didn't know what to say. He had never seen Izzy looking so lost and forlorn. She was usually strong and resilient. He wanted to say something to encourage her, but words failed him and so he walked away to search the house for anything they could use.

When he came back with some tatty sheets, Izzy was standing looking out of the window.

"What's that?" she asked.

Ratty looked where she indicated, just able to make out what appeared to be lights in the distance. There was also a faint humming sound, carried on the wind like a sibilant lullaby and he remembered the man mentioning a generator.

"It looks like a farm or something," Izzy said.

It was the 'or something' Ratty was worried about.

Both too tired to worry about it now, Ratty took the Swiss army knife from his pocket. It had been a birthday present from his granddad. Looking at it reminded him he hadn't seen his granddad in ages and he felt a sudden pang of sadness.

Cutting the worst of the mouldy patches out of the material, he laid the sheet flat, and even though she pulled a face, Izzy crawled beneath the mouldy bed linen, too tired to complain.

Lying next to her, Ratty could smell the coconut aroma of Izzy's hair; amazed that he was so close to her, he began to think that getting lost in the fog might not be so bad after all. He debated whether to put an arm around her, but decided against it. He lay listening to her breathing and the house settle until his eyes began to close and sleep laid claim.

He didn't know how long he slept, but it was still dark when he was abruptly woken by a noise and his eyes sprang open like shutters. For a moment he was disorientated, wondering where he was; then the memory returned.

The light of the moon was just enough to allow him to see and his eyes surveyed the room, settling on the dark area where the ceiling had collapsed. He held his breath, straining his ears when he heard voices outside.

Thinking it might be a search party out looking for them, he started to rise.

Then he remembered the men with guns, and he decided to stay still.

He wasn't prepared to risk the second option.

Whoever those men had been, he instinctively knew he didn't want to be found by them. His heart felt as though a blacksmith pummelled it. Goosebumps prickled his arms.

Paralysed by fear, he stared at the door.

At his side, Izzy stirred but didn't wake.

Ratty shivered.

Downstairs, the front door creaked open.

Chapter 5

Ratty couldn't move. He wanted to wake Izzy, but he was afraid that if he woke her, she might scream and alert the men to their presence.

The situation was made worse because he couldn't tell where the voices were coming from, or what they were saying. Lying as still as he could, even his breathing seemed too loud and he was terrified they would hear it. What if the men had seen their exhaled breath emanating from the window like a smoke signal? Perhaps that's why they were here. He knew it was a foolish notion, but he couldn't help it. He was in a strange place; it was dark and he was scared.

Downstairs, a floorboard creaked.

Ratty's heart stopped beating and his balls went into hibernation.

They were in the house.

But what if it really was a search party? It was only natural that their parents would be missing them and be looking for them. The thought made sense, and he had almost convinced himself that the men were here to rescue them, but he couldn't get the vision of the fox out of his head.

One of the stairs groaned as weight was applied to it.

They were coming up.

As if confirming his worst suspicions, he heard one of the men speak. "I'm going to have a look upstairs. If I find them, get ready to grab..."

"Hold it, Jock. Roger that control. Over. Come on, there's a disturbance in the village. Everyone's needed."

The stair groaned again and Ratty lay listening as the men walked away, his lips sucked into his mouth, pensive before he relaxed and let out a sigh of relief. It was a search party all right, but he didn't .feel that it would be in his best interests to be found.

***

When Ratty woke, sunlight had replaced the moonbeams. Izzy stirred at his side. Her arm was draped over his chest and he was loath to move in case it broke the spell, in case he was still dreaming. He closed his eyes once more, savouring the moment. He had hardly slept after the men had gone. He had been too scared that they would return.

"Is that your stomach rumbling?" Izzy asked, bringing him out of his reverie.

Ratty opened his eyes. "Yes, sorry. I thought you were asleep?"

"I couldn't sleep. You snore like a pig." She took her arm back.

"Thanks!" But he knew she was lying, otherwise she would have mentioned last nights events. He decided that it was better not to tell her about it in case it freaked her out.

"I'm starving. How are we going to find our way home?" Throwing back the sheet, she stood up.

Ratty couldn't think how to reply.

Daylight didn't improve the decor of the abandoned house; in fact it showed up more of its faults. Cracks streaked across the bare plastered walls and cobwebs rounded out any sharp edges like grim coving. Bare floorboards creaked under Izzy's foot, the sound less distinct in the cold light of day than it had been at night.

Casting off the sheet, Ratty stood up and went to look out of the window. He looked down at the veil of fog, trying to see if anyone was hiding outside the house. Although the fog was dense, he couldn't see anyone, and he relaxed slightly.

The sun had already risen, but he wasn't wearing a watch so he didn't know what time it was. He looked across to where he had seen the lights the night before, but couldn't see anything save the omnipresent fog and a smudge of trees that looked like shadows in the mist. Izzy came to stand at his side.

"You look filthy," he said.

46

"So do you," she replied.

"We'd better make a move. At least the daylight will let us see a bit better." Looking at the fog, he was unconvinced by his own words.

Izzy reached in her pocket and took out a cigarette. She lit it and blew out a steady stream of smoke. "We're in the shit."

Ratty bit his lip. He wanted to say something inspiring; something to alleviate their predicament, but the words just wouldn't come. "Yes, I think we are," he eventually said. "Come on, let's get out of here."

The fog lingered outside the front door like a vampire, waiting to be invited in. Stepping into it, the cold chill returned and both of them shivered. Ratty had taken stock of where they were relevant to where the lights had been shining and he thought he knew the way, but now he was back in the fog, all sense of direction was lost. North, south, east, west, it was all immaterial, they were just points on a compass he didn't have. He didn't even know if heading toward the lights was the best option, but it was the only one they had.

He felt Izzy grab his hand, and he took support from her touch. "This way, come on," he said, starting to walk in what he hoped was the right direction.

***

Chase woke feeling bleary eyed. She had woken numerous times during the night, partly because she was sleeping in a strange house, but also because she was sure that she had heard someone screaming and shouting. She had even got out of bed to look out of the window, but it was too dark to see anything so she guessed she had imagined it. Being haunted by the uneasy feeling there had been a mistake and she shouldn't be here didn't help.

Throwing back the sheet, she slipped out of bed, the cold floor on her bare feet making her shiver. Walking to the window, she drew back the curtains, surprised to see the fog was still here, circling the village like a wolf closing in for the kill. The sun sat above it like a bloodshot eye. Shivering at the thought, she dressed and shouted to Jane who gave a mumbled reply. Chase laughed and went down to the kitchen.

The cupboards were almost bare but she found a jar of coffee, milk, bread, butter and jam that was all fresh. After making a drink, she took one up to Jane.

"Come on lazy bones," she said, entering Jane's room and opening the curtains.

"Bright light, bright light," Jane squealed, drawing the sheet over her head.

"It's another glorious day in Paradise."

"Hallelujah, praise be to the Lord," Jane mumbled.

"Now, now. I've made you a cup of coffee. Drink it before it goes cold."

"So this wasn't some bad dream. We really are in the country."

"Yes, now get up." She tugged the bed sheet down to reveal Jane's face.

"A little bit further and you'll see paradise all right."

Chase shook her head and raised her eyebrows in exasperation. "Don't you ever think about anything else?"

"What else is there?" Jane sat up, the sheet slipping down her bare torso.

Chase laughed. "Gravity's a bitch."

"These are the real deal."

"Well they haven't improved with age, now put 'em away and drink your coffee." She walked out of the room, grinning.

Downstairs, she studied the fireplace before tackling the ashes. There was a full bucket of coal and a pile of logs stacked by the hearth and she set about making her first real fire. By the time Jane came downstairs, the room was full of smoke without flames and Chase had given up.

"Sugar, you'll freeze to death if you can't light a fire. Open that window and let me show you how I can get anything hot." She winked and began to redo what Chase

48

had started. Within fifteen minutes, a fire was roaring in the hearth and Chase went through to the kitchen to toast some bread.

When Chase came back with the toast, Jane said, "You should just throw your toast in the fire in future, it's burnt more than those logs were."

"Choke on it."

Shaking her head, Jane said, "What will you do without me?"

"I'll manage."

"That's what I'm afraid of. Are you sure you want to stay here? This just isn't you."

Chase looked down the hillside, admiring the view. "It is now."

Jane crunched on her toast. "Good job I like it burnt."

***

After breakfast, Chase put a fireguard around the fire and then they both went to explore the village and to buy some supplies. It was a warm day and the trees rustled and swayed as though in reverence.

Chase noticed curtains twitching in some of the houses, as though disturbed by a slight breeze. She didn't mention it to Jane. Halfway down the lane, they passed the grey haired old lady Chase had seen in the hall. She was weeding her garden.

"Hello, again," Chase said.

The lady looked up and nodded imperceptibly before turning away.

"Friendly old soul," Jane mumbled.

Chase shrugged. "The city hasn't got the monopoly on weirdoes."

At the bottom of the lane they turned left onto a narrower lane that led to a general store called 'Necessities'. Entering the shop, a bell jangled above the door.

The first thing Chase noticed was that all of the products on the shelves were in the same white-labelled tins with only the name of the contents printed on the label. It made the store appear sanitary, like a medical room.

"Weird," Jane mumbled, voicing Chase's thoughts.

In response to the bell, a middle-aged woman stepped from the rear of the shop. Her hair was long and straggly and her eyes were dark and threatening. She wiped one hand on her apron. In the other she had a knife. She smiled when she saw Chase and Jane and she stabbed the knife into the wooden counter, letting the handle sway like a deadly metronome.

"Anything you want, just let me know, my dears," she drawled.

"Thank you," Chase said as she perused the shelves. Perhaps it was the knife, but the woman made her feel uncomfortable. What was it about knives around here?

Although strangely packaged, the shop was well stocked, seeming to provide most of the necessities, if not the luxuries, needed to survive.

"Why's everything in this white packaging?" Jane asked.

"It's the fog my dear. Since the fog arrived, the army has been supplying our food."

"What do they do, dip it in the fog to give it this shade of white?" Jane picked up a tin and inspected it.

The woman either didn't seem to notice Jane's remark, or she ignored it. "They call them army rations. Come from an emergency supply I was told, just for occasions like this."

Chase frowned. "So how long has the fog been here?"

"It gets hard to remember. A long time."

"So how do you get out, you know, to visit people?" Jane asked.

"Get out. We don't get out, my dear. It's the fog, you see."

"So why hasn't the fog disappeared?" Chase asked, interrupting Jane.

"I don't rightly know, my dear. You would have to ask someone else. They did tell us something..." She scratched her chin, her dark eyes distant, lost in thought.

"Now will you reconsider coming home?" Jane pursed

50

her lips.

"I am home, Jane. Please, we agreed."

"But the fog!" She leaned closer and whispered, "And the people!"

"Well there must be a good reason." She looked back at the woman behind the counter who still seemed to have a remote, frowning look on her face, as though struggling to remember something.

"It's not just the place that's fogged around here." Jane looked at the woman and shook her head.

Abruptly the woman snapped out of her reverie. "Now what was it you wanted?"

"Answers," Jane said.

"Do they come in a tin or a packet my dear?" the woman asked. "If we haven't got them, I can always ask them to bring some next time they come with the deliveries."

Chase and Jane stared at the woman, waiting for her to laugh. She didn't.

Jane looked at Chase and frowned, rolling her eyes.

"No, answers to questions," Jane said.

"You're welcome to look if we've got any. Now, if you'll excuse me, I've got some work to do. Just give me a shout if you need me, otherwise just help yourself and take what you want." She yanked the knife back out of the counter and walked into the back of the shop, out of sight.

"Was she serious?" Jane asked.

"I don't know. I... I don't think so... was she?"

"Loony tunes." Jane made circles with her forefinger at the side of her head.

"Perhaps she was just joking."

"Well she isn't Norman Wisdom because I aren't laughing."

"Come on, let's go. I'll come back later for some food." She needed some fresh air. For some inexplicable reason, the woman had disturbed her.

As Chase opened the door, the bell jangled again and the woman walked back into the shop.

"Can I help you?" she asked.

.

Chase shook her head. "Thank you, but we're just leaving."

The woman frowned. "Leaving? You haven't come in yet!"

"We *were* just inside. Don't you remember?"

"Crazy," Jane mumbled. "Come on, let's get out of here."

Inclined to agree, Chase let the door shut behind her.

"Ah, I see you've met Ms Woods."

"Excuse me!" Chase turned to face the young man who had spoken. He had a slim build with rugged good looks. His nose looked slightly off centre, as though it had been punched and his blue eyes held her attention with their clarity. He had medium length, tousled brown hair and a warm, compassionate smile. She noticed his eyes momentarily linger on Jane's prominent bosom, and she silently cursed her friend's plentiful bounty.

"My name is Adam White. Doctor Adam White." He extended his hand and Chase shook it, feeling a flush of embarrassment.

"Black and white," Jane murmured into Chase's ear, making a connection between their surnames. "If you've got to have a man, I suppose you could do worse."

Chase felt her cheeks flush a deeper shade of red in case Dr White heard. "Erm, yes, Ms Woods, is that the lady's name?" Chase asked.

"Yes, I'm afraid she suffers from a mild form of dementia." He must have seen the worried look on Chase's face as he said, "I can assure you, it's nothing to be afraid of. She's harmless."

Chase had never heard of a mild form of dementia.

"I bet that's what they said about Jack the Ripper," Jane sneered.

"You must be Chase Black," he said, ignoring Jane's comment.

"Is it that obvious?"

Jane sniggered. "Small town England where the village grape vine is quicker than the Internet."

"Something like that," Adam agreed.

52

"Well yes, you are right and this is my best friend, Jane."

"Pleased to meet you." He gave Jane a perfunctory nod and turned back to Chase. "I'm sorry I couldn't be at the gathering yesterday, but I had an urgent matter to deal with."

Gathering! The word conjured up images of witches in her mind.

"Someone stub their toe, doc?" Jane asked.

Adam laughed. "You'd be surprised. We have our little dramas now and again."

"Yeah, like watching television soaps like Emmerdale. I bet it's hot to trot when the surgery opens."

Adam grinned, revealing perfect teeth. "I'm sure you think we're a little out of touch here, but we do have our moments, like tea at the vicar's, dancing round the maypole, oh yes, it has its moments." He winked at Chase and she laughed in response.

"That hit my funny bone, doc," Jane said, folding her arms across her chest and walking toward a bench at the edge of the lane where she sat, scowling.

"Your friend's hard to please."

"She's not a country girl. I think she misses the smog, it's her drug."

"And you?"

Chase blushed again. "I think I'm going to be happy enough here."

Adam nodded his head and smiled. "I'm glad about that."

"So am I." After his earlier inspection of Jane's bust, she thought he was going to be a typical male lecher. But perhaps she was wrong.

"You will have to visit me at the surgery, so I can get your details and sign you onto my register."

"Yes, I'll come in soon."

"Promise?"

"Promise."

Adam smiled again and walked into the shop.

"That was a bit rude," Chase said as she walked toward Jane.

"So sue me. I can't help the way I am. Men just bring out the worst in me."

"Well, if I didn't know better, I would think you were jealous that he seemed more interested in me, than you. But you could try to be nice. Remember, I've got to live here when you've gone."

Jane tutted indignantly. "How could you think such a thing? Can we go now?"

Chase laughed. "Come on then, let's see what else there is to see around here."

"Oh joy!"

They walked further along the lane, not speaking to each other. Chase thought about the doctor. She thought he was quite attractive and she felt a momentary pang of guilt as she remembered Mat. Even though it had been nearly four months since he had disappeared, there was no closure on the relationship; she still loved him and she felt guilty having feelings for someone else.

She suddenly wondered how Mat would find her out here? That's if he ever came back. Perhaps it would serve him right if she did meet someone else. Let him worry for a change.

At the edge of the village, they came to a public house that listed as though drunk. A sign swung from a pole above the porch: The Slaughtered Dog.

"Charming. Isn't anything about this place normal?" Jane shook her head.

"Compared to some of the places you go, this place is the Vatican!"

"Well, at least we can get a drink."

They walked to the front door and Chase gave it a push, but it wouldn't open. She looked at her watch. "Too early."

"Great, perhaps this is the Vatican."

"It isn't going to work you know."

"What isn't?"

"This hard-assed act of yours. You know I'm staying."

"Well, you can't blame me for trying."

"I'll never get a chance like this again. Things like this

54

just don't happen everyday. Can't we just enjoy it. It might be a while before I see you again."

"Don't say that."

"Well, it's true."

"At least I know I'll be leaving you in capable hands."

Chase playfully punched Jane on the shoulder. "How does Gina put up with you?"

"That reminds me." She unclipped her mobile phone from her belt and shook her head. "Still no signal."

"Perhaps there's a problem with the network."

Jane put her phone away and sighed. "I need to find Drake or Moon to find out how I'm getting back to civilisation."

"Jane wanting a man, now there's a first."

"Hey sugar, leave the jokes to me."

"Wait till I tell Gina."

"Now you know she wouldn't believe a word of it."

"*No one gets out of paradise*," Chase said, imitating Ms Woods, the shopkeeper.

Jane shook her head and rolled her eyes.

Chase laughed. "You're right though. I don't know how to find Moon or Drake. It's a bit strange how they disappeared. We'll have to take a look around and see if we can find them."

"Great, bring it on. More sight seeing."

"You love it really."

"For you, sugar. Only for you."

They headed back toward the village hall, hoping there would be someone there who might be able to help them. The church had an adjoining graveyard that they circumnavigated to get to the hall. As they passed, Chase peered over the low surrounding wall. A lot of the graves seemed old, the inscriptions on the headstones obscured by mould and lichen. Angels and cherubs were dotted here and there, seemingly frozen beneath a Medusa stare. None of the graves had fresh flowers on them, which she found somewhat odd for what she assumed was a close-knit community. The fog drifted lazily at the edge of the graveyard, wispy threads breaking off from the main body and gliding among the graves, increasing the eerie feel, even in daylight.

Suddenly, Chase thought she saw a figure in the fog, motionless, all in white like a ghost, watching her. Before she could mention it to Jane, the figure disappeared into the fog like a wraith.

Chase shuddered and folded her arms across her chest. Perhaps she had just imagined it?

The door to the hall was open and Chase knocked. Receiving no reply, she entered, followed by Jane. A few tables were still laden with the remnants of the buffet, but the drinks had gone. Paper doilies were scattered over the floor like giant snowflakes.

"Hello, is anyone here?" Chase felt suddenly anxious.

Movement on one of the tables caught her eye and she turned just as a paper doily drifted down from the table to join the others on the floor.

Something moved on the tabletop. Chase froze, narrowing her eyes before she squealed.

"What is it? What's the matter?" Jane demanded.

"On the table. It's a rat," Chase said, backing away.

Jane cautiously walked toward the table. "Rat my ass. It's a squirrel."

Chase stopped backing away and laughed with relief as she saw the bushy tail of a grey squirrel scampering across the table. It stopped, eyeing Chase for a moment before it took up a remnant of the buffet food in its tiny paw and sat back on its haunches, watching the two of them as it ate.

"You'll never get very far in the country if you can't tell the difference between a rat and a squirrel."

As though in agreement, the squirrel chattered and scampered out of the door.

"You've upset the locals now." Jane laughed.

"Well, it did look like a rat if you only caught a glimpse of it."

"A good job it wasn't a cat because I'd hate to see what you'd make of that!"

"Screw you."

"I wish."

At that moment a man coughed and both girls jumped.

"Vicar!" Chase blushed as she noticed who had drawn their attention. The vicar was instantly recognisable by the dog collar constricting his neck below his double chin. He was balding, what hair he did have slicked back across his crown. His cheeks were ruddy, as though through exertion or alcohol.

"Sorry to startle you like that. It's just I thought I heard voices."

"Yes, we were just looking for Mr. Moon or Drake," Chase said.

"Ah, yes. I remember seeing you last night. You've moved into High Top Cottage, I believe."

"Yes, I have."

"Well, I hope you know what you've done." He shook his head, as though lamenting.

"Pardon?" Chase said, unsure what the vicar was implying.

"Yes, the congregation has been dwindling lately. I think the fog has made them lose faith. But now, perhaps I can encourage you to join my flock?"

"Fat chance," Jane mumbled.

The vicar cocked his ear toward Jane. "You'll have to speak up a bit."

"I said, good chance. She's an old Sunday school girl, aren't you Chase."

"Ah good, that's what I like to hear." The vicar smiled and nodded graciously.

Chase pulled a face at Jane that the vicar couldn't see. "So do you know where we can find Mr. Moon or Drake?" she asked, turning back to face the vicar.

"Haven't got a clue, my dear. They appear now and again. I'm sure they'll turn up. Now, where were we, ah yes, the congregation."

Chase sighed and Jane sniggered as they listened to the vicar sermonising on the state of the church, the state of the parishioners and the state of the hall. It was fifteen minutes later before Chase managed to make their excuses and leave - and she still didn't know how to find Moon or Drake.

They spent the rest of the morning exploring. Chase couldn't get over how quaint the cottages looked. It was as though they were part of a bygone age, and she still couldn't believe she had won one of them. It was a dream come true.

When they had explored the village, they ventured around the rear of the hill, following a leaf shaded lane through a copse of trees until they came to a dilapidated farmhouse. The outbuildings had been left to rot, the frame of the large barn a series of decaying beams like rotten teeth; rusty metal panels creaked and groaned in the wind. The farmhouse windows had been smashed, the roof had caved in and the front door swung on its hinges, beckoning.

"What a waste," Chase said, admiring the building.

Jane frowned.

"I bet it was beautiful before being abandoned. Come on, let's have a look inside."

Jane pulled a face. "What for?"

"Why not?"

"Do you really need to ask? It's crumbling."

"Where's your sense of adventure?"

"Back with my sense of humour."

"Well, I'm going inside." She walked toward the door.

Jane sighed and traipsed along behind her, kicking her heels like a petulant infant.

The door creaked as Chase pushed it open and stepped inside. Broken glass crunched underfoot like the dry carapaces of long dead insects. Flowery wallpaper peeled from the walls, the design faded like an old tattoo. The smell of decay filled the air, wet and fungal.

Remnants of furniture littered the room; the skeletal frame of an armchair, a smashed bureau, and a cabinet overturned like a coffin, the hinged door of which was open and inviting morbid inspection. Unable to resist, Chase approached, curious. Her action was more to show Jane that she would be all right on her own, but it didn't stop her feeling apprehensive about looking inside. She knew it was stupid. After all, it was only a cabinet. She gripped the edge and leaned over.

Something stirred in the shadows.

Chase jumped, her heart fluttering.

In a flurry of motion, a white, ghostly spectre flew screeching toward her face. A beady black eye glinted as a razor sharp blade made to cut her. Chase stumbled back, tripping over her own feet. She fell to the floor, shielding her face as the spectre swooped.

Chase screamed and closed her eyes, her heart dancing a fandango.

"Shoo, get away," Jane said.

Puzzled, Chase couldn't understand why Jane wasn't screaming too, and she cautiously dropped her hands from her face and opened her eyes in time to see the pigeon fly out of the window.

"Stupid bird," Jane muttered. "And I'm not on about the feathered one. Didn't you know that it was only a bird?" She looked at Chase and shook her head. "What are you like?" Reaching down she helped Chase to her feet.

Chase blushed. Her fertile imagination had cultivated the seeds of illusion.

Dusting herself down, she shrugged. "It could have happened to anyone."

"Only someone stupid enough to want to come into a derelict building!"

Ignoring her, Chase said, "Come on, let's see what's in the next room."

"Don't you ever learn?"

Chase grinned and wrinkled her nose. In the next room, there were two doors, one at the far end and one on her right which led to the stairs; it was blocked by debris from when the roof had collapsed, but it was the makeshift bed in the corner of the room that grabbed her attention. Next to it was a small camp stove and some jars of food.

"Jane, look at this."

Jane walked through the door. "What is it now, another

rat?"

"I think someone's living here. Look."

"Well, I've seen people live in worse places."

"But you don't expect it, you know, not out here, in the country."

"Well, let's just make like an omelette and beat it."

"I wonder who it is?"

"Who cares, come on sugar, let's go."

A door creaked at the rear of the house. Someone coughed, a deep and phlegmy sound.

Chase froze.

"Come on, let's get out of here," Jane whispered. "Now." She tugged at Chase's arm.

Chase backed out of the room, trying to be as quiet as she could, but she was sure her heart was beating loud enough to be heard.

For once, even Jane looked worried.

Exiting the house, they ran along the lane. Chase glanced over her shoulder and was relieved when she didn't see anyone in pursuit; not that she really expected to see anyone. They hadn't done anything wrong so why would anyone come after them? She was being foolish and she slowed to a walk. Jane stopped altogether and leaned over with her hands on her waist as if she was going to be sick. Wiping sweat from her brow, Chase took deep breaths and sat beneath the shade of an oak tree at the side of the lane. She couldn't remember the last time she had run so fast.

"Who do you think was living in that derelict building?" Chase asked between breaths.

"Who cares? But if they want to live there, it's not someone you or I would want to know."

"Perhaps we shouldn't have run away."

"Run away! I call it a tactical withdrawal. In other words, we got our metaphorical tails out of there."

"Yes, but it does seem a bit stupid now, doesn't it?"

"Sugar, if you want to live in the middle of nowhere, stupid is as good as it gets."

Chase rolled her eyes.

"Perhaps it was the man with the knife?" Jane ventured.

"That's comforting."

"Well you asked."

Chase sighed. "Well, we're going to have to go and buy some food. My stomach's rumbling like a freight train and I could do with a drink. Come on, shake your metaphoric tail." She laughed as Jane scowled at her.

"Can't a girl catch her breath first?"

"In that top, you'll catch more than your breath."

Jane pushed her bosom out even more. "If you've got it, flaunt it."

Chase smiled. Inside she was cringing. It wasn't that Jane embarrassed her, but from what she had seen, she didn't think Paradise was the right place to let it all hang out.

Chapter 6

As Chase and Jane walked down the lane to the general store, the sun was high in the sky. The occasional curtain still twitched, as though moved by inquisitive whispers, but the village remained quiet, as though still sleeping. A bird whistled a mournful tune in the distance, but nothing replied.

"Happening place isn't it," Jane said, shaking her head.

"It's called getting back to nature. People pay a premium to live in a place like this."

"Well, I'd want a refund. Nature is for the golden oldies. Me, I want the bright lights, not a retirement home."

Chase disagreed. She loved Paradise. It was quintessentially English, and it had an attractive doctor that she wouldn't mind being ministered to by. She smiled to herself, the wicked thoughts making her blush. She hoped Jane didn't notice.

As they entered the shop, Ms Woods came scuttling out of the back room. Chase was thankful that this time, the shopkeeper was unarmed.

"Hello my dears, are you new around here?" Ms Woods asked, wiping her hands on her apron.

"We came in this morning," Chase replied, perusing the shelves.

"No, not this morning. Shop was shut this morning. Are you new around here?"

Chase looked at Jane and pulled a quizzical expression.

"Bats in the belfry." Jane shook her head.

"Oh you've seen them, have you," Ms Woods said. "I've told the vicar but he won't believe me. Come out at night they do, swooping and flitting. Nasty, horrible things. You can hear them... only come out at night though."

"What do?" Chase asked.

"Bats."

"Oh, I see."

Jane laughed.

Chase picked up a shopping basket and selected some of the white labelled tins from the shelves: beans, spaghetti, tinned carrots, pasta sauce, potatoes, tomatoes, curry sauce. She also took a couple of cartons of orange juice out of the fridge. They were deliciously cool and she rubbed one of them across her brow.

"You'd better hope none of those labels come off," Jane said, "otherwise, you could end up with curry on your spotted dick."

Ignoring Jane's remark, Chase went to pay for the shopping, eager to leave the shop and its clinical atmosphere. She felt anxious around people with mental problems. It was as though they existed in another reality, one that didn't have borders of acceptability, right from wrong, past from present; they lived in the twilight zone of their own minds. She still couldn't understand how Ms Woods was allowed to carry on working, not when her brain seemed to be blowing fuses like candles on a birthday cake.

"Will that be all?" Ms Woods asked.

Chase nodded and took out her purse.

"Oh no. Don't worry about that. It's all free due to the fog. Emergency rations, you see."

Chase looked surprised. "Free!" Perhaps Ms Woods mental problem was worse than she thought, and if it was, she couldn't take liberties and walk off without paying.

Before Ms Woods could reply, Jane dropped more items into the basket. "If it's free," she said, shrugging.

"Go right ahead," Ms Woods said. "All I have to do is tick the items off on my list." She picked up a pen and a clipboard and started to stab the pen into the board, her tongue poking out of the corner of her mouth like a bloated leech.

Chase took a step back, momentarily uneasy. "Let's get out of here," she said, turning and hurrying outside with her shopping. She felt guilty walking out of the shop without paying and she expected Ms Woods to come charging after her with the knife, shouting, 'Thief, stop, thief." Looking back at the shop, she saw Ms Woods had stopped stabbing the clipboard and was now writing on her arm, pressing hard enough to draw blood, her countenance like a grotesque gargoyle. Chase shook her head, startled. She wondered whether to try and stop her?

"Did you see that?" she asked.

Jane nodded. "Now you must see how stupid it is to want to live here? It's dangerous. There's something *wrong* about this place. Come home with me."

"Home to what? There's nothing there for me any more."

"There's more than there is here."

Chase shook her head. "I've been given an opportunity and I'm not going to waste it."

"Well just promise me you'll think about it. And remember, there'll always be a home for you with Gina and me."

Chase grinned. "In your bed you mean?"

Jane bit her lip and turned away.

Looking back, Chase saw Ms Woods waving at her, a rivulet of blood and ink rolling down her arm like a grotesque exclamation mark.

***

Walking up Slaughter Hill, Chase noticed the village was still quiet; everyone was still indoors. *Or in hiding.* She didn't know where the strange thought came from, but it sent a chill down her spine and gooseflesh erupted along her arms like volcanoes.

It was certainly a strange village, but she was loath to talk to Jane about it, as she would use it as more ammunition to try and get her to leave. She absently wondered where the name Slaughter Hill had come from; the image of virgin sacrifices to a pagan God suddenly invaded her head, and she was glad that she wouldn't be on that particular list.

Back at the house, Chase prepared a quick pasta meal with a tin of sauce. The smell made her feel slightly

64

nauseous and again she wondered if she was coming down with something.

As Chase cooked, Jane stoked the fire. She shouted from the living room, "If the food's free, perhaps it isn't so bad living here after all!"

Chase grinned and stirred the sauce. "You'll be wanting to move out here yourself next."

"I wouldn't go that far."

"Oh I don't know. At least you and Gina would give the locals something to talk about."

"I think you and the doc will give them plenty to be going on with."

Chase blushed the same colour as the sauce she was stirring.

The meal was bland and unexciting, and when they had finished, they both retired to the living room. The fire roared away in the hearth, giving out waves of heat. Chase watched the flames, mesmerised until she fell asleep, overcome by a tiredness that penetrated down to her bones.

It was dark when she woke and the fire had burnt down. Soft moonlight filtered through the window and she sat up, wondering how she could have slept so long? She yawned and stretched, easing life back into her body.

"Jane, wake up." She looked at the chair where she had last seen Jane, but it was empty. Walking to the foot of the stairs she shouted up, but her call fell flat as the walls absorbed the sound like water in a sponge.

Thinking that Jane might be dead to the world, she walked up the stairs, knocked on Jane's door and entered. The room was empty. Chase frowned. Where the hell is she? The wardrobe door was open and Chase walked toward it and peered inside. All of Jane's clothes were gone. There was nothing left to suggest anyone had even been here.

Her heart started beating faster and she ran to the front bedroom. Pale moonlight illuminated the walls, giving the room an ethereal quality, but Jane wasn't there.

What the hell was going on?

For a brief moment, she thought that Jane might be

playing a trick on her, but she knew Jane wasn't like that.

"JANE." Panicking, she ran down the stairs, calling her friends name. Perhaps she had fallen and knocked herself out, she thought. But that wouldn't explain why her things were gone. Outside the back door, the garden was a wash of cold, silvery light, nocturnal blooms nodding in the slight breeze that caressed her face. "Jane, are you out here?"

A dark shadow flitted across the moon, swooping and pirouetting as it cast its silhouette across the garden like a demented shadow puppet show.

The bats had come out of the belfry and Jane was gone.

Chapter 7

She searched the house for any sign of Jane, but there was nothing. Even the dishes had been washed and put away. It was as though she had never even been here. All trace of her had been removed. Think, damn it, she thought. Where could she have gone? Why didn't she wake me? More to the point, why didn't I hear her and wake up anyway? Thoughts surged through her mind like a raging river, but no answers washed up.

The house was cold. The fire had gone out a long time ago. It slowly dawned on her that she was alone in the house and a chill swept through her. At night, now she was alone, the character of the house was different, changed. As though it sensed her fear, the walls closed in; the ceiling pressed down. The effect made her feel claustrophobic and she ran out of the front door to breathe in a deep lungfull of fresh air. Walking to the bottom of the garden, she looked back at the house. The lights she had switched on illuminated the windows with a crystal veneer, a facade for the hollowness that lay within. When she had company, the house was warm and inviting, but now, it was cold, aged with secrets. She knew houses had a character of their own, the walls imbued with the identity of who lived in them; this one seemed to have a Jeckyl and Hyde character and again she wondered who had previously lived in it.

A thought occurred to her, and she went back into the house and up to her bedroom. Rummaging in her handbag, she took out her mobile phone; a text message was waiting for her but there was still no signal available to make calls. Chase frowned, puzzled. Accessing the message she read:

Chase. Moon showed up. Told me I had the chance to leave, so I took it. Didn't want to wake you. Be in touch, Jane x

Chase read the message several times. It didn't seem right. The syntax was wrong. Jane never wasted time spelling all of the words out properly. It should have read something like:

```
Chs. Moon shwd up. 2ld me Id th chnc 2
lev, so I hv. Dnt wnt 2 wke u. B in
tuch, Jne.
```

Jane's text messages were usually such a cryptic nightmare you needed the Enigma machine to decode them. This just wasn't right.

"Damn it. Jane, where are you?" A seed of fear was growing in her gut, and her heart beat rapidly. She bit her thumbnail, thinking. After a moment she grabbed a green parka jacket from the hallway and left the house.

Clouds shrouded the moon, the darkness pressing down. As she walked along the lane, something rustled in the hedge and her heart skipped a beat. There were only occasional streetlights to guide her way, and as she approached one, her shadow crept up behind her like a stalker.

The night felt oppressive. She felt vulnerable and exposed. Her footsteps seemed unnaturally loud, echoing. She wondered why sound was amplified in the dark, why the night became a stage for the minds invention. She quickened her pace. The houses on the hill were in darkness; she could almost believe she was the only resident of Paradise. Perhaps Jane was not the only one to have left?

At the bottom of the lane, she headed toward the pub. The sign outside creaked as the breeze played it. The Slaughtered Dog. Slaughter Hill. The names seemed out of place in Paradise.

A single light burned in the porch, circled by moths like the dark droplets of a macabre chandelier. She could hear the beat of their wings as they flitted around the bulb, a papery, dried leaf cadence. Opening the door, she nervously walked inside.

The first thing she noticed was how dimly lit the interior was; darkness crouched in the corners. The optics behind the bar glinted with the reflections of the dim, nicotine stained lighting. Round wooden tables sprouted from the wooden floor like bizarre mushrooms in an Alice in Wonderland pastiche. Walking toward the bar, she sensed more than saw that people were sitting silently in the corners of the room, hidden in the shadows. She could feel their eyes, watching her and she swallowed, trying to wet her dry throat. What am I afraid of? she wondered.

A man sat behind the bar. He had a heavyset face and bushy eyebrows shading small, beady eyes. His thin hair was lifeless, greasy, and his checked shirt was stained with something that resembled blood, but which was more likely tomato sauce. He stood up as she approached and she noticed there was a walking stick leaning against the wall that he didn't use, limping slightly as he ambled down the bar to where she stood.

"Yes?" he grunted.

"Hello, I'm looking for..."

"Miss Black, how nice to see you again."

Chase turned to see Moon standing behind her. He wore a cocksure smile like a mask. She hadn't heard him enter so she assumed he had already been in the bar, hiding in the shadows, which would have been easy enough as he was wearing a dark suit.

"Mr. Moon, just the person I'm looking for. It's about my friend, Jane."

"Ah yes, she seemed quite eager to return home when I called at your house earlier."

"You came to the house?"

"Yes, you were fast asleep. I imagine it's a result of all the excitement. Yes, your friend..." his smile faltered slightly as he said the word 'friend', "We arranged for her to be flown home. I advised her not to wake you as you looked worn out."

"She wouldn't have left without telling me." Her voice rose slightly.

"I'm sure you will see her again soon. Now, how are you settling in?"

"What time did she go?"

"Let me see, it would have been about five-thirty, or thereabouts."

"And what time is it now?"

Moon looked at his watch. "Ten-fifteen."

"I slept all this time!" It was not a question. "Jane wouldn't have left without waking me, I know she wouldn't."

"What are you implying, that she was abducted against her will?" Moon laughed without mirth. "Now, now miss Black, I can assure you she was only thinking of you. Now let me buy you a drink, and perhaps George here can rustle you up something to eat, you must be hungry?"

Although she hadn't thought about it, as soon as Moon mentioned her being hungry, it acted like a catalyst, making her stomach rumble. It was almost as though by voicing it, he had made her hungry.

"I would hazard a guess you are a white wine drinker?"

"Forget the wine. I need to speak to Jane."

Ignoring her, Moon ordered two white wines and George shuffled down the bar to pour the drinks.

"And George," Moon called after him, "Rustle up a nice salad and baked potato for our newest resident, let's make her feel at home, there's a good chap."

Chase noticed George glance back; the dim lights glinted in his eyes making them look feral and she shivered.

"Come, let us sit down," Moon said when George returned with the drinks. He walked to one of the mushroom tables where he seated himself.

Chase followed, the chilled wine cradled in her hands. She felt slightly light headed even before taking a sip. Sitting down, she could sense people around her, like cats stalking prey; the scraping sound of a chair being moved was like fingernails drawn down a chalkboard. She winced. Somebody coughed, and quiet chatter bubbled out of the darkness. Looking down at the table, she noticed it had been slashed, gouged. Remembering the man in the hall with the knife, she tried to make words out of the gashes, but Moon put his drink down and leaned forward, casting a dark shadow that obscured the table.

Chase sat back, feeling threatened. "I will need to go home myself, to pick things up." She needed to see Jane. Even if it was only to ask her why she left without a word. Moon was lying. He had to be. But why? She couldn't believe her best friend had just gone. It just didn't feel right. She couldn't have left. She just couldn't. It made her think of Mat. He had left her too. Why did everybody leave her?

"You are home," Moon said, fingering his wine glass.

"No, I mean my former home. My *real* home. This is still all too new to me. It's too much."

"This is your real home. You can't leave," Moon said, leaning back in his chair.

"What do you mean, I can't leave?"

"There are no more flights scheduled for a while."

"Well goddamn schedule one then. There are things I need to do." She could feel rage bubbling below the surface.

"I can assure you when a transport is available, I'll let you know."

"Well that's not good enough, I need-"

"Miss Black. Chase, how nice to see you again."

Chase looked up to see the doctor, Adam White standing beside her. He was dressed casually in a blue, short-sleeved shirt and gray trousers.

"Would you mind if I joined you?"

"Doctor White, be my guest," Moon said, his hands steepled together on the table.

"How are you settling in?" Adam asked, sitting next to Chase.

"I was fine until Jane disappeared. Now Mr. Moon has told me that I can't leave the village." She felt like a virtual prisoner, trapped by circumstance beyond her control.

"Well, if you'll excuse me." Moon stood up.

"Hold on a minute." Chase started to stand, but the room began to spin, the walls turning, twisting. She felt a cold sweat steal over her and she swayed slightly, feeling as though she was standing on a ship in stormy seas.

"Chase, are you all right?" Adam asked.

"I... I feel a bit giddy."

"Here, sit down and take a few deep breaths." Adam held her arm as she sat back down.

"Well, I'll leave you in the doctors capable hands. Now if you'll excuse me."

Chase opened her mouth to protest but the room began to spin again and she closed her eyes and cupped her face in her hands, lowering her head. She felt slightly nauseous and when she looked back up, Moon had disappeared like a ghost. She silently cursed him for leaving her with unanswered questions. If she didn't know better, she would swear he had caused her to fall ill to avoid answering questions about Jane, and to ignore acknowledging her request to return home.

You are home.

"How are you feeling now?"

"A little better," she said as the room slowly stopped revolving.

"Well, I'd like you to come and see me on Monday. I'll give you a check up."

"Yes doctor." For the first time in a while, she smiled.

"Your meal," George said, noisily dropping a plate of food and a knife and fork on the table.

Chase had forgotten about the meal; she didn't feel hungry now. "Thank you," she said, annoyed by George's surly attitude.

"Don't mind me," Adam said. "You go on and eat, I like watching people eat."

"It takes all sorts," Chase replied, smiling as she picked up her knife and fork and began to eat. Her appetite returned with each bite until she unexpectedly found herself faced with a chewy and slightly gristly mouthful. She would have spit it out, but with Adam watching her she thought it would be too rude so she swallowed it and looked down at her plate. It was hard to see in the dimly lit room, but it looked as though the potato was riddled with black bits. She poked one of them with her fork, separating it from the potato.

Having most probably been cooked in the microwave, the black object retained much of its shape and she realised with horror and revulsion that it was a slug - and she had just eaten one. The sick feeling returned and the colour drained from her face; she quickly took a gulp of wine to wash her mouth out.

"Is everything all right?"

"Yes. I'm just not hungry." She didn't know why she lied. Looking across at the bar, she saw George watching her with a humourless grin. Did he know? Had he done it on purpose? No, she was just imagining it. He wouldn't do that, not on purpose. It must have been a mistake. *Just like moving here*, a little voice teased.

She noticed Adam staring at her.

"I suddenly don't feel very well. Would you mind walking me home?"

Adam looked at Chase, then down at the plate, then back at Chase. "Of course not. It would be my pleasure."

Chase stood up and Adam swept past her and opened the door before she reached it.

"After you," he said, bowing.

Stepping outside, Chase noticed the clouds had dispersed, the moon casting its baleful glare across the fog that shimmered on the periphery. "How long has the fog been here?" she asked as they walked.

"Almost two years."

"*How long*?" she spluttered. Had she heard him right?

"Almost two years."

"Isn't that a little strange?" She couldn't believe what she was hearing and although not cold, she shivered.

"More than a little I'd say. The scientists and weathermen said it was something to do with adverse atmospheric conditions and global warming. High pressure, low pressure, it was all double Dutch to me, I'm afraid. It's something to do with living in a damp valley."

Chase shook her head. "Well, did they say how long it would be here?"

"When can you ever get a straight answer out of people?

Take doctors for example." He grinned, his teeth ominously white in the glow of the moon.

Chase smiled. "How long have you lived here?"

"I was born here. Studied away, and then returned to open the surgery. Not a very exciting locale, but it has its moments. I couldn't stand living in a city for the rest of my life."

"Don't you get bored?"

"I don't have time to get bored. There's always something to do, that's the beauty of my job. Even when I'm not in the surgery, people approach me for advice with their ailments. Not that I mind. You have to expect it in a small, close knit community like this."

They walked in silence for a while. Although Chase felt comfortable with Adam, she was still on a learning curve, testing boundaries and gauging his character. She wondered whether he would try to kiss her, and if he did, would she resist?

"Why do you think my friend would leave without telling me?" Chase asked, eventually breaking the silence. She still couldn't accept that Jane had just left.

"I couldn't really say. Ah, here we are, home sweet home."

Chase was going to invite him in for a drink - there were so many things she wanted to ask - but Adam was already turning away. There would be no kiss tonight. She didn't know whether she was relieved or disappointed.

"Have to rush. Just make last orders. See you on Monday. Don't worry about an appointment. I'm sure I can squeeze you in. I'll tell my receptionist to expect you."

She watched him walk down the path and onto the lane, leaving her in the ominous shadow of the house on Slaughter Hill.

Chapter 8

"How could we have got lost?" Izzy wailed.

Ratty was just able to make her out in the fog, her dishevelled appearance making her appear vulnerable. He knew she was looking to him for answers, but he didn't have any. He silently cursed his lack of insight. This was his chance to impress her, but he was as lost and baffled as she was.

"People will be searching for us by now. Smitty and the others will have told them what happened. They will have search parties. Perhaps we should just stay where we are so they can find us?" Izzy said, lighting another cigarette.

Ratty didn't reply. He didn't think their friends would have told anyone what had happened, because then they would have to admit where they had been, and then they would be in trouble. No, they wouldn't do that. There was a great divide between teenagers and adults, and when you overstep the line, shit happens. Ratty knew they wouldn't cross the line, not when their own skins were at stake.

For the last few hours, they had been following a large metal pipe through the fog, but when it suddenly passed through a wire fence, they lost their arterial lifeline. The fence was about seven feet high, and topped with barbed wire, so they couldn't climb it.

"Now what?" Izzy said, exasperated.

"Well, we'll have to follow the fence. Come on, let's go." Ratty sounded braver than he felt. The fence was another part of the mystery. Was it to keep something in, or something out? Pulling Izzy after him, he decided to go left.

The humming sound he'd heard during the night was now discernible again, a steady, throbbing buzz like an angry swarm of wasps hovering in the fog, waiting to strike. The thought made him apprehensive; perhaps Izzy was right and they should just stay where they were. Perhaps by walking deeper into the fog, they were only making things worse, getting more and more lost and making it harder for anyone to find them. But then he remembered the men with guns. No. It was up to them to get out by themselves. He didn't want those men to find them, because he felt that if they did, something bad would happen.

The ground underfoot was becoming boggy and they squelched through mud. Ratty almost lost his trainer as his foot sank into the quagmire; for a moment it seemed as though the ground didn't want to let him go, as though it was conspiring against him and it blew a malodorous raspberry as he tugged his foot out.

"Great idea to come this way," Izzy whispered. "I knew we should have stayed where we were."

Ratty didn't know whether she was squeezing his hand so tightly because she was angry or because she didn't want to lose him, but he didn't mind either way. Just having her close was more than he could hope for. They had been friends since infant school, but it was only recently that Ratty's feelings had changed. He now wanted to be more than just friends, and although he got the feeling that Izzy felt the same, he was nervous about testing his theory. If he was wrong, he would die of embarrassment. The opportunity to kiss her had arisen a couple of weeks ago, but he had chickened out at the last minute. Everything had been perfect. They had been in the cinema, and Izzy had looked gorgeous. She had been wearing a mini-skirt and a cropped T-shirt with the message *Living Doll* printed on it that displayed her growing charms to the full, and just looking at her made Ratty ache. Fortune had it that they were seated next to each other, and out of the corner of his eye he had noticed her keep looking at him while the film was playing. Once he turned to look back at her and she had smiled and leaned closer, her lips shiny with lip-gloss. His heart had started beating fast, his eyes drifting to the swell of her chest and he blushed and turned away. And that had been that. Opportunity had knocked, and he had stupidly ignored it. Idiot!

He wondered whether the opportunity would present itself again? And if it did, would he be brave enough to accept?

The fence ran straight, making it easy to follow. Even the ground became solid again which made the going easier and Ratty felt a glimmer of hope.

And then he heard the voices, indistinct at first as the fog muffled them.

Although he didn't know why, Ratty felt scared. He dropped to the ground, pulling Izzy down with him. She scowled and opened her mouth to protest, but Ratty gagged her with his hand.

Putting a finger to his lips to indicate silence, he motioned toward a hedge a few feet away. Izzy frowned but followed as he crawled toward the foliage. Overhead, the branches of a skeletal tree reached out of the fog like claws.

A sudden breeze thinned the fog a little and Ratty could make out a road, leading to what appeared to be a security checkpoint in the barbed wire fence. A barrier barred the entrance and what looked like a jeep was parked at the side of the road. The voices were coming from inside a security hut, but they were still too vague to interpret. Before the swirling fog enveloped it, a faded sign at the side of the road said: *Paradise 4 miles.*

Ratty recognised the sign. He used to see it when he visited his granddad. The road was the only way in and out of Paradise.

"Izzy, if you follow that road, you can get home," Ratty said, pointing away from the barrier.

"*We* can get home, you mean."

Ratty shook his head. "My granddad lives in Paradise. I haven't seen him for almost two years. I want to know what's going on." He remembered the men in the farmhouse being called away to a disturbance in the village and a knot of fear pulled tight in his stomach. Something definitely wasn't right.

"But you can't. Look, come with me and we'll get help, tell someone."

"No, I can't."

"Don't be stupid, Ratty. They've got guns."

Ratty gritted his teeth. "My dad's doped up because of this. I want to know why? There's something going on, and I want to know what?"

"But you're just a kid."

Ratty didn't let her see how much that hurt him. Is that all she saw him as? Now he was even more determined. "Izzy, just go."

"I can't. Not on my own." He heard the fear in her voice as her words trailed off.

Looking at her, he felt his determination waver for a moment as tears sparkled in her eyes.

"Izzy, I need you to go and fetch help. Please. Keep to the side of the road. If anyone comes, hide. If you hear anything, hide." He squeezed her hand (wanted to hug her, but thought better of it), smiled and began to crawl toward the barrier. He wanted to look over his shoulder, but he knew that if he saw her looking lost and forlorn, he wouldn't be able to leave her.

The voices grew louder as he approached the barrier. He kept his eyes peeled, alert, his muscles tensed for fight or flight. Something pierced his elbow and he almost screamed, grimacing as he pulled out a long thorn. His eyes watered and he gritted his teeth before creeping onto the concrete road. The fog shrouded him; in normal circumstances he knew it would conceal him, but these weren't normal circumstances and he knew they had devices that pierced the fog. Are they watching me now? He shuddered at the thought.

The barrier was about three feet away when he heard the door to the security hut open; lights chased the darkness and someone stepped outside.

Ratty held his breath. The light glared off the fog, dazzling him as he tried to melt into the road. The person that stepped from the hut was momentarily visible as an amorphous mass walking toward him; illuminated by the light, the fog swirled and eddied, making visibility difficult.

Ratty held his breath, trying to remain as still as possible. The figure was only feet away, blanketed in a thick swirl of fog. The staccato rhythm of footfalls on the tarmac drew closer... closer. He wanted to stand up and run, but fear rooted him. Gulping in a lungfull of air as silently as possible, he held his breath. His head spun and myriad images flashed before his eyes like binary code. But this was no game.

He heard the serrated rasp of metal on metal, followed by the pitter-patter of liquid splashing near his face. The caustic smell of urine filled the air and he realised the figure had come outside to relieve himself. He pulled a disgusted face, hoping none of the splashes hit him. After a moment, the figure sighed, zipped himself back up and walked away, hidden in the fog. The door opened, closed and the light went off, leaving darkness in its wake. Ratty looked back toward Izzy, waiting for a break in the fog and his night sight to return. When the gap came, he saw she was gone and he was alone.

There was no turning back now.

Steeling himself, he crawled toward the barrier.

Chapter 9

The house felt cold and empty without Jane. Even after Chase successfully lit a fire, the cold remained. Daylight streamed through the windows, highlighting motes of dust in the air as she busied herself with cleaning. When she opened the living room door, the smoke from the fire was sucked back into the room, causing her to cough. She flapped her arms around to clear the air and cursed the fire, cursed the house, cursed Moon and cursed the competition she couldn't remember entering.

The cup of tea she made to calm herself left a bitter taste in her mouth. When she had finished, it weighed heavy on her bladder and she had to use the toilet.

She had planned to phone Jane when she woke up, but there was still no signal available and she made a mental note to find a payphone.

It was only now she was by herself that she noticed there was no television in the house. The last time she had spent any considerable time without a television was when she was on holiday in Ibiza, but she hadn't needed one then; she'd been too busy partying. Now she hadn't got one, she missed it. The television was like a familiar friend when in a strange place. Turn it on and there was always someone there you knew: the cast of Coronation Street, Eastenders, Hollyoaks, they were people you invited into your house, a make-believe family, but now she hadn't even got that. What was she doing here, in this strange place where she didn't know anyone?

After two hours of cleaning and scrubbing with the cleaning supplies she had found beneath the sink in the kitchen, she decided to see if she could find a payphone. It was not like Jane to leave without a word, and the niggling worry had gnawed away at her all night, not letting her sleep.

Opening the front door, she was surprised and upset to see a dead squirrel lying outside the door. It was on its back, its tiny claws gripped with rigor mortis. It looked like the squirrel that had been stealing the leftovers from the hall when she had arrived in Paradise, but then she imagined all squirrels looked the same. She found it strange, but apart from road kill, she had never seen a dead animal in the wild. She always assumed they had an elephant's graveyard, a sacred place where they went when they were due to die. Not wanting to touch the squirrel, she picked up a stick and prodded it, just to make sure it really was dead, and not sunbathing. The squirrel didn't react, even when the stick punctured its eye. Chase grimaced and whispered a silent apology. She would bury it when she returned, but now she wanted to find a phone.

She was surprised it was warmer outside the house than it had been inside, and she was glad that she had opted to wear a blue knee length skirt and a purple cotton shirt that helped keep her cool.

Walking down the lane, Chase noticed the gray haired old woman was in her garden again, but she decided to ignore her.

"How are you settling in?" the old woman asked.

Surprised at being addressed by the previous acquiescent old lady, Chase didn't know what to say. She stared at her, amazed a smile could crack her deadpan veneer. "Erm, fine, thank you. And how are you?"

"Oh I'm tickety-boo." A mischievous glint sparkled in her eyes. "You'll have to call in for a cup of tea later, so we can be properly introduced."

"Oh, I erm..."

"That's settled then. Call round at three this afternoon and I'll have some nice cakes ready as well. Don't be late. My name's Belinda by the way, and you're Chase?"

It sounded more like an accusation than a question. Chase half-heartedly nodded in assent. Suddenly remembering what she had come out for, she said, "By the way, is there a pay phone anywhere I could use?"

81

Belinda nodded and pointed down the hill. "Bottom of the lane, turn right and it's on your left."

"Thank you," Chase said, turning and walking away.

"Not that it works though."

"Pardon?" She whirled around.

"I said it doesn't work."

"Well, is there another one?"

"No. Just the one."

"Well, have you got a phone?"

"Oh yes. It's in the hall."

"Well, I know it may seem a bit rude, but could I use it? I'll pay you, it's just I've got to make a call."

"Of course you can. That's what neighbours are for."

Chase opened the gate and started to enter the garden, feeling relieved. She would phone Jane and get to the bottom of all this.

"But it's broken," Belinda said.

"Broken! Then why did you say I could use it?"

"Because you didn't ask whether it was working or not. Just whether you could use it."

"Well, obviously I only wanted to use it if it was working, not if it was broken." Chase felt annoyed and slightly confused. Why couldn't she have just given her a straight answer and told her the payphone and her own phone were broken? Why the verbal cat and mouse?

"See you at three. And don't be late," Belinda said, turning back to her gardening.

Chase gave an exasperated sigh and turned away clenching her fists. She slammed the gate behind her and carried on down the lane without looking back. She didn't want to get into arguments with her new neighbours, but she could make an exception.

At the bottom of the lane she turned right and spotted the red phone box, half hidden by overgrown foliage. Stepping inside she lifted the receiver but there was no ring tone. Slamming it back in the cradle, she went outside and sat on the grass verge, cradling her head in her hands. Her head was spinning and she took deep breaths to calm herself. She felt slightly sick and before she knew it, she was coughing up bile that she spat on the grass. A cold sweat washed over her and she shivered, suddenly cold in the morning sunlight.

A bird whistled in the tree above her. She felt like shooting the blasted thing. It had no right to be so damn cheerful. The noise grated on her nerves and she stood up and walked away. Further along the lane, she came to a large pond opposite the surgery and she remembered Adam asking her to call in. As she wasn't feeling very well, she thought it was a good idea to see him anyway. He was a doctor, after all.

Walking through the front door, she was faced with a studious looking brunette receptionist seated behind a small counter. A nameplate on the counter identified her as Miss Patricia Smith.

"Can I help you?" Patricia asked, pokerfaced.

"Yes, Adam - Doctor White asked me to call in. My name's Chase Black."

Patricia looked at a book on the counter and ran her finger down it. "Ah yes. He said you would call. If you go through to the waiting room, I'll call you when he's free."

Patricia cocked her head to indicate where the waiting room was and Chase went through to wait. There were three people already waiting. They all looked up as Chase entered (she thought they held her gaze longer than common decency dictated), and she felt embarrassed by their attention as she seated herself. There was a pale old man who kept snuffling, his weathered skin like parchment. Next to him sat a teenage boy who picked his nose. Finally there was a middle-aged woman with her hair swept up in a severe bun dressed in a gingham suit. The woman reminded Chase of a matriarchal headmistress.

Clinical posters adorned the walls and a fish tank sat in the corner of the room, although she couldn't see any fish among the plastic plants or around the skull which opened at the jaw to release a stream of bubbles before snapping shut. Someone had placed a sticker on the front of the tank: Gone Fishing.

She tried not to make eye contact with the other patients, although she could still feel them looking at her. Scanning the posters on the wall, she caught glimpses of words: report, symptoms, HIV, government, disease, cancer, cure, study, sample, test...

The teenage boy stood up and began pacing back and to, his hands behind his back. He had a serious demeanour and his lips were peeled back. As he paced, he kept clicking his teeth together like a wind-up set of false ones sold in a joke shop. Chunks of his long hair were missing and his eyes were dark and soulless.

Averting her eyes, Chase noticed the pale old man. He was fastidiously playing with something in his lap. At first, Chase couldn't make out what it was, but then she realised that it was his flaccid penis and she covered her mouth with her hand, shocked. She couldn't believe it. The old man looked across at her and grinned, revealing yellow teeth.

Chase felt sick.

"Miss Black, the doctor will see you now."

Relieved to see Patricia standing in the doorway, indicating she could go through, Chase quickly stood up and shook her head. What the hell was wrong with these people? As she crossed the room, she felt the patients' eyes watching her and she shivered. Behind her, the old man snorted loudly and coughed up phlegm and Chase hurried into the hallway to a door with Adam's name stencilled on it. With a rapid knock, she entered without waiting to be invited and closed the door rather too quickly; it banged loudly and she winced.

Momentarily blinded by bright light streaming through the slatted blinds, she felt the nausea return.

"Chase, nice to see you."

Rubbing her watering eyes, she was unable to make anything out too clearly. Objects were unfocused, blurry, like a Rorschach test she had to interpret. The air was tainted with a stringent aroma that didn't help as it stung her nostrils. Slowly the shapes sharpened in clarity, became recognisable shapes and she saw Adam seated behind a desk. He indicated a chair and she sat, grateful to take the weight off her feet.

"So how are you feeling today?"

"Actually, not too good." Should she mention the weirdoes in the waiting room? Or did he already know about them? Was that why they were here?

"Oh," he leaned forward with his elbows on the desk, his eyebrows arched. "And what's the matter?"

"Well, I've been feeling a bit sick. And I keep feeling dizzy."

"Anything else? Any pain anywhere?"

"No, well, just a little tender around my bosom." She blushed, embarrassed.

"I see. Well, I'll take your blood pressure and a blood sample."

"Blood sample!" She didn't like needles. It was her only phobia.

"Don't worry, I promise it won't hurt. Trust me."

Chase smiled sheepishly. "Is it that obvious?"

"Only to me. I see it all the time. But come on, roll your sleeve up and we'll start with the easy stuff."

After taking her blood pressure and temperature, he had her lie on a padded bench to take a blood sample. Chase couldn't look. She felt the needle invade her body, sucking like a steel vampire as he siphoned her blood. She felt the room begin to spin, felt as though she was passing into another plane of reality, one where nothing was solid, where her brain was spinning inside her skull, disjointed; her eyes wouldn't focus, she was falling from the realm of the physical to the metaphysical but she fought it, sure that if she let herself pass through, she would be lost.

"There you go. All done."

Chase put her hands to her face. She looked as pale as she felt.

"Sit up and put your head between your legs," Adam said, transferring her blood to a phial.

She glimpsed how much he had taken and the room began to spin again. Putting her head between her knees eventually returned her equilibrium and she felt well enough to stand up. Adam stood beside her, a concerned look on his face.

"Feeling better?" he asked.

"A bit."

"Well, take your time, there's no rush." He returned to his desk and made some notes. "I'll have the results in a couple of days, if you want to make another appointment on the way out."

Although he had said she could stay to recover, Chase took that as her cue to leave.

She stood and walked toward the door.

Adam said, "If you would like, we could meet for a drink tonight?"

Chase felt her heart skip a beat and she smiled before turning back to look at him. "Yes, I'd like that."

"About seven in The Slaughtered Dog?"

"OK." She walked out to make her next appointment with Patricia and even the waiting patients (which had now grown to five), couldn't wipe the grin off her face as they glared at her.

Outside, the fresh air came as a welcome relief after the stringent aroma and she walked across to the pond. Marginal iris' and grasses rustled in the breeze while Angels Fishing Rods arched out over the water. A clump of gunnera on the opposite bank shaded the water like large, primordial umbrellas. A white water lily had just flowered and Chase noticed a small frog sitting on one of the lily pads like a living piece of John Ditchfield pottery. As she watched, movement caught her eye and a shape glided across the water. Turning to look, she recoiled in horror. It was a snake. She had never seen a snake in the wild before, never mind swimming. She knew they were out there, but she never expected to see one. But then she never expected to move to the country.

As she watched, it zigzagged across the surface of the water, sleek and shiny.

It had a green back with vertical black bars along its sides and a yellow neck patch. Slowly and silently it approached

86

the frog before striking with such speed and agility that Chase stepped back in shock, her hand at her mouth. It swallowed the frog in two gulps, constricting its throat to accommodate the meal before gliding away into the marginal plants like the memory of a bad dream.

There were serpents in Paradise.

Chapter 10

The episode with the snake and the frog had upset Chase more than she realised. She knew it was only nature at work, performing the cycle of life, but she didn't like it. It was too brutal. Combined with the patients in the surgery and her distress at not being able to contact Jane, she felt sick. Something wasn't right. People didn't act like that and Jane wouldn't have gone without telling her. Why hadn't she heard her leave? Chase was a light sleeper at the best of times. Mat used to joke that he was scared to fart in his sleep in case it woke her.

Perhaps she had made the wrong decision in moving to Paradise, too hasty in her wish to leave the city? She considered going back to the house and reading through the contract before she remembered Moon hadn't given her a copy! There was no proof of anything.

There had to be a telephone somewhere that she could use? She tried to recall whether she had seen one in the public house the night before, but it had been so dark inside the building that she hadn't been able to see much of anything. She considered the church hall, then remembered the vicar - if anyone could help her, it would be the vicar. Weren't they the pillars of the community?

Walking through the lanes toward the church, she heard something rustling in the hedge; she imagined the snake (absently wondered if it was poisonous) following her and she increased her pace, her eyes alert for any movement.

The church was a small stone building with a spire that reached up to the heavens. You had to walk through the small cemetery to reach it, and as she walked toward the church, Chase absently regarded the tombstones. She noticed some of the older graves were covered in weeds, the gravestone inscriptions weathered and hidden by lichen.

Some graves contained generations of families, all piled on top of each other in a macabre genealogy ladder. Other graves were more recent, the soil freshly tilled. The graveyard was unkempt, left to grow wild. The smell of grass filled the air, but there was also the putrescent aroma of decay, as if something had been left to rot.

She could see the fog hanging on the perimeter of the graveyard like a curtain, a barrier from the world, and she had the uncanny feeling someone was watching her from within its cold embrace, and the hairs prickled at the nape of her neck. Hesitating, she thought she saw movement out of the corner of her eye, and she spun around to see strands of fog stretching tentacle-like from the main mass, as though someone had run out of the ethereal cloud. Narrowing her eyes, she scanned the area, but couldn't see anyone. She trembled. Suppose it was a ghost? But that was stupid. There was no such thing. She laughed at her foolishness, but the fog was now losing its charm, becoming something sinister.

Eventually she put the movement down to the wind, fully aware that her mind was capable of playing tricks on her, especially as she was alone and vulnerable at the moment.

With a shake of her head, she carried on walking.

The door to the church was ajar, and Chase pushed it and stepped inside. The interior was cool and she trembled at the sudden climatic change, rubbing her arms to warm herself. It's no wonder the congregation's fallen, she thought. Perhaps if they had a bit of heating...

At the back of the church a stained glass window depicting the crucifixion of Christ cast shards of colour across the wooden floor. The blood dripping from the wounds looked too red and vivid, as though it was real blood, and not just coloured glass. Chase looked away. Walking between the pews, her footsteps echoed eerily from the eaves. At the front of the church, the altar was adorned with two white candles and a large, gold cross. The candles were lit, the guttering flames causing shadows to dance around the walls; a white linen cloth hanging from the front of the altar billowed slightly like a spectre.

Chase frowned as she studied the altar cloth. She couldn't feel any discernible breeze, certainly not enough to stir the heavy cloth, so why was it moving? As she cautiously approached the altar she heard a noise, a soft sigh. Her heart missed a beat. Something wasn't right here. Standing in front of the altar, she steeled herself and grabbed the cloth. Heart in her mouth, she quickly tugged it aside and a figure fell out and rolled across the floor. Chase jumped back in alarm before she recognised the vicar. An empty whisky bottle rolled out with him.

What the hell was he playing at?

The vicar looked up at Chase with bloodshot eyes; she was sure there was fear in his gaze. Mumbling to himself, he scuttled away, crab-like, sending the bottle spinning.

"Are you OK?" she asked. She hurried across and crouched down, placing a hand on his shoulder.

"Get away from me," the vicar hissed, smacking her hand away. "And I looked, and behold a pale horse: and his name that sat on him was Death, and Hell followed with him."

"Here, let me help you up." Chase was shocked by his outburst, but she was also concerned for him.

"I am beyond help. We are all beyond help. And he opened the bottomless pit; and there arose a smoke out of the pit, as the smoke of a great furnace; and the sun and the air were darkened..."

"I know what you need. A good, strong cup of coffee."

"... by reason of the smoke of the pit. And there came out of the smoke locusts upon the earth: and unto them was given power, as the scorpions of the earth have power."

Chase shook her head. The vicar was obviously drunk. She considered getting help, but she didn't want to jeopardise his position or embarrass him. "Have you got a kitchen where I can make you a drink?"

The vicar grinned. "Behold I show you a mystery; we shall not all sleep, but we shall all be changed..."

"You really should drink some coffee."

"... In a moment, in the twinkling of an eye, at the last trumpet: for the trumpet shall sound, and the dead shall be raised incorruptible, and we shall be changed." He started to giggle, rocking backward and forward on his haunches.

Chase shook her head, sighed and walked away toward a door at the side of the church, which she hoped would lead to the rectory.

"We have left undone those things which we ought to have done; and we have done those things which we ought not to have done; and there is no health in us..."

Walking through the door, Chase closed it behind her, shutting out the vicar's rambling sermons. She didn't like to admit it, but he was scaring her.

Finding herself in a small annex, she walked through another door and eventually found a kitchen. Picking up the kettle, she carried it to the sink and turned the tap, wrinkling her nose as the water ran brown as though it hadn't been run for a long while. A stagnant smell emanated from it and she turned her head away to breathe in fresh air. When the water ran clear, she filled the kettle, found a jar of coffee in the cupboard and brewed a black coffee, which she carried back to the vicar who was still sitting on the floor of the church. Passing him the drink, she sat on the end of a pew and looked at him, shaking her head and sighing.

The vicar stared wild-eyed at her, looked at the cup in his hands and then threw it against the wall where it shattered, showering the pews with coffee. "Drink no longer water, but use a little wine for thy stomach's sake and thine often infirmities," he boomed.

Chase flinched. "Bloody hell," she mumbled. She never imagined she would be nursemaiding a vicar. Weren't they the ones meant to offer comfort?

Walking back to the kitchen she found a cloth and a dustpan and returned to the church to try and clear the mess as best she could. When she had finished, she stepped back, eerily noticing that the coffee had stained the wall with a brown mark that bore an uncanny resemblance to the devil shaped bloodstain on the letter from Moon. Thinking that the image looked sacrilegious in a church, she tried scrubbing it, but the stain just got more vivid, as though she was uncovering a picture hidden by years of grime, so she gave up, hoping that when it dried out, no one would notice.

Although it was a struggle, and she ended up almost carrying him, she coaxed the vicar through to the rectory where she eventually managed to put him to bed. She sat with him for a while until she heard him snoring. She reasoned that he would wake up with a well-deserved sore head.

Although she felt guilty about snooping through someone else's house, she needed to find a telephone. Through a door in the kitchen, she discovered a larder full of recognisable brand name, tinned food. There were a few of the nondescript white cans from the local store, but they had been discarded in the bin. Not that she could blame him. She knew from her own experience that the white tinned food tasted a little bland. There were also a number of whisky bottles in the larder that she viewed with distaste.

In the antiquated lounge, she noticed photographs on a Victorian bureau. They showed the vicar and a cheerfully rotund woman (the vicar didn't have his red cheeks in the photographs). Both of them wore wedding rings and happy smiles. The present state of the house didn't reflect a woman's general housekeeping, and she wondered where the woman (who was most likely his wife) was now? Had she left due to her husband's drink problem? If she had, then Chase couldn't blame her.

She found what she was looking for in the hall, but when she lifted the receiver, the line was dead. Why were none of the phones working? And how had she received a text message on her mobile when there was no signal available to make calls? Ideas bloomed in her mind, but she quashed them before they were fully grown. Exhaling a frustrated sigh, she slammed the receiver down and checked back on the vicar. He was snoring away and leaving him to sleep it off, she walked back through into the church. Out of the corner of her eye, she glimpsed the devilish stain, and for a moment she could have sworn that the silhouetted head turned toward her, but when she looked straight at it, nothing had changed. She was scaring herself, although the residents of Paradise weren't helping. They were strange. More than strange, they were scary. Was it inbreeding?

She left the church feeling depressed, scared and lonely.

Walking up Slaughter Hill, she noticed Belinda was no longer in her garden. She was relieved. She couldn't face seeing her, not after the vicar.

When she entered the garden of High Top Cottage, she felt a sense of relief. It was then that she noticed the dead squirrel had gone. Remembering the snake, she shivered and scanned the garden where predators could lurk. Did snakes eat squirrels? It didn't matter whether they did or not; she rushed inside the house and slammed the door shut. For the first time, it felt like home when she shut the door, and she felt safe, as though the house had now accepted her. Putting the squirrel to the back of her mind, she thought about how much time she had left before she had to meet Adam and she decided to have a lie down. It had been an exhausting morning.

In the bedroom, she lay on the bed and stared at the ceiling, pondering on the day's events when she noticed the entrance to the loft. She hadn't really noticed it before. Curious, she slipped off the bed and walked across the room to the dressing table where a long wooden pole with a hook on the end was leaning against the wall. She had wondered what it was for. Now it's purpose was evident. Using the pole to push open the hatch, she used the hook to pull down the loft ladder that descended in a cloud of dust.

Coughing and wafting the dust away, she climbed the ladder and peered into the dark loft. Just able to make out a light pull, she tugged it, flooding the room with light from a bare bulb in the rafters. Cobwebs hung like macabre decorations from every available crevice and she decided not to venture any further when she suddenly caught sight of a box, half hidden in the corner. Curious, she stepped into the loft and crossed the creaking floor, squirming as she brushed away the cobwebs.

The box was an old wooden packing crate and she lifted the lid to reveal a few old clothes. Sifting through them with an air of trepidation, she half expected to see a large spider scurry out. Finding nothing else in the crate, she shut the lid and turned to descend the ladder when she noticed a hole in the wall. She only really noticed it because the light failed to penetrate around the edge, making it stand out from the rest of the brickwork. A cobweb hung over the hole like a gossamer veil and she was going to ignore it when she noticed there was something in there. Crouching down to get a better look, she was wary of putting her hand in. The cobweb meant there was a spider somewhere, but curiosity got the better of her. Screwing her face up in disgust, she brushed the cobweb away and hurriedly slipped her hand inside, snatching out the object and dropping it on the floor as she wiped her hands on her jeans, a tremor of disgust making her shake.

When she had calmed down enough, she retrieved the object to find that it was a diary. Blowing dust from the cover she carried it down into the bedroom, pushed the loft ladder out of the way and closed the hatch with the pole.

Lying on the bed, she opened the diary and began to read.

April 17th

Thought it was about time I started writing about what's going on, as I can't always remember things. Fog has been here for 3 months now. Damned strange.

Damn arthritis is playing up as well so it's hard to write too much.

Don't reckon much to the food rations. Had better in the War. Unless it's just me, they taste a bit funny. Can't complain though. Not when it's free and I only get a pension to live on. They've even got dog food for Samson, which smells better than the food I get, so perhaps I should eat that instead?

April 19th

Fog is still here. Heard some scientist giving a half-baked explanation for it. Bullshit with a capital B. They say we can't leave the village, as though we're under house arrest! They've even got guards posted to stop us. I didn't fight for my country to be stopped from leaving my village.

Stopped smoking today. After fifty years, just like that. Didn't even realise I wanted to stop!

Funny, but when the wind blows right, you can sometimes hear a funny humming sound in the fog. Some folks have started saying that there's ghosts in there. Stupid buggers. There's always a rational explanation.

April 25th

Not for the first time, I wanted to contact my relatives on the other side (think of the fog as a veil between this world and the next, the real world and the make believe, perhaps there are ghosts in the fog, or are we the ghosts?) but *they* wouldn't let me. Said they hadn't got the resources. Why are all the damn phones dead? I'm beginning to hate this damn fog.

June 4th

We had a village meeting to discuss the fog today (or was it yesterday?) that was attended by Drake who couldn't answer any of our questions. Funny bugger. He's always mooching around. He's no scientist though, that's for sure. Couldn't answer diddly squat. (Some of us are planning a great escape, so I'd better start hiding this diary. Mr. Jones wants to build an escape tunnel! Silly old bugger).

Arthritis hardly playing up at all today.

95

I took Samson for a walk, but he ran away, hiding from me.

July 15th

I can even throw sticks for Samson now without any pain. Doc says it's 'very encouraging'. More like a bloody miracle if you ask me. But I'm not the only one. Other people have noticed improvements in their health as well. Perhaps it's the fog? Perhaps it's not so bad after all!

August 22nd

Noticed the landlord, George has stopped using his walking sticks. He says he has never felt so good. Perhaps the fog does have restorative powers? Damned strange. Not that I'm complaining.

Mr. Jones, Grace Hopkins and Robert Hunter lead the escape committee. I think the plan is for everyone to make a mad dash for it. Divide and conquer.

September 7th

Felt peculiar today. Had to lie down. Even Samson noticed, as I was pretty off-hand with him. Poor dog didn't know what he'd done wrong when I started shouting at him. Have to make it up to him and give him a good long walk (it's funny, but I can't remember what I was shouting at him for!).

Escape committee has been disbanded. Mr. Jones has disappeared. Folks say he made a dash for it on his own, but everyone's now too scared of the ghosts in the fog to follow suit.

October 21st

Took Samson for a walk this morning, but only I came back! Samson ran into the fog, chasing a damned rabbit. I called him, but he didn't come back. I heard a yelp. It was Samson. Following the sound, I eventually found him. DEAD. Some bastard had shot him clean through the head. Too upset and angry to write any more today.

October 28th

Went to ask the so-called scientists what the bloody hell was going on. They fobbed me off with excuses. They tried to tell me it was most probably an accident, caused by someone with a shotgun. I know the difference between shotgun wounds and bullet wounds as I saw enough during the war. This was a bullet wound. A man called Moon seems to be in charge. I'll get bloody answers if it kills me. Buried Samson today.

After the burial, I walked to the fog; damned if I didn't see one of them ghosts, white as a sheet, just standing there, watching me. Put the willies up me, that's for sure.

November 3rd

Moon is still 'unavailable'. Bullshit. He's just avoiding me. Damned fog. I keep forgetting things. Putting things down and then can't find them. Old age I suppose! And then there was old Bob. I saw him yesterday. Wouldn't be a problem, but he's been dead for three years, I think...????

December 16th

Rages are getting worse. Samson cowers when I walk in the room. But isn't Samson dead? Asked Bob about it, but he doesn't say much!

Damn it. What's wrong with me?

January 8th

I had an argument with Ms Woods in the general store today. Could have killed the silly old tart. Funny though, because I can't remember what it was about!

February 1st

That damned fog. Going stir crazy cooped up in this village. Woke up with blood on my hands today. No idea where it came from.

April 17th

There's a man hiding in the old farmhouse. Scruffy bugger, I call him the Raggedy man. I think he's scared of something (perhaps I imagined it, but he looked as though he was scared of me).

April 18th

Grace Hopkins is dead. Folk say she was murdered. Some say the ghosts killed her. Did I used to have arthritis? I can't remember. What's wrong with me?

May 16th

The vicar came to see me today. He wanted to talk. Preach more like. I punched him. Am I damned now? Forgive me Father, for I have twatted a man of the cloth. Fuckerfuckerfuckermother. Says he forgives me my sins. What sins?

May 23rd

What's wrong with everyone?

Raggedy man spoke to me today. He says he knows what's going on, and then he ran off! Damned strange as I didn't know anything was going on! Is it?

May 26th

Samson's dead. I killed him, didn't I? No. They killed him. Didn't they? Who are they? Them? It?

June 9th

Vicar's wife died today. I saw her die. I killed her. We killed her. They killed her. It killed her. Can't remember properly. Is she dead? Can't find Samson. Where's Samson?

June 12th

Raggedy man knows.

There were no more entries after June. Chase read the diary again, but it still didn't make any sense. First the dog was dead, and then it wasn't. Then there were people dying or disappearing. What did it mean? Was it someone playing a joke? Or was it the ravings of a lunatic? Neither option was very appealing. Perhaps the author was mad and had been locked away - but what if he came back! The last entry was only a month ago. She shivered and went downstairs to lock the doors. She made a mental note to ask Adam if he knew who had resided in the house previously. And where they were now?

When she entered the lounge, her breath hitched in her throat: there was someone at the window, peering in. She only caught a glimpse of them, the image burned on her retina like a photographic negative before whoever it was ducked out of the way. Expecting a knock at the door, she waited, but no one called. She thought of the diary; thought of the Raggedy man. Hadn't she also seen something in the fog? But it couldn't have been a ghost, because she knew there was no such thing.

Cautiously she peered out of the window, but she

couldn't see anyone. Even though she had only just checked them, she checked the doors again, and the windows. She wasn't going to go outside to check if anyone was there. Perhaps she had only imagined it, her imagination fuelled by the diary and its peculiar entries, but she wasn't going to take the risk.

She yanked the curtains across, feeling too exposed in the window.

An uneasy feeling settled over her and she wished her phone was working so she could call someone, just to hear the reassurance of a friendly voice. She felt like a stranger in a strange land as she read the diary again. *The vicar's wife dead, murdered?*

A helicopter flew low overhead, the noise reverberating through the house. Peeking through the curtain, Chase watched it disappear over the fog - The damned fog, wasn't that what the author of the diary had called it! She was beginning to agree.

Letting the curtain fall back, she shook her head.

The reference to the old farmhouse must be the one that Jane and herself had found, on the far side of the hill. That was where the Raggedy man lived. *The Raggedy man knows.* Knows what? She wished Jane was here. Even more she wished Mat was here. There was too much going on; her mind was in a spin, the world spiralling out of control. She suddenly felt sick. Knowing that she wouldn't be able to make it to the bathroom, she rushed into the kitchen and threw up in the sink.

Chapter 11

Although her stomach still felt uneasy, Chase recovered. Once or twice she thought she heard a faint humming sound in the distance, like a swarm of angry bees, but she put it down to her imagination, which was now running riot. She wished she'd never found that damn diary.

She also wished that Adam was coming here rather than meeting her in the pub because she was still wary of venturing outside. Whether there was someone lurking outside was now irrelevant; her mind assured her there was.

It was now 6.45. She didn't like being late for dates (she suddenly realised that's what it was, a date, and she blushed, glad that no one was around to see), but she didn't know whether she could pluck up the courage to leave the house.

She had already got ready to go out, but now she wondered whether a short, black skirt and a tight halter-top were appropriate, especially as she wasn't wearing a bra. It might give Adam the wrong idea. Should she really be showing so much flesh? After all, this wasn't the city. People seemed more conservative in the country and they might think she dressed like a tart. She didn't want to give the wrong impression, but she did look good, so eventually she decided to stick with what she was wearing, and to hell with what people thought.

It was still light outside, and she berated herself for being nervous about leaving the house. Nothing bad was going to happen to her - certainly not in daylight, anyway!

Keeping that thought in mind, she picked up her bag, took a deep breath, unlocked the door and left the house.

She scanned the hedgerows, her heart racing. Seeing there was no one around, she began to relax and she locked the door and headed down the lane.

At the thought of meeting Adam, butterflies danced in her stomach and she felt like a nervous schoolgirl. How long was it since she'd been on a date? She hoped he was worth it. To hell with Mat. She had a life to lead, too. Even though she tried not to, she cast sidelong glances at the trees and bushes, still wary of being watched.

Walking past Belinda's house, she noticed the curtains twitch and she absently remembered that she hadn't kept her appointment for tea. Not that she was too concerned. It wasn't a definite date.

The rock cake that suddenly hit her on the head came as a painful surprise. Chase winced and spun around, alarmed to see Belinda standing in the doorway of her house with cakes in her hands, her pinched face red with fury. She was wearing a dress that had seen better days, the pattern almost indiscernible after countless washes, and she wore slippers fashioned to look like rabbits. Her grey hair was long and straggly, giving her an even more alarming appearance.

"Burned they are. Ruined. And it's all your fault," Belinda screeched, throwing another cake that Chase ducked to avoid.

"I'm sorry!" Disturbed by Belinda's behaviour, Chase blushed. She didn't know what to do.

"*Sorry,* I'll give you *sorry* my girl." She threw another cake like a grenade, crumbs flying like shrapnel as it hit a tree.

Shaking her head in disbelief, Chase began to run down the lane. She was terrified. The look on Belinda's face was murderous. A passage from the diary ran through her head: *I killed her. We killed her. They killed her. It killed her.*

What the hell was going on?

She looked over her shoulder, relieved to see that the screeching harridan wasn't following her. In different circumstances, the situation might be funny. But after what she had read in the diary, it was anything but. She slowed her pace, wheezing slightly.

When she eventually reached the Slaughtered Dog and entered the bar, she was breathing heavily. She knew she must look a state, but she wasn't bothered. She just wanted the safety afforded by other people, even if she didn't know them.

I killed her. We killed her. *They killed her.*

Even though it was still light outside, inside the public house it was dark and dismal. She approached the bar brushing crumbs from her hair. George was sitting where she had seen him last time. He was still wearing the same stained, checked shirt and she was now convinced that it really was blood. He regarded Chase with a scowl before hobbling toward her.

"Yes?" he grunted.

"I'll get these."

Chase turned to see Belinda standing behind her and she recoiled in alarm, her mouth open. She didn't know what to do. "Honestly, I forgot all about tea!" she blurted, taking a wary step back.

"Tea?" Belinda said, scowling. "I just want to buy you a drink to say welcome to the village. Don't you want one?"

Chase was confused and scared. "No, no of course not. I mean, yes, yes, I'll have, erm, white wine please." She didn't feel she could refuse. And she definitely wasn't going to mention the cakes.

"White wine George. And one for me as well."

George poured two white wines and slopped them on the counter. Belinda picked hers up and began to drink while George stood holding his hand out, waiting to be paid. Obviously not everything in Paradise was free.

Time passed excruciatingly slowly as George stared at Chase and she didn't know what to do. She noticed Belinda didn't appear to be making any move to pay for the drinks so she took the money from her own purse and paid. It was all too surreal.

"There, isn't that better," Belinda said, delicately fingering the stem of the glass as she looked Chase up and down.

Chase had a vision of Belinda smashing the glass into her face and she backed away slightly, putting a bit of distance between them. Nonchalantly she stared around the bar, hoping to see if there was anyone around who could come to her assistance if anything happened, but it was too dark to see.

"Am I boring you?" Belinda asked, her expression hardening into a scowl.

Chase turned to face her. "No, of course not. I was just meant to be meeting someone here."

"And who might that be?"

"Doctor White."

"Doctor White! Are you ill?"

"Ill?"

"Yes, you know, is there something wrong with you?"

"No, not that I know of." Knowing that she really had been unwell lately, and that she was lying, made her blush slightly.

"Why else would you see a doctor then? Two blacks don't make a white. Two wrongs don't make a right."

"Pardon?" Chase didn't understand. Was Belinda alluding to Adam's and her surname?

"I said isn't it your round."

"But I bought the last one." As soon as she'd said it, she regretted it.

"Well that's rich. Did you hear that George. You go out of your way to make someone welcome, and they throw-"

"Sorry I'm late."

Chase turned at the sound of Adam's voice. He was wearing a brown jumper and dark, corduroy trousers, and she had never been so relieved to see anyone in her life.

"I had a call out at the last minute. Have I missed anything? I hope you're making our newest resident feel welcome, Belinda."

"Doctor White. Would I do anything else? Now if you'll excuse me, I've got some cakes in the oven." She gave Chase a vitriolic sidelong glance before walking out of the bar.

"I'm glad to see you're settling in and getting to know people. You look fantastic by the way," Adam said.

Chase didn't know what to say. She nodded acquiescently and downed her drink. She didn't feel fantastic. Should she tell Adam what had happened?

Adam frowned. "Are you sure you should be drinking alcohol like that?"

"I don't usually, but I needed that. By the way..." Here goes, she thought, trying to find a way to broach the subject of Belinda's peculiar behaviour.

"I mean... no, forget I said anything." He twiddled with his thumbs.

"Forget what? What's wrong?" Looking at Adam, she forgot all about Belinda.

"Nothing. Honestly. Just forget it."

"I wish you wouldn't say that. I can't forget it now. Is there something wrong with me?" The room suddenly seemed to lurch, as though someone had shifted reality. She put her hands on the bar to steady herself, but quickly withdrew them when she found it felt sticky.

"It depends how you define wrong."

"And how would you define it?" The room began to spin.

"Well, I shouldn't really tell you here. It's not ethical. You're booked in to see me tomorrow, so let's leave it until then."

"And I'm seeing you now. I can't go away worrying that something's wrong with me."

"Yes, you're right I'm sorry, I shouldn't have started this, but perhaps we should sit down first."

They walked over to a table and Chase collapsed gratefully into the chair. The room was still spinning, but at least now she didn't have as far to fall if she succumbed.

"Chase, you're pregnant."

"What?" Had she heard him right?

"You're pregnant."

"That's what I thought you said. I don't believe it. Are you sure?" She shook her head and the room lurched again.

"Yes. Positive."

"But the last time I had sex was four months ago." It

didn't seem possible! She was sitting here with a man she liked, and he was telling her she was going to have Mat's baby! Her clothes suddenly seemed very out of place. She felt sick. Now she needed a drink. A large one. A very large one.

"Chase, are you okay?"

"Yes, it's just... I don't believe it. Are you really, positively sure?" He must have made a mistake.

Adam nodded.

"But I was on the pill."

"Well, it isn't one hundred percent safe."

She looked down at her stomach and placed both hands on it. There was a slight increase in her size, but she'd put that down to bingeing after being made redundant; although she hadn't had a period in while, she had never been regular. She couldn't believe what she was hearing and tears welled in her eyes. She didn't know whether she was happy or sad. Where was Mat when she needed him?

"Let me get you a drink. A soft drink," he added, walking away to the bar.

Chase couldn't take her eyes off her stomach. She had a quick mental image of the alien breaking out of John Hurts stomach in the Alien film and gooseflesh peppered her arms. Was there really something growing in her stomach? Had she all ready harmed it (was *it* a boy or a girl?) by drinking to excess and frequenting smoky public houses? Was it going to be okay? She wanted her Mum. She wanted her friends with her. She wanted Jane. She wanted Mat. She wanted anyone she knew well enough to discuss it with. The questions she had planned to ask Adam about who had previously lived in High Top Cottage were now irrelevant. She was going to have a baby. Mat's baby. Where the hell was he when she needed him? Had he found himself another girlfriend? A pang of jealousy shot through her as she imagined him with someone else.

Returning with the drinks, Adam sat down and smiled. "Feeling any better?"

"I thought you said the results would take a couple of

days."

"I know but I rushed them through as I knew you were concerned."

Chase sipped the orange juice Adam had bought her. She felt as though she was in a dream and would wake up any minute. Mat would be lying next to her, snoring slightly, his wavy hair sticking up in all directions. She closed her eyes, willing herself to wake.

"Are you okay?"

Chase opened her eyes. Nothing had changed. "Yes, just a little tired. I think I need to go home."

"Would you like me to walk you?"

"No thank..." She remembered Belinda. Mad Belinda the rock cake thrower. "Well, if you don't mind?" She decided not to question Adam about Belinda. Her head was already spinning.

"No, of course not."

Leaving the Slaughtered Dog they walked up the lane without speaking. Chase had too much on her mind. Pregnant. She couldn't believe it.

Belinda's house was in darkness, the curtains drawn; Belinda was nowhere to be seen. Chase was grateful for that. She didn't think she could handle any more problems.

"Do you know where the name Slaughter Hill originated?" Adam asked.

Chase shook her head.

"Legend has it that there used to be a coven of witches that lived in a cave in the hill. They were friendly witches, and the locals used to call on them for potions and cures when they were sick. But then one of the witches turned bad. Spurned by her lover, she cast a spell, bewitching the men of the village to do her bidding. They became her sexual slaves, but the women of the village were understandably jealous and late one night they crept up to the cave and chopped all the witches heads off - they couldn't risk another witch turning bad. The bodies were sealed in the cave and the heads were buried at the junction of a river, but sometimes, late at night, people say you can hear the witches fluttering through the sky, looking for their heads."

Chase shivered and surreptitiously looked up at the sky.

Adam laughed. "It's only a legend though."

"Well thank you for sharing that with me. I'll sleep easy now!"

"Sorry!" Adam sheepishly shrugged his shoulders.

When they reached High Top Cottage, Adam said, "Would you like me to come in?"

"Is that why you told me the story?" she joked, forcing a smile. She shook her head. "Not tonight." She needed time by herself to think.

"Well, come into the surgery tomorrow, and we'll have a chat. Call in any time you like, I'll tell Patricia to expect you."

Chase nodded, unlocked the door and walked inside. She waved Adam goodbye and he gave her an encouraging smile before disappearing down the lane. Closing the door, she locked it and then checked that it was secure before walking through to the lounge. Sitting on the settee, she closed her eyes. Her life was in turmoil.

She wasn't sure whether she fell asleep, but a sudden noise made her open her eyes.

Darkness had descended; long shadows had slipped uninvited into the room. Once familiar objects took on unnatural shapes in the nocturnal gloom. Dismissing the noise as the tail end of a lucid dream, she was about to close her eyes again when she heard a rattling noise in the kitchen that made her heart stop.

Someone was trying the door handle.

Someone was trying to get into the house.

She tried to remember whether or not she had locked the door, certain that she had, but panicking in case she hadn't. Remembering Belinda, she wished she had a telephone to call someone for help.

Why are all the bloody phones dead?

Too scared to move, she tried to will the person to go away, but she heard the door handle turn again, squeaking and protesting as someone tried to force the door open. She wanted to scream, but that would tell whomever it was, that she was in - and that she was terrified. She didn't want whoever was out there to know she was scared, as they would feed on her fear, gaining a psychological advantage.

The eaves creaked, sighing as they settled down for the night. Or was someone in the house, walking in the bedroom above, the floorboards protesting as weight was applied to them? Why hadn't she checked the house when she returned from the pub? Anyone could have got in while she was away. But why would they?

Panic churned her stomach like a turbulent sea, making her feel sick. She thought about the baby and felt a sudden maternal instinct for something she hadn't known was there a few hours ago. She was going to be a mother. And someone was trying to break into her house. Rage began to replace the fear, nudging it aside as strength flowed back into her limbs. She stood up, cautiously making her way through to the kitchen in time to hear a key turning in the lock.

The door began to open.

Chapter 12

Chase felt giddy. Everything was happening too quickly.

Her heart was beating fast, as though trying to escape from its cage of ribs.

She knew how it felt.

In the ambient light, she could see the door handle turning, the door beginning to open.

Her heart momentarily missed a beat.

Preservation instinct took over as she grabbed a serrated knife from the draining board. The weight of the knife was comforting and she clenched it in her fist, prepared to defend herself against the intruder.

The back door swung open, banging against the wall and a shadow crossed the threshold, followed closely by the physical body that hesitated in the doorway.

Chase steadied herself, sucking in a deep breath.

The figure was too dark to make out; she reached for the light switch, prepared to see Belinda standing there, armed with rock cakes, or worse. Much worse.

She tightened her grip on the knife.

Flicking the switch, light flooded the room, chasing the shadows away and Chase let out a loud cry as she confronted the intruder: a gangling teenager covered in mud who looked more scared than she was.

His mouth dropped open and he stumbled back. "Where's my granddad? Who are you?" the boy demanded before he saw the knife and took a further step back, his expression fearful.

"What are you doing breaking into my house?" Chase demanded in return, her voice shaking almost as much as her legs.

"Your house! I've got a key. This is my granddad's

house. What have you done to him? You..." he visibly gulped, "You haven't killed him, have you?" He looked at the knife and took another step back.

"Don't be stupid." Chase lowered the knife slightly.

"GRANDDAD," the boy shouted.

"Look, there's no one here, especially not your granddad. This is my house. I won it."

"Won it! Don't talk stupid. You can't have. My Granddad lives here." The boy's face was a mask of confusion.

Chase remembered the diary. "Did your granddad have a dog?"

"Samson. Where is he?"

"Look, I don't know what's going on, but you'd better come in."

The boy eyed her warily and Chase put the knife back on the draining board.

"I won't hurt you. Look, come in and shut the door." She backed away and after a contemplative moment, the boy stepped inside, although he didn't shut the door.

"Come into the lounge." Chase was anxious to sit down as the adrenaline that had flooded her body ebbed away, leaving her feeling drained.

Without seeing if he followed, Chase walked through to the lounge, collapsed onto the settee and watched the boy cautiously enter the room, his eyes darting nervously around, as though he expected someone to jump out on him.

"My name's Chase."

"Peter. But people call me Ratty."

"Well, Pete... Ratty, sit down."

Ratty shook his head.

"Okey dokey." Chase sighed and quickly explained the circumstances of how she had moved in; about the competition, about Jane, about Moon. She didn't mention bizarre Belinda, or her pregnancy, which was an intimate matter that she hadn't come to terms with herself yet. She showed Ratty the diary, watched his pained face as he read it, and then listened in silence as he explained about the fog and the hunters or whatever they were. She didn't believe it, putting most of his tale down to youthful exuberance.

He must have been mistaken, perhaps scared at being lost and embellishing the tale to make it more interesting and to deflect from his fear. Youth was the great pretender.

When he had finished, Ratty sat down, as though telling the story had taken a weight from his shoulders and he could now relax, safe in the knowledge that the information was in the hands of an adult.

"So what are you going to do?" he asked.

"Do?" Chase frowned. "Well, I think I should tell someone that you're here. Your parents will be worried about you."

"No, I mean about the fog and the armed men."

"Ah, that." She nodded her head. "Well, it's quite a story."

"Story! It's not a story. That's what happened." His lower lip trembled.

Chase could see Ratty was becoming agitated. "Would you like something to drink? Perhaps something to eat, you look famished."

Ratty licked his lips. "Well, perhaps just a glass of water and a piece of toast."

"Water and toast! I'm sure I can rustle up something better than that." Walking into the kitchen, she quickly shut the back door and locked it. She still hadn't forgotten about Belinda, and as she prepared a meal of pasta with tomato sauce and vegetables, she kept glancing warily out of the window, but only her own pale reflection stared back, ghostly and surreal. She hadn't mentioned to Ratty that she had also seen a figure in the fog, afraid that it would only fuel his fertile imagination.

But something was going on. Of that she was sure. Thoughts bounced around her head like a pinball.

When the meal was ready, she poured a glass of orange juice and called Ratty through.

He stepped into the kitchen, warily eyeing the back door that was now shut before fixing his eyes on the food and

112

sitting at the table.

As though his fear was forgotten, he devoured the meal in a matter of minutes and drank another two glasses of juice before wiping his mouth and saying he was full.

Chase finished her own meal, thinking about what Ratty had said. He certainly seemed to know the house, and he did have a key. He also knew about the dog, Samson, but it didn't make any sense. Why did he think his granddad still lived in the house? The last entry in the diary had been in June, one month ago. Where had the author gone after that? Had he moved away and just forgotten the diary? Or was he dead? She didn't like to voice this last option to Ratty. He looked serious enough, and she honestly believed *he* believed his story. But, thinking of Belinda, she knew looks could be deceptive. Perhaps he was delusional. Perhaps he had run away from a secure home. Or perhaps she was just being stupid, having been left badly shaken by Belinda and the news of the pregnancy.

What she needed - what *they* needed - was a good nights sleep. It was too late to tell anyone Ratty was here now, and she didn't fancy going out in the dark, not when Belinda might be out there somewhere. Just in case, she checked her mobile phone again, but there was still no signal available.

"What do you say to a good nights sleep?" she suggested, throwing the phone down.

As if warmed to the idea, Ratty yawned "But what are we going to do? Where's my granddad?"

Chase didn't know what to say. "There must be a reasonable explanation."

"You do believe me, don't you?"

Chase looked at him across the table and smiled. "Of course I do. Now come on, you can have the spare room."

Having shown Ratty to the spare bedroom, Chase retired to her own room and propped the dressing table chair under the door handle, jamming the door shut, just in case Ratty really had escaped from a secure unit. She knew she was being foolish, but after the day she'd had, being foolish was the least of her worries.

***

Tears rolled down Ratty's face as he slept and he woke in the morning feeling upset and miserable. He dressed quickly and ran downstairs, hoping to see his granddad sitting at the table, his granddad who had charmed him with wartime tales, his granddad who had been commended for bravery, his granddad who had single handedly taken a German machine gun post, his granddad who used to playfully scare him with ghost stories, his granddad who helped him with his homework.

But he wasn't there.

Even his belongings were gone. The furniture, the photographs, the mementoes, the ornaments, the pictures Ratty had drawn for him aged six and which had been framed and hung on the wall, the clothes, the smell, it was all gone. It was as though he had never existed. All that was left was a memory, and even that was faded. He couldn't remember his granddad's face, couldn't remember what the twinkle in his eye looked like, couldn't remember what the smell of his pipe tobacco was like. He was angry with himself, angry that he could forget what the person he loved, looked like. Screwing his eyes up, he tried to conjure up his granddad's image in the darkness behind closed lids, but all he saw were spots of luminescence, and even those disappeared, replaced by tears that he quickly wiped away.

Movement upstairs: the squeak of a bedspring. The creak of a floorboard. The sound of someone being sick. The flush of a toilet. Ratty held on to the hope that it would be his granddad that walked down the stairs, but it wasn't.

"Morning. Did you sleep well?" Chase asked, walking into the kitchen wearing jeans and a T-shirt.

Ratty shook his head. "I want to know where my granddad is?"

"So do I."

"He wouldn't leave, not without telling us."

"Have you eaten anything?"

Ratty shook his head.

"Right, first things first. A cup of tea, then breakfast. I don't know about you, but I don't function without my morning cuppa."

Ratty watched her as she brewed the kettle. He was still wary of the strange woman in his granddad's house. What was she doing here? It didn't make any sense. How could she win the house in a competition when it belonged to his granddad? His head spun with questions.

"By the way, were you here earlier in the day yesterday, looking through the window?" Chase asked.

"No. Why?"

"Oh, it's probably nothing. Do you know any of your granddad's neighbours, like the woman down the lane, Belinda?"

"Yes, I know her. She's that old lady."

"And what's she like?"

"Oh, you know. Old but nice, I suppose. Why?"

"No reason really. Here you are, would you like sugar in your tea?"

Ratty shook his head and gratefully accepted the steaming brew.

"Is there any chance you're mistaken, you know, about your granddad? Could he have moved out and you perhaps forgot he'd moved somewhere else?"

Ratty glared at Chase. "I would know if my granddad had moved. Do you think I'm stupid or something?"

"No, no, of course not. It's just... I don't know, strange."

"You can say that again."

"Those men you said were in the fog."

"Hunters," Ratty said, sipping his tea.

"Hunters. Did you catch any of their names?"

"No. Why don't you believe me?"

"I do."

"No you don't. I can tell. But then why should I believe you? Why should I believe that you won my granddad's house in a competition? Don't you think that sounds just as stupid to me?"

Chase considered this for a moment. "I suppose when you put it like that, it does."

"And it's not just my granddad. Your friend's gone too!"

"She's only gone home."

Ratty shook his head. "You're stupider than me then if you believe that. Can't you see there's something going on? They're covering something up. They brought you here for a reason."

Chase laughed. "Now you are being silly. Why would they want to do that? It's not as if I have anything important. I've got no money, nothing they could want. You've been watching too many films."

"And you haven't been watching enough. These things happen."

"Not to me they don't. Now what would you like for breakfast?"

Ratty stared out of the window. "I'm not paranoid, but they're after me," he whispered. "Walls have ears. That's what they say, isn't it?"

"They also have sausages. And that's what we're having for breakfast. Sausage, egg and beans. How does that sound?"

"Like you want to change the subject."

"I could swear you sound like an old man, worrying."

Ratty sighed and shook his head.

"Well you've got plenty of time to worry about things when you get older. You should learn to relax and not get these silly ideas in your head."

"If I live that long."

"Now that's enough of that. Look, we'll get this sorted out after breakfast and get you home. Then you'll see how silly you've been."

Ratty didn't reply. He watched a crow strutting across the garden before someone knocked at the front door, startling the bird into flight.

Ratty noticed the knock at the door startled Chase as much as it had the crow (she looked like she would fly away too, if she could), and she almost dropped the frying pan she had taken out from below the sink.

Ratty followed her out of the kitchen, noticing that she hesitated before finally opening the door.

"Miss Black," a man drawled.

"Drake. What are you doing here?"

"Just calling to see if you've heard from a young boy who's gone missing. We thought he might turn up here, as this is where his granddad used to live."

"What have you done with him," Ratty vehemently said, stepping from behind Chase so he could see the imposing figure stood in the doorway.

"Peter Rathbone. We've been *looking* for you."

Ratty noticed Drake's permanent harelip sneer grow more pronounced.

"Where's my granddad?"

"Yes, what is going on?" Chase asked.

"Going on, Miss Black, that's what I was going to ask you. Are you usually in the act of harbouring runaways? Didn't you stop to think that someone would be looking for him? Worried even? Why didn't you tell someone he was here?"

"Runaways." Ratty glared. "Who's a runaway?"

"Now, now Peter. I've come to take you back. Your parents are worried about you."

"And I'm worried about my granddad," Ratty replied, putting on a show of bravado he didn't feel when faced with the behemoth before him.

"Teenagers!" Drake raised his eyebrows in disbelief. "Now you know your granddad left the village to live with you and your parents as he was getting too old to look after himself."

"What are you on about? You're lying. Chase, he's lying. This is my granddad's house. He lives here."

Drake shook his head and gave a derisory nasal snort. "I'll bet he's been telling you all sorts of nonsense, hasn't he. It's a good job you're old enough to know better, Miss Black."

Ratty couldn't believe what was happening. He could see from the expression on Chase's face that she would rather believe Drake. His story was more acceptable.

"There you go Ratty, I told you there was nothing to worry about," Chase said, smiling benignly at him.

"Nothing to worry about. You really are stupid."

"That's enough of that," Drake barked, clipping Ratty round the ear and grabbing him by the arm.

"Hold on a minute." Chase stepped forward to intervene.

"No, *you* hold on," Drake spat menacingly. "Don't you know it's a crime to harbour a runaway minor? Do you really want to press the matter, Miss Black? Do you really want to be prosecuted for what you've done? Well, *do you?*"

"I... I didn't realise. I'm sorry."

"Well, I just hope his parents don't want to take the matter further."

"But I'm *not* a runaway," Ratty protested.

"So what are you doing here, Peter? Why aren't you at home, where you should be?"

Ratty wanted to flee, but Drake still had a grip on his arm. "Let go of me," he shouted.

"We don't want to lose him again, do we? I'll take him with me and let his parents deal with it."

Ratty looked at Chase, imploring her to believe him, but he could see that it was too late. The illusion that is the wisdom of age had defeated him.

"Go with Mr. Drake, Peter. Everything will be okay, I promise."

Ratty noticed that Chase called him Peter, and he knew he was lost. She had succumbed to Drake's brute threats. He screamed, struggling to break free, but Drake gripped him too tightly.

"Don't worry, Peter. I'm sure Mr. Drake will let me come with you, just to make sure everything's all right."

"No, Miss Black, Peter's parents are eager to have him home. We don't want to complicate the matter any further and I think you've done enough damage already."

"I see." Chase shrugged her shoulders in resignation.

"I'm sorry, Peter, but I'm sure when this is all over, they'll let you come and visit your granddad's old house? And me, I hope, just to let me know everything's OK."

"Say thank you, Peter," Drake said, shaking Ratty.

"Fuck you." Ratty spat in his face.

"Now do you see what his parents have to cope with?" Drake said, wiping his face and pulling Ratty outside.

"Do you have to be so rough with him?"

"It's the only thing they understand. Have a nice day, Miss Black."

Ratty didn't know what the hell was going on, and from all accounts, neither did Chase.

He looked back at the house, hoping to persuade Chase not to let Drake take him, but she had already shut the door.

***

Tears rolled down Chase's cheeks. She didn't know why she was so upset. She hardly knew the boy. It was just something about the way he was hauled away that worried her. She leaned against the door, half slumped, ashamed at the weakness she had shown in front of Drake. She should have spoken out more. Demanded to accompany them. But that wasn't how she was. She was too weak, too used to skirting conflict to take a head-on stand, especially against someone as menacing as Drake. That was why she needed Jane.

She hugged her stomach and waited for the tears to stop before going into the kitchen and starting the breakfast she had intended to make for Ratty. Why would Ratty have lied about his granddad? Why would he say his granddad was still living in Paradise when he wasn't? It didn't make any sense. The thoughts turned over in her head as the overcooked sausages split like cauterised fingers in the frying pan.

Turning off the heat, she slopped the sausages onto a plate with half the fat from the frying pan, quickly put her trainers on and ran out of the house. She couldn't let Ratty go, not with Drake. Whether or not he was lying was irrelevant. He had been visibly scared, and she knew only too well how that felt.

Running down the lane, she threw a cursory glance at Belinda's house. The curtains were drawn and smoke curled from the chimney but there was no sign of Belinda.

At the intersection at the bottom of the lane, she looked both ways, but there was no sign of Drake or Ratty. She glanced at the fog in the field beyond, at the church in the distance, toward the surgery, but there was no one around. Where could they be? she wondered, biting her bottom lip. It was like a ghost town.

Movement in the hedge to her left drew her attention. Leaves rustled as something disturbed them. Frowning, Chase approached the hedge, expecting a bird to fly out when she suddenly caught sight of a dirty face, masked by the foliage. The eyes were hollow pits, the cheeks drawn and thin; there was something about the face that she couldn't quite put her finger on.

"Hello, are you coming to see me?"

Startled, Chase turned to see Adam jogging toward her. He was dressed in jogging bottoms and a sweatshirt and he was sweating slightly and seemed out of breath. "No, I... erm, have you seen Drake and a young boy?" She didn't mention the person hiding in the hedge in case she had just imagined it, in case she was succumbing to the madness that seemed to grip the village.

"No." Adam shook his head.

She glanced back at the hedge, but just as she'd feared, the face had disappeared.

"How are you feeling today? Have you come to terms with the news I gave you?"

She whirled back on Adam. "You mean about being pregnant? You can say it you know, and no, I haven't."

"Well, if you want to talk." He shrugged. "Remember you've got an appointment."

"Yes, I know." After a moment she said, "Actually, you can help me. Do you know who used to live in High Top

Cottage before me?"

"Yes, that was Albert Rathbone. Nice old chap."

"What happened to him?"

"Happened, what do you mean?"

"It's easy enough. Where is Albert Rathbone now?"

"I think he went to live with his son."

Chase nodded. "That's what Drake said."

"And you don't believe him?"

"Yes... no... I don't know what to believe any more. You see, Drake came to the house for Peter Rathbone."

"Peter, he was here?"

"Yes, he came to the house. Do you know him?"

Adam frowned. "Only through the missing person report I had. And where is he now?"

"That's what I want to know." She quickly explained about Ratty turning up at the house, although she omitted to mention his outlandish story.

"Well, you head toward the church and I'll go the other way to see if we can find them."

"Will he be safe with Drake?"

Adam frowned. "Of course he will."

Chase was fond of Adam, but she felt strange, knowing that he knew she was pregnant with another man's baby. She wondered if he could love a woman carrying another man's child and she blushed. This wasn't the time to be thinking about her love life - or lack of.

"We'll meet back by the pond in twenty minutes. OK?" he said, jogging backward as he spoke.

Chase nodded and walked toward the church, hoping that he hadn't noticed her blush.

She intended to question the vicar, but she remembered the last time she had been in the church. Would the vicar be drunk again? Would he even remember her last visit, and if so, would he be embarrassed?

Sunlight dappled the road through the patchwork of leaves above and in the distance she noticed two people standing further up the lane, and although she should have felt relieved to see someone, she wasn't. Even at this distance, she felt there was something wrong with them, something that the eye couldn't see. She knew she was being foolish, but she couldn't help it. As she watched them, she thought that she saw one of the figures roughly push the other one over.

Walking out from beneath the shade of a tree, sunlight stabbed her eyes, making them water and she blinked and rubbed them. When she looked back up and her vision had refocused, the two people had disappeared, but a demented chuckle was delivered to her on the wind like a warning.

Increasing her pace, she hurried to the church and ran inside, causing the vicar, who was walking down the aisle, to look up, startled. For a brief moment she thought that she saw a look of fear on his face, but it dropped away as quickly as it appeared. He looked sober and even managed a weak smile. Did he remember? she wondered. Or is he just putting on a brave face?

"Hello again. It's Chase isn't it?" He held out a pudgy hand, which Chase shook, slightly repulsed by his sweaty palm.

"Yes. How are you?" She didn't want to broach the subject about the last time she had seen him, but she felt there was a sense of embarrassment about him, as though *he* remembered.

"I'm glad I've seen you."

"Oh, why's that?" She was expecting an apology, a need to purge the soul.

"How's your friend?"

"You mean, Jane?"

The vicar nodded.

"I don't know really. She's gone home." She wanted to mention she had come around the other day to use the phone to call her, but that would give flesh to the unspoken issue, giving it life, making it real.

"Really? I was sure I saw her yesterday with Drake and Moon."

"Well, you must be mistaken. If she was still here, she would have contacted me."

"Would she? What if she couldn't?"

"And why on earth wouldn't she be able to? What are you implying?" Chase felt a knot of fear twist in her stomach, or was it the unborn baby moving? How big would the foetus be after four months? Why was he putting doubt in her mind?

"Unto the woman he said, I will greatly multiply your sorrow and thy conception; in sorrow thou shalt bring forth children." The vicar bowed his head and shook it.

Chase didn't like the implied meaning of the vicar's rhetoric. Did he know she was pregnant? But how could he?

"I don't understand what you mean," she said. Was everyone around here mad?

Casting furtive glances around the church, the vicar motioned for Chase to follow him outside, which she apprehensively did.

His long gown fluttered like wings as he strode purposefully between the headstones toward the far corner of the graveyard, near to the bank of fog. When he stopped, he gestured to a grave with his arm. "There is no truth in him. When he speaketh a lie, he speaketh of his own: for he is a liar, and the father of it."

Chase looked down at the fresh grave the vicar indicated and read the simple inscription on the headstone:

ALBERT RATHBONE
1920-2002

Chapter 13

Chase stood with her mouth open in disbelief before finally finding her voice. "It can't be. This isn't the man who lived in High Top Cottage. Drake told me he was living with his son. So did Adam!"

The vicar shook his head and took a hip flask out of his pocket. He offered Chase a drink, which she refused with a shake of her head before he took a large swallow himself.

"I don't understand what's going on." She couldn't take her eyes from the inscription.

"And ye shall know the truth, and the truth shall make you free."

"What truth?"

"This. The truth." He gestured at the grave, then at the fog.

"Tell me what you mean." She sank to the floor, thinking of Ratty and his insistence at the tale he had told her. Remembering the look on his face as Drake hauled him away, she began to cry.

"Don't you get it yet?" the vicar said, taking another swig from his hip flask. "We have made a covenant with death, and with hell are we at agreement."

"Just tell me what you mean." Chase had had just about enough of the vicar's oblique preaching.

The vicar shook his head. "And God shall wipe away all tears from their eyes; and there shall be no more death, neither sorrow, nor crying, neither shall there be any more pain: for the former things are passed away."

"Please, just tell me what the bloody hell's going on. What do you mean?" She wanted to slap him. She remembered that according to his diary, Albert Rathbone had done just that: *Forgive me Father, for I have twatted a man of the cloth.* She now knew how he felt.

The vicar took another drink. "It means if you're stupid enough to seek the truth, don't expect to like what you find. Albert Rathbone searched for the truth."

Chase looked down at the grave and a chill climbed up her spine with icy claws.

"If you still want answers, go to the old farmhouse on the far-side of the hill and seek an audience with the fool. God save us." Shaking his head, the vicar walked away, mumbling to himself.

Chase stayed looking at the grave for a few moments. She didn't understand any of it. The more she thought about it, the more tangled the story became and the more she regretted letting Drake take Ratty away.

Who was the fool? Was it the Raggedy man who Albert Rathbone had made a final reference to in the diary: *Raggedy man knows.*

With a head full of questions, she walked out of the graveyard. There was only one way to find out.

The sun had now risen high in the sky, the light diffused by the clouds that had drifted over the horizon, making it hard to see where the fog stopped and the cloud started as it all fused to become a smothering blanket of whiteness.

As she left the graveyard, she noticed Adam's receptionist, Patricia, walking toward her carrying a bunch of flowers. Seeing Patricia reminded her she was meant to be meeting Adam by the pond and she bit her lip, wondering whether to just carry on to the abandoned farmhouse, or whether to keep her appointment?

Patricia was frowning.

"Hello again." Chase smiled, although inside, she was churning up.

Patricia stopped walking and glared at Chase. "I was taking these to the graveyard," she said. "But I think I'll just give them to you instead."

She held the flowers out and Chase looked at them: White lilies.

"Sorry, but why would you give them to me?" She frowned.

Patricia scowled. "Because they're for dead people."

Chase didn't realise her mouth was open until a fly flew into it, making her gag and spit. "I beg your pardon?" She wasn't sure she had heard properly.

"Dead people. Dead people. Dead people," Patricia sang.

Chase took a step back and Patricia took a step forward.

"Dead people. Dead people..." She flung the flowers at Chase before skipping away toward the church, still chanting her macabre litany.

Chase stared at the flowers scattered at her feet, shaking her head in disbelief. First Belinda had thrown rock cakes at her, and now Patricia had thrown flowers. What next? What the hell is going on? She wondered.

***

Beneath the black sky, the farmhouse looked even more decrepit. Nervously, Chase approached the swinging front door. The last time she was here, Jane had been with her, bolstering her bravado. Now she was alone. All alone. Thunder rumbled in the distance, a celestial drum roll that shook the ground and startled her.

Unsure whether to enter the building, Chase stood on the threshold, holding the door open as another peal of thunder played percussion to the raindrops that began to fall, sizzling as they hit the rusted metal panels on the barn. In the darkening atmosphere, the interior of the building appeared to come alive with shadows. A rancid smell filled the air. A sudden wind blew past her, snatching the door from her grasp and slamming it against the frame. The house shuddered. Hesitantly, she opened the door back up, noticing objects suspended from the rafters of the room swinging like incense holders. She narrowed her eyes, trying to make out what they were before a flicker of lightning illuminated the scene, and she wished that she hadn't see it after all: dead animals; rabbits, squirrels and pigeons hung up like a grotesque mobile hanging from a crib.

Chase felt sick; she remembered the dead squirrel in her

garden. She backed away from the door, clumsily tripping over rubble on the floor, her balance suddenly precarious, causing her to flail her arms like a windmill as she began to fall. Snatching at empty air, she fell backwards to the floor, her head smashing onto a brick. Pain suffused the horror and a flicker of lightning illuminated a dirty, gaunt face peering down at her before the darkness of oblivion claimed her consciousness.

"So are you going to tell me what's going on?" Ratty asked as Drake dragged him through the fog.

"You ask too many questions," Drake growled. "Just like your granddad, before I killed him."

Ratty flinched. "You're lying."

"Why would I? But you'll be seeing him again sooner than you think."

"You wouldn't dare. My friend will have told people where I am by now."

"Really!" Drake seemed unfazed.

As the wind picked up, it parted the fog like curtains revealing they were at a barrier in a perimeter fence guarded by men in army attire, their guns levelled at the floor as they saluted Drake. Imaging devices covered their features, making them look like bug-eyed insects.

Passing through the barrier, Ratty was dragged to a small, squat building. Drake punched a code on an electronic keypad and the door slid open. Ratty was about to protest, but Drake pushed him inside and the door slid shut with a laughing emission of compressed air.

"Get out of that one, Houdini," Drake bawled from outside.

Inside the building it was dark and Ratty picked himself up off the floor and reached out his hands to feel his way around. His shins banged into something and he muttered a curse before crouching down and feeling what he had bumped into. It felt like a bed. He squashed his hands down on a hard mattress, testing it when his fingers brushed against warm flesh. He recoiled in shock, a small squeal of fear issuing from his mouth.

"Please, please don't hurt me," a voice screamed.

"Izzy, is that you?"

"Ratty. Oh my god, Ratty, it's you." Ratty felt arms encircle him as Izzy hugged him and a tear rolled down his cheek. He was glad she couldn't see him in the dark. He wanted to kiss her, but he didn't dare in case she felt his tears.

"What are you doing here?" he asked when she finally released him.

"I was following the road, like you said, but they found me. I didn't hear them coming, but they had those goggles on, you know. Ratty, I'm sorry. What are they going to do to us?" She sniffled.

Ratty shook his head. "I don't know." Slowly his eyes adjusted to the dark and he could just make Izzy out as she sat on the edge of the bed. She had her face in her hands and he could tell she was crying.

He sat down next to her and put his arm around her shoulder. "I won't let anything happen to you, I promise." He only hoped he could keep his promise.

He thought about Chase. Why hadn't she believed him? What was it about adults that made them think they had the monopoly on the truth? Did you have to reach a certain age before they took any notice of you? Before, in their eyes at least, you left behind childish things.

"There's definitely something weird going on," Ratty sighed. "I went to my granddad's house in Paradise, but he wasn't there. Instead, there was a woman who said she'd *won* his house in a competition! Can you believe it?" He shook his head in disbelief, not telling her that Drake had said his granddad had been killed as he didn't believe it - didn't want to believe it. "Have you heard anyone saying anything? Something that might tell us what's happening?"

Izzy shook her head and wiped her eyes. "I was brought straight here and then a man called Moon came and talked to me. He wanted to know how I got here. Why I had gone into the fog? Where you were? Things like that."

Ratty nodded his head. "They must have known we were missing, because I think they were looking for us."

"Then why won't they take us home?" She started crying again.

"Because now we know they're here. I don't think they want people to know about them and what they're doing."

"But we don't know what they're doing!"

"Yes, but if we go home and start talking, people are going to ask questions. Didn't you ever find it strange that the fog has been here for so long, but has never been on the news? It didn't even get a mention in the local paper. No, these people must have high connections to cover up what they're doing so well."

"You're just being stupid. They couldn't make a village disappear."

"Then why don't you explain it?"

She hesitated. "I can't."

"Well, whether you believe it or not, in a sense, Paradise has disappeared. It's there, but it isn't visible. No one has been in or out for nearly two years. It's like the story of Sleeping Beauty, only instead of a forest, there's fog stopping people entering."

"And are the people sleeping?" Izzy asked, sarcastically.

"No, but they seem, I don't know, different." Ratty didn't rise to her bait.

"What do you mean?"

"Well, I never really talked to any of them as I wanted to get to my granddad's house, but I saw a couple of the villagers and there was something about them."

"In what way?" Izzy frowned.

"Well, they were, I don't know, it was like when you see someone and you have to cross the road to avoid them, because you can tell there's something wrong with them, mentally, you know, like Mental Mickey who puts an elastic band around his dick to stop himself wetting his pants. It's in the way they look and act."

"So what did the villagers do?"

"That's just it, they didn't *do* anything. They didn't have to. I avoided them because... I don't know, I was scared I suppose." He didn't like admitting it.

"That's just stupid."

"You wouldn't think that if you'd been there."

Izzy shrugged her shoulders. "What on earth did you have to be scared of?"

"I don't know, but I'm sure as hell going to find out."

Chapter 14

When Chase recovered from the concussion, it was dark. She slowly opened her eyes and moved a hand to rub the spot where her head had struck the brick. There was a large bump and she winced as she touched it. Her second instinct was to protectively hug her stomach and hope the baby was all right - She still couldn't believe it. A baby!

She realised she was still lying on the floor, but she was no longer outside the farmhouse: she was inside, the macabre, rotting mobile of carcasses swinging above her head. Slowly the realisation dawned that someone must have dragged or carried her, as she doubted she had crawled inside by herself. Panic flooded her system, starting in the tips of her fingers and spreading through her body like liquid nitrogen, freezing her blood.

She could feel her heart hammering away; could see the slight crystallisation of her breath creating ghosts in the cold air as she fought to control her breathing. She didn't want to move, too afraid. Her eyes darted nervously around the room, and she inclined her head slightly, taking in the skeletal armchair and the upturned cupboard. Was that someone in the corner, watching her? She wanted to run, and she started to stand up, but a wave of nausea swept over her and she collapsed back down.

Looking back toward the corner, the figure, if that's what it was, had slipped away.

The carcass mobile twisted in the breeze, spreading the scent of death. The smell seemed stronger near the floor and she gagged.

Movement caught her eye, startling her. A shadow within shadows.

A rabbit carcass swung into the one next to it as someone slipped past, setting in motion a morbid Newton's cradle that swept across the room. The beams of the ceiling creaked as the pendulous weights swung to and fro, dead, glassy eyes sparkling in the darkness as though the hosts had been reanimated.

A floorboard creaked as pressure was applied.

"Who's there?" Chase whispered.

No one answered.

Outside, an owl hooted and she heard the beat of wings as it flew past.

"I know there's someone there." Her eyes scanned the room, looking for the slightest motion.

"*Here*," a voice hissed, causing Chase to jump.

"What do you want?" Her throat was dry; she could hardly get the words out. Peering toward where the voice emanated, she saw someone was sitting in the skeletal armchair, his features hidden.

"Want? What do *you* want?"

Chase tried to sit up but her head throbbed when she moved. "Answers," she said.

"Answers, solutions, revelations."

"Just answers."

"*Just* answers. Questions sometimes lead to answers."

Chase bit her lip. There was something about that voice! She tried to see the figure more clearly, but he was cloaked in nocturnal shadow.

"Ask me a question."

Chase could hear him tapping his foot on the floor. She licked her lips; tried to swallow. "What's going on, here in Paradise?"

"Paradise, nirvana, heaven, utopia. Do you believe in paradise?"

"I thought you were going to give me answers, not more questions."

"*Do you believe in paradise?*" he hissed.

"It depends what you mean by paradise, the village, or the dream?"

"Paradise, inhabited by mankind before the first sin. What was the first sin?"

132

"I don't know. Look, I want answers, not puzzles."

"*Answer my question,*" he hissed again. "What was the first sin?"

"I don't know, something in the bible about eating an apple."

"An apple. The tree of life. Knowledge. Snow White. And so endeth today's lesson." The man stood, shook his garments around him and walked out of the room, laughing.

"Wait, come back." Chase gained her feet, fighting the nausea and giddiness that swept over her. "You haven't answered anything."

A disembodied voice came back out of the darkness: "Oh, but I have." A door slammed.

This is bullshit, she thought, staggering to the back door, holding the back of her head in an attempt to alleviate the pain. But the Raggedy man had gone. "Asshole," she mumbled.

What had he given her but more questions? Apple. Tree of life. Knowledge. Snow fucking White. What was this crap? Her head hurt - it hurt even more if she tried to think. Fighting back the pain, she started for home (although now she was beginning to doubt it ever would be a home, at least not to her).

Now she new why the vicar called the Raggedy man the Fool. She wanted to kick the vicar's holy ass. He must think she was a fool too, telling her to go and see him.

In the dark, the ambience was foreboding. Nocturnal predators skittered through the undergrowth, hunted through the trees, stalked on the breeze. She sensed, more than saw them. Felt their eyes, tracking her. In the darkness, shapes twisted, distorted from the recognisable into the startling, into the bizarre, into the terrifying. Tree trunks, contorted by shadows, became old hags. Bushes became huge, lurking beasts with teeth and tusks. A patch of light through the trees became a spectre, the leaves adding the illusion of dark sockets for eyes and giving contour to the illusory shape. Branches became claws, reaching out to grab her.

Somewhere in the night, someone screamed and Chase

flinched.

A twig snapped. Someone was following her. She surveyed the trees that lined the path, but darkness held dominion.

She quickened her pace, but that created more noise as she disturbed the undergrowth; which made her heart beat faster; made the fear swell; caused her to let out a little whimper of fright; made her feel more vulnerable.

Something flew past her face, black as pitch and she thought of the witches searching for their heads.

She wanted to scream, but she couldn't. If she started, she wouldn't be able to stop. Something shimmied up a tree, disturbing leaves as it danced along a branch. Something called out with a feral shriek; something replied with a death cry as it was attacked.

Up ahead was a house, its windows in darkness. But it was civilisation, and it came as a welcome relief after the primordial backwoods. She felt herself relax slightly, her heart beginning to slow its frenetic beat. Then another house appeared, then another, these ones illuminated behind curtains that hid whatever macabre play was being enacted within. Shadowy figures were visible, silhouettes behind the curtains. Some of the figures were animated like marionettes in a shadow play; others were motionless. She heard conversations emanating from some of the houses, voices raised in argument.

Hurrying up the lane to High Top Cottage, she saw lights burning in Belinda's house, heard muffled conversation, and heard the crash of breaking pottery, a shout, a squeal, and a laugh. Chase shivered and hurried to her house. Unlocking the door, she slipped inside and locked it behind her. She didn't turn on the light, feeling that it would advertise she was home (for some reason she couldn't explain, she didn't want people to know she was here). Walking through to the lounge she slumped onto the settee, exhausted. Thoughts and ideas drifted through her mind like clouds, forming into recognisable shapes and possible answers before dissipating as she dismissed them.

She heard someone laughing outside, the sound carried on the breeze so she couldn't tell where it originated. It wasn't a comical laugh, more like a demented chuckle that made the hairs on her arms stand on end. Was that a gunshot? She bit her lip and crept to the window to look out over the village, her arms folded protectively across her chest. After five minutes of seeing nothing, she returned to the settee and sat back down.

As she sat thinking, it seemed as though the walls were closing in, the giant who had originally buckled the walls having returned to compress them more. She felt the weight of the house pressing down on her, making her feel claustrophobic. But it was preferable to going outside.

***

A knock at the door woke Chase from her slumber. Daylight flooded through the window, and she wiped sleep from her eyes. How long had she slept? Rising, she yawned and walked through the hall to the front door. Her hand hovered over the lock as she hesitated.

"Chase, are you in there?"

It was Adam. Unlocking the door, she pulled it open and smiled at him, momentarily embarrassed by her shabby appearance as she was still wearing the same clothes from the day before.

"I was worried about you," Adam said. "Yesterday, I waited by the pond for you, but you never turned up."

"Sorry about that. Did you find Ratty, I mean, Peter?"

Adam shook his head. "Not a trace. I'm sorry. I take it that you didn't either?"

"No. Please, come in." She stepped aside to let him enter before leading him through to the kitchen, absently noticing her reflection in a mirror in the hall and realising she looked a state. Running her hands through her hair, she accidentally touched the bump that had resulted from her fall and she winced.

"Are you okay?"

"Yes. Would you like a drink?"

Adam frowned before nodding his head. "Tea would be nice."

She filled the kettle, but remembering the vicar's brown, dirty water she didn't make herself a drink: *Drink no longer water, but use a little wine for thy stomach's sake and thine often infirmities.*

In his drunken preaching, was the vicar telling her not to drink the water? But why? What was wrong with it? An apple. The tree of life. Knowledge. Snow White ate a poisoned apple. Connections suddenly clicked into place. Were the vicar and the Raggedy man telling her not to eat or drink anything in Paradise?

She watched Adam as he drank the tea. He noticed her and said, "Is there something wrong? You haven't poisoned it have you?" He grinned.

Chase smiled. "Of course not. Is it all right?"

"Lovely. Best drink of the day."

Chase nodded her head and sat down. "I don't know how to ask you this, but is everything all right, you know, with the people around here?"

"All right! What do you mean?" He frowned and set the cup down on the table.

"Well, it's just that some people are, I don't know, acting a little... strange."

"Strange!"

"Yes, you know, quirky."

"Quirky! I don't know what you mean." He shrugged his shoulders and picked his cup up again.

"Well, take your receptionist. For no reason at all, she threw some flowers at me. Then there's Belinda who lives down the lane. She threw rock cakes at me. Then the people waiting in your surgery were a little peculiar. Then there's the lady in the general store..."

"Chase," Adam shook his head, laughing. "You must have imagined it."

"No, it happened."

"Really. Well, in your condition, you are, how shall I put

it, going through hormonal changes. You may experience bouts of depression or be prone to crying more. For no reason at all, things may anger you or upset you, but if you think about them rationally, you will see there was nothing to get upset about."

"Wouldn't you call someone throwing things at me something to get upset about?"

Adam smiled. "Now are you sure that's what really happened?"

She felt like punching him. "Of course I'm bloody sure."

"Okay, calm down." He raised his hands in a placating manner. "Just take deep breaths. Perhaps you should have a drink." He went to the sink and filled a glass with water that he handed to her.

Accepting the glass, she licked her lips. She *was* thirsty; beads of liquid rolled down the frosted glass.

"Go on, take a sip."

Lifting the drink to her mouth, she felt the cold glass on her lips.

"That's it. Drink."

Tilting the glass, she saw the liquid pouring toward her mouth.

"Drink."

Felt the cold water on her lips.

"Drink."

Felt the water in her mouth, cold and satisfying. All it would take was one swallow.

"Drink."

One swallow and she would be sated. *Drink no longer water, but use a little wine for thy stomach's sake and thine often infirmities.* Hearing the vicar's voice in her head, she spit the water out of her mouth and threw the glass toward the sink where it smashed, sending shards of glass across the room.

Adam's mouth dropped open in surprise. "Chase, what's wrong?"

"I'll tell you what's wrong. I don't want a drink and I don't want you humouring me."

"Humouring?"

"And I don't want you repeating every damn thing I say."

Adam sipped his tea. "Repeating?"

Chase shook her head. "Please, just go. Leave me alone."

Standing up, Adam placed a hand on Chase's shoulder. "I can see you're upset. If you need to talk, you know where I am. I'll see myself out, but please, come and see me. I'm worried about you."

She watched him go, feeling momentarily guilty about shouting at him. It wasn't Adam's fault, and he was the only friend she had around here. She decided she would apologise the next time she saw him.

Hearing the front door shut, she walked through to lock it behind him. She had never felt so insecure, so unsure of what was going on around her, causing her to confuse what was real with what she imagined. Had those people really thrown things at her? She needed to talk to someone other than Adam, and the only people she had were the vicar and the Raggedy man. Neither option was very appealing. Both of them spoke in riddles to avoid a direct answer, as though the truth was too dreadful to voice.

The vicar had hinted that some things were better left unknown, but she needed to know. She needed to find out why she was here. Had there really been a competition, or was Ratty right when he called her stupid? Had she really fallen for a ploy, drawn to the house like a moth to the flame, unable to resist such a prize when everything else around her was going wrong? Jane had been more cautious; perhaps she was right to have been, but it seemed too ridiculous to think she was here for any other reason.

Oh, Jane, where are you?

She couldn't face Adam again at the moment, but she needed answers.

Walking out of the house, Chase headed for the church.

Chapter 15

When Chase arrived at the church, the doors were locked. She walked around the side, trying not to look at the bank of fog as she was sure there was someone in there, watching her. Peering through the dirty windows, she thought she glimpsed movement between the pews. She tried to clean a small circle in the glass to see more clearly, but the grime was old and defied her attempts to move it.

"Hello, is anyone there?" She knocked on the glass.

A figure dashed across the church.

"Vicar, is that you?" No one answered, and she wondered if he was drunk again? Shaking her head and frowning, she walked further around the church and along the side of the adjoining hall until the fog encroached. Despite her trepidation, she stepped into the fog and felt her way around the hall, the brickwork wet with condensation. She was surprised at how thick the fog was as she was unable to see anything more than a few feet away. At the back of the hall she came to a door that was unlocked. Even before she entered, she could smell rotting food, and she stepped inside to find the remnants of the buffet still lying discarded on the tables and floor. The word, *hell* that the man had gouged into the wall at the reception caught her eye and she shivered. Why hadn't anyone tidied up?

Walking past the tables, she approached a side door. Cautiously opening it a fraction, she peered into the church. Shadows danced around the walls, cast by the candles on the altar. Opening the door enough to pass through, Chase slipped into the church and pressed herself against the wall. Something didn't feel right.

Wooden columns held aloft the high, vaulted ceiling, obscuring her view of the front of the church. As she crept along the wall at the side of the pews, she caught glimpses of a figure, crouched before the altar. The figure didn't move, as though deep in prayer. Almost level with the altar, Chase still couldn't see the figures face so she didn't know who it was. Realising how stupid she would look to someone, creeping along the wall, she stepped out, unsure whether to disturb the person if they were praying.

She coughed, trying to attract their attention without being too forward. The figure didn't respond. Didn't even move. She coughed again, louder, the sound echoing from the eaves. Still nothing. The candle flames flickered, casting the figures shadow like a dark net across the floor. Taking a step toward the figure, Chase coughed again, realising she was being overly zealous in her attempt at getting their attention. Still no response. Praying or not, she thought it was rather rude of the person to ignore her.

"Excuse me." She reached down and touched the person's shoulder, surprised when the figure slumped to the floor. Concerned and worried, Chase looked down and a scream gathered momentum in her throat.

It was the vicar.

But it wasn't a dark shadow on the floor.

It was blood.

Someone had cut his throat. Blood glistened wetly around the fatal wound; the edges of the skin had parted like a grotesque zip. Blood covered the front of his clothes and speckled the floor in a gruesome dot-to-dot. She couldn't see a knife; he hadn't killed himself (no one slashed their own throat, did they?), and because the blood was still wet, she knew he had only recently been killed. Was the killer still here? Was that who she had seen running between the pews? Her eyes scanned the room and she backed away from the body, leaving macabre footprints in her wake. She gagged, fighting the urge to be sick.

The candles flickered, smoked, and went out as a wind blew down the aisle. A door slammed, the sound echoing around the church and Chase jumped, looking frantically around before fear propelled her toward the exit. Something fell and hit the floor behind her, but she didn't look back, too afraid. She heard footsteps, running, almost disguised in synchronisation with her own. Finding the door was locked, the scream broke from her mouth and she frantically struggled to slide the bolts across, the footsteps growing closer as the lower bolt jammed. Panicking, she slammed the bolt with the heel of her palm, ignoring the pain as she slammed it again and again until it moved with a protesting squeal. The footsteps were directly behind her as she flung the door open, the sunlight stinging her eyes. Running outside, she risked a glance behind in time to see the church door slam shut with a sound like thunder.

Although the vicar was beyond Adam's ministrations, she ran toward the surgery, her heart thudding like a drum. Fear propelled her flight, and by the time she reached the surgery, she was sweating and breathing heavy. As she dashed through reception, Patricia looked up from filing her nails into claws.

"Miss Black. Can I help you?"

Ignoring her, Chase ran through the waiting room where two people sat in silent contemplation of the empty fish tank.

"Miss Black, come back..."

Without knocking, she opened Adam's door and ran in, panting. Adam was sitting on his desk, taking a young girl's blood pressure.

"... The doctor is seeing someone," Patricia said, grabbing Chase by the arm, her sharp claws digging in and making Chase wince.

"*He's dead*," Chase screamed, trying to shrug Patricia off.

The young girl Adam was ministering too, looked up at Chase with panic etched across her face. She squealed, stood up and backed away with the sphygmomanometer still wrapped around her arm like a suckling alien. Her long, black hair fell across her face, but she made no attempt to brush it away. Black circles around her eyes marred her pale face.

"Chase, calm down, what is it?" Adam grabbed Chase by the shoulders to restrain her, his face full of concern.

"Adam, I tried to stop her," Patricia said.

Adam nodded and mouthed 'it's okay'.

"The vicar, he's dead. Someone's killed him."

"The vicar! Are you sure?" He looked sceptical.

"Of course I'm sure. He's at the church and I think the killer's still there."

Adam frowned. "Now calm down and tell me what you saw."

Chase took a deep breath. Her throat felt sore from screaming, as though she had pulled something deep in her throat. "Well, I went to see the vicar, but the church was locked and I went around the back, the door was open, I went in and he was dead, crouching in front of the altar." She spoke quickly, the words running together so they became one word. She didn't know whether Adam had understood what she said, because he was just staring at her, his expression blank.

"Come on, he's dead, someone's killed him. We've got to get help."

Adam nodded his head. "OK, let's go and have a look." He didn't look convinced.

"I can't go back there," Chase squealed, shaking her head. "We need to contact the police."

"Well, if he's dead, he isn't going to hurt you, is he!"

"Don't get fucking sarcastic with me. The killer might still be there."

"Well, I'm sure no self-respecting killer is going to hang around at the scene." As he spoke, he approached the young girl who was cowering against the wall.

"Keep her away from me," the girl said as Adam took the sphygmomanometer off her arm.

"Don't worry, she won't hurt you, will you Chase."

Shaking her head, Chase let out a loud, exasperated sigh. "Of course I won't hurt her." Why would she think that?

"Come on, let's go and have a butchers then." He walked toward the door.

Chase didn't like the way he used the word 'butchers'. He was being obtuse and sarcastic. As they walked out of the

142

surgery, the two people in the waiting room still contemplated the fish tank, seemingly oblivious to the commotion.

As if out of respect or disbelief, they walked toward the church in silence with Patricia and the young girl following at a discreet distance. When they arrived, the doors were still shut. Chase swallowed as Adam opened the door and walked inside. "Be careful," she whispered.

Adam nodded and closed the door behind him. Turning around, Chase noticed Patricia and the young girl whispering to each other. Both of them stole furtive glances in Chase's direction.

Chase swayed from side-to-side, nervous, impatient, her arms folded protectively across her chest. What was taking him so long?

When the church door creaked open, she flinched and took a cautionary step back.

Adam appeared in the doorway, motioning for Chase to follow him inside. She took another step back, biting her lip. She really didn't want to go in there. She didn't want to see the vicar again. It was the first dead person she had ever seen and she recalled how pale his face had been, drained of blood, ghostly, like the fog.

"Come on." Adam leaned out and grabbed Chase by the hand.

"No, I don't want to go in there," she protested. She didn't think she could face it, not again.

Shaking his head, Adam pulled her inside.

As they walked down the aisle, Chase looked anxiously around the church, avoiding the altar. She really didn't want to see the vicar. Why was Adam making her come back inside? Did he get some obscene pleasure out of scaring her? What if the killer was still here? Didn't he realise how dangerous it was? She just wanted to get the hell out of here and call the police.

"Well?"

Chase looked at him. "Well what?"

"Where is he?" He swept his free arm out, indicating the

altar.

Chase frowned. What did he mean? She looked toward the altar and her mouth opened in surprise. There was no one there. No body. No blood. Just a wet patch where a vase of flowers had fallen to the floor.

The room began to spin, getting faster and faster as reality disconnected, and Chase felt herself falling, as though spinning down a plughole into unconsciousness.

***

Ratty listened to the voices outside the room, straining to decipher the conversation. Izzy sat huddled at his side, shaking. He wanted to comfort her, but he felt useless. It was his fault she was in this mess.

He could feel the pressure of her breast crushed against his arm and it thrilled him, but he couldn't believe he was thinking about such things at a time like this. Izzy needed him to be strong, not horny.

As the door opened, Ratty stood up. He could see two figures silhouetted in the doorway. One was immediately recognisable as Drake due to his size.

"Bring them to my office," the other figure said before striding away.

Drake entered the room, grabbed Ratty and Izzy by their arms and pulled them outside. He was wearing green army trousers and a black body warmer over a green jumper, giving him a military demeanour.

Izzy squealed and Ratty flinched. He wished that he could help her but Drake's fingers were like a vice, digging into his biceps.

They walked up an incline and the mist slowly dissipated, allowing Ratty to see they were walking between parallel, prefab buildings, the windows of which were dark. At the end of one of the buildings, they entered through a security door into a bright reception area. A man in a blue uniform sat behind a desk. He warily eyed Ratty and Izzy until they turned a corner, out of sight.

People hurrying along the corridor seemed to give Drake a wide berth, as though out of fear or respect. Ratty decided it was fear. Stealing a glance at Izzy, he saw the same look on her face; she looked more dishevelled than ever. Her hair was dirty and matted to her head while her face was caked in mud and his heart sank. He felt like crying, but he knew he had to be strong.

At the end of the corridor a middle-aged woman was sitting behind a desk. Her brown hair was tied up in a bun, making her narrow face appear serious and grave. Drake nodded to her and let go of Izzy to knock on a door. Without waiting for a response, he opened it and pushed Ratty and Izzy through.

Inside, the room was dark, the shutters down. A bearded man was seated at a desk, his hands steepled beneath his chin as he watched them enter. His face was expressionless, deadpan, as nondescript as the dark suit he was wearing. There was a laptop computer on the desk, the screen saver reflected in the man's eyes, a phantasmal flicker-show.

"So this must be Peter Rathbone. Isabelle I've already met. My name is Nigel Moon." He moved his hands from his chin and placed them behind his head, his fingers interlocked. He leaned back, his eyes narrowed into slits.

"Why did you lock us in that room?" Ratty demanded, an attempt at bravery that fell flat as Moon out-stared him.

"It was for your own safety," Moon eventually said. "There's a lot of dangerous equipment around our facility. We wouldn't want you to get hurt, would we? What would your parents say?"

Ratty didn't like Moon's tone of voice. He seemed more threatening than concerned.

"So we can go home then?" Izzy looked expectant, eager.

"Of course you can. But first I need to ask you a few questions."

Ratty frowned. "What questions?"

"Well, what are you doing here for a start?"

"We got lost in the fog," Izzy said.

"I see. And what were you doing entering the fog?

Haven't you heard how *dangerous* it is to go wandering around like that?"

Ratty flinched as Moon stared at him.

"It was an accident, that's all." Izzy lowered her head, the expectant look fading.

"An accident. I see. So what do you think now you've seen our little facility?"

Izzy opened her mouth to speak but Ratty interrupted her. "We don't think anything. We just want to go home. We won't even tell anyone you're here."

"You won't? Now why's that?"

Ratty shrugged. "Because you don't want people to know you're here."

"And what makes you think that?" Moon leaned forward like a predator, ready to pounce.

"Nothing, I don't know what you're doing and I don't want to."

"But you already seem to know some of it. I wonder. Can I trust you to keep our little secret?"

"You can trust us, honest," Izzy said, still looking at the floor.

"I can, can I. And what do you think, Mr. Drake? Can we trust them?"

Drake sneered, his harelip giving him a macabre countenance.

"Well there we have it. For the time being, I think we will have to keep you here."

"But you said we could go home." Izzy looked up. Tears were welling in her eyes.

"Yes you can, eventually. When we have finished our work, it won't matter what you know or what you've seen."

"But I want to go home now. We won't tell anyone anything. I promise." Izzy started to cry.

"You can't keep us here," Ratty said, his voice trembling.

"And why's that Peter?"

"Because you're not allowed to."

"I see. Did you hear that Mr. Drake. I'm not allowed to keep them here. Now let me see, where's that piece of paper?" He rummaged over his desk. "Here it is. Ah yes." He briefly held the piece of paper in front of Ratty. "Would you like me to read it to you? Of course you would." He coughed for dramatic effect. "Due to the recent volatile behaviour of Mr. Rathbone, it has been deemed necessary to place his son, Peter Rathbone in the custody of Storm Enterprises for his own safety... Would you like me to read on?"

"You can't do that," Ratty protested. "My mum wouldn't send me away."

Moon skimmed his finger down the page. "Ah, here we are. Mary Rathbone. That's her signature I believe. She indicates that in the circumstances, it is in your best interests to be placed into care while she ministers to her husband."

"No, I don't believe you."

"It's all there in black and white. Signed sealed and delivered. So I can keep you here as long as I want." Moon grinned.

"What about me?" Izzy said. "That doesn't stop me going home."

"Where's that other piece of paper. Ah, here it is. Isabelle Adams social report. Unsociable. Moody. Depressed. Liable to excessive mood swings. Classic case of drug dependency."

"You what? That's not me," Izzy protested.

"Well your parents would beg to differ, especially after the drugs they found in your bedroom."

"Drugs, what drugs?"

"Your parents agreed to a period of rehabilitation, courtesy of Storm Enterprises."

"You're lying. They wouldn't believe that."

"But they do. Teenage angst can easily be modified into drug dependency in the eyes of those who don't know the truth."

"But why? Why keep us here?" Ratty asked.

"Because after you tell people what you've seen, people will start asking questions, and we can't have that, not now."

"But we won't tell anyone," Izzy sniffled.

"I know, because you won't have the chance. Take them away, Drake."

"You can't do this," Ratty shouted.

"Can and have, Peter."

"Well, what about when you do let us go? What will stop us telling people then?"

"Well, then it'll be too late. The experiment will have finished and we'll be gone. People won't even know we've been here."

"Experiment? What experiment?"

Moon tapped his nose and shook his head.

"People already know something's going on. Fog doesn't hang around for nearly two years."

"People will believe whatever they're told. They prefer it that way. Let someone else worry about it. Paradise is too far off the beaten track for people to bother about. It's a village selected for its high propensity of older residents, most of which have no relatives outside of the village. It's a unique place in that the people who live there, stay there. Generations of the same family live side by side, never falling far from the nest. Any relatives outside the village, like your father, are, shall we say, placated. We didn't stick a pin in a map. Paradise is ideal for our experiment. Secluded and close-knit with little possibility of outside interference."

Experiment! The word conjured images Ratty would rather not see.

"Then why has someone been brought in to live in my granddad's house from outside the area?"

"Ah, Miss Black. Now that's another matter entirely..."

148

Chapter 16

Chase woke with a start. She opened her eyes and looked around to find she was lying in a double bed in unfamiliar surroundings. She frowned, confused. Where was she? And how did she get here?

Throwing back the duvet, she saw she was wearing checked pyjamas, which were at least two sizes too big for her. Sitting up, she rolled the pyjama sleeves up and slipped out of bed. The curtains were drawn, but enough daylight filtered through to allow her to see clearly. At the foot of the bed were a wardrobe and an ottoman on which her clothes had been neatly folded. She undressed quickly, momentarily inspecting the small swell of her stomach before dressing in her own clothes.

The recollection of the vicar suddenly flashed through her head like a bullet and she keeled over, clutching her abdomen as though she had been shot. She thought she was going to be sick. When the pain and nausea subsided, she walked to the door and quietly opened it to look out on a dark landing with two doors leading off it and a staircase leading down.

The sound of a toilet being flushed made her start and a door opened. Adam stepped out, smiling as he rolled the sleeves of his black top down.

"Back with us I see. How are you feeling?"

"The vicar, did you find the body?"

Adam shook his head. "Come on, let's go downstairs."

"Did you find the vicar?"

"Yes. The vicar's fine."

"But I saw him..."

"Chase, you're emotional at the moment. A lot has happened to you in the last week. You've moved house and found out you're pregnant. These two events both rate highly on the stress scale. Having them both together, it's no wonder you..."

"But I saw him." She didn't understand?

"The mind is capable of playing cruel tricks."

"But he was dead." Hadn't she seen him? She thought about the diary and the madness within its pages.

"Come on, let's go downstairs. You need a drink."

Chase meekly followed him, unable to believe what she was hearing. Could she really have imagined it? Was her mind conspiring against her? Was that image of the vicar in her head just a phantom, a moment of madness?

They walked through a small hall and into a pleasant lounge. Chase collapsed onto the settee. Her head was spinning.

"Did the pyjama's fit okay?"

Chase blushed. "Fine."

"Don't worry, I'm a doctor remember. I've seen it all before."

Not mine you haven't, she thought, inspecting the ornaments on the mantelpiece to avoid looking at him.

"Would you like a drink?"

Chase nodded and watched him leave the room. Looking around, she admired the paintings on the wall. They seemed to be abstract images of Paradise; there was something dark about them, as though someone whose palette consisted of only black and gray had painted them.

A few moments later Adam returned holding two cups of tea. "I hope you're not going to break this one," he said, hesitating before handing her the cup.

Chase shook her head. She was too thirsty to refuse anything at the moment. Sitting down on a double settee, she sipped at the drink, absently looking out of the window. Adam's house was lower down the hill and his garden was overgrown with weeds. She could just see the church spire above the nettles. Had she really seen the vicar or not? Was he dead? When she dropped her gaze, she noticed Adam was staring at her.

"How are you feeling now?"

150

"Better. Thank you."

Adam smiled. "Tea, best drink of the day. I don't function without one."

"Me neither." Although she was still confused and distressed, Chase smiled back.

"I'll bet you're hungry aren't you?"

Chase nodded. When had she last eaten?

"Well, we could always go to the pub and get a bite to eat."

Chase remembered the last meal she'd had in the pub and she shook her head.

"Well I'm no Jamie Oliver, but I can rustle up a mean spag bol."

"That sounds lovely."

"Well, you sit there and relax and I'll go and make it. Put the television on if you want."

Chase looked at the television in the corner of the room. She hadn't noticed it before. How long was it since she had last seen one? It seemed like forever. Turning it on, she settled back on the settee as Hollyoaks started.

"The pictures a bit grainy I'm afraid," Adam shouted. "I think it's atmospheric, caused by the fog!"

Chase wasn't bothered. It was heaven to see people she knew, even though they did have ghost images following them across the screen. She sipped at her tea and settled back.

When Adam called her through to the kitchen, she was loath to leave the television behind but the smell of food caused her stomach to grumble and she followed the Pied Piper aroma.

Two steaming plates of spaghetti were set on the table, along with two glasses of wine. "Just the one won't hurt after what you've been through," Adam said, pulling out a chair so she could sit.

"Thank you."

"No, thank you. It's not often I get to entertain." He placed a comforting hand on her shoulder and smiled before sitting down on the other side of the table.

As she ate, Chase absently noticed the empty cans of chopped tomato on the draining board. Unlike the white cans sold in the village shop, they were the regular brand named variety found in most supermarkets.

"Don't you shop at the local store?"

Adam looked at her and screwed his nose up. "No, I erm... no." He looked embarrassed.

"Don't blame you. They aren't exactly top cuisine."

Adam laughed. "Exactly."

When she finished the meal, Chase said, "You weren't lying." She wiped the back of her hand across her mouth and licked her lips.

"Wasn't I?" He frowned.

"You really do rustle up a good spaghetti Bolognese."

The frown relaxed into a smile. "Why thank you."

"No, it should be me thanking you. You're the only person I feel at all comfortable with. You're the only one that's made me feel welcome."

"That's because you are. Unless you haven't noticed, there aren't many pretty young girls around here."

Chase blushed.

"Would you like to retire to the lounge?"

Chase nodded and they walked through and sat on the settee, taking the bottle of wine with them. Even though he had advised only one glass, Adam poured Chase another, which she quickly drank. She felt slightly light headed as the alcohol took affect and she forgot all about Mat, Jane, Ratty, Drake, the Raggedy man and the vicar.

"You're like a fresh breeze around here," Adam said, watching her.

Embarrassed, Chase lowered her head. Adam put his hand on her shoulder and she flinched. When she looked up, Adam's face was next to hers, his rapid breath on her cheek. She blushed. Her heart fluttered. Damn it, kiss me, she thought, and he did. Chase didn't resist. She closed her eyes and let herself melt into his arms. For a brief moment, she thought it was Mat she was kissing.

The kiss was tentative, testing the boundaries of

acceptance before they momentarily broke the contact, eyeing each other before they kissed again, holding the lip connection for longer. She felt one of Adam's hands caressing her back; it felt so good - his other hand slipped around to her stomach and the baby kicked.

Shocked by the movement, Chase pulled away and snatched Adam's hand off her stomach.

"What's wrong?"

"This. I can't. I'm sorry." She stood up, embarrassed. Rubbing her stomach, she felt guilty, as though she was being unfaithful – as if the *baby* knew she was being unfaithful.

Adam stared at her. "You've no need to feel sorry. It's me who should be apologising."

"No. It's not you."

"I don't mind you know. About the baby I mean."

"I know. I just need a little time."

"I understand. Well, I won't be going anywhere. Now what would you like to watch on the television?"

After a period of embarrassed silence, Chase spent an enjoyable evening at Adam's. They talked about what they liked to watch (he was as much a soap addict as she was, and he updated her on the storylines she had missed), what they liked to eat, their favourite films, and best holidays. She hadn't talked so much in ages and after he had walked her home, her throat was sore.

Back in her own house, it felt empty without a television and she retired to bed where with the help of the two glasses of wine, she slept undisturbed.

The next morning, Chase woke bright and alert. She smiled as she opened the curtains. It was another sunny day. The fog was still there, but today it had a romantic quality; it was something poets would write about. Dressing quickly in a pastel blue, knee length dress, she realised for the first time how much her stomach had grown. Where could she buy maternity clothes out here? Brushing her hair she walked down the stairs and noticed a letter on the floor in the hall.

Picking it up, she realised it wasn't a letter, just a scrap of paper. Unfolding it, she read the scrawled handwriting:

Are you ready for the next lesson?

It must have been from the Raggedy man and she was momentarily scared. He had been to her house. He knew where she lived. As the floodgates of remembrance opened, the horror came surging back. For a brief moment, she had been able to believe everything was normal; that perhaps everything was going to turn out all right. But the note shattered her illusions as easily as an axe breaking twigs.

She remembered the vicar. Chase didn't know what was real and what was illusion any more. Walking into the lounge, she screwed the note up and threw it into the fireplace where she set it alight, watching it curl and burn before sailing up the chimney like a dark request to Santa Claus. *That's what I should have done with the first letter,* she thought.

Walking through to the kitchen to boil the kettle, she tried to forget about the note, but as she poured the water into the cup, it settled on her conscience like a vulture on a carcass. *Are you ready for the next lesson?*

No longer thirsty, she poured the water down the sink; watched it swirl away. Why couldn't everything be normal? Why couldn't she have her dream; why did someone have to spoil it? She was angry more than fearful. Angry that just when she thought things might be going all right, the Raggedy man had intruded.

Picking up her shoulder bag, she stormed out of the house, determined to get to the bottom of it all. Walking past Belinda's house, she increased her pace, looking straight ahead in case Belinda was in her garden. If she saw her, she thought she might just turn around, go home, lock the door and hide.

At the bottom of the lane, she saw a face she recognised. It was the young girl who had been in the doctor's surgery when she had burst in. Feeling the need to apologise, Chase approached her.

The girl was sitting on a bench at the junction of the lane, reading a book. She was dressed in jeans and a Linkin Park T-shirt. Her black hair was long and unkempt, hanging like a dark veil over her cheek. When Chase's shadow fell across her, she looked up, startled, the veil of hair taking flight as she flicked her head, revealing a pretty face etched by the dark remnants of sleepless nights.

"Don't hurt me, please." The girl dropped the book on the floor and slid along the bench. Her blue eyes were wide and fearful.

Chase frowned. "Why would I want to hurt you?"

"You don't want to, please don't do it."

"I don't want to what? I don't know what you're on about!"

"Please."

Taking a step toward the girl, her arms held out to placate her, Chase smiled to try and calm her down.

It didn't work. The girl backed further away until she ran out of bench and fell onto the floor. "Please, please, don't kill me," she squealed.

Chase backed away. "Kill you?" Was she serious?

The girl started crying.

"What's wrong?" Chased asked.

"Everything... everyone!"

"What do you mean?"

"There's something... something. I'm sorry..." Her eyes focused on a point behind Chase.

"Is there a problem here?"

Chase turned to see Drake standing ominously behind her. He was dressed in dark trousers and a tight jumper that hugged his muscles.

The young girl gave a little squeal, stood up and ran down the lane.

"Do you always have that effect on women?" Chase asked, rounding on him.

"What was going on?"

"We were talking, that's all." She wished she *did* know

what was going on. She was now *sure* that it was Drake she had seen lurking around outside the wine bar in the city, and the thought alarmed her. It raised the question of what he was doing, but she was too afraid to ask because she might not like the answer.

Drake spat on the floor.

"How's Ratty... I mean, Peter?" she asked, wanting to change the subject.

"He's back with his parents, where he belongs."

"So how is he?"

"Like I said, he's back with his parents."

Chase sighed. Why couldn't anyone give her a straight answer?

"Are you going somewhere?" Drake glared at her.

"Nowhere specific."

Drake thoughtfully nodded his head. "Well, I'd be careful if I was you. A person can get hurt wandering around here."

"Is that a threat?"

"Just a warning."

"Well, don't worry, I'll be *very* careful."

"I'm sure you will, Miss Black, I'm sure you will."

Chase watched him walk away in the same direction as the young girl. There was definitely something strange going on in Paradise. Like Ratty had said, she was stupid not to have seen it earlier. Now everyone was a threat. Who could she trust?

Bending down, she picked up the young girls book: Paradise Lost, by John Milton. She didn't fail to spot the irony as she put the book in her shoulder bag.

Having decided to return to the old farmhouse for the vague 'next lesson', she took a detour past the church. She had to see for herself if the vicar was there, if only to prove to herself that she wasn't going mad. Approaching the front door, she felt apprehensive. If the vicar was there, then she was going mad; if he wasn't... She didn't know which option she preferred. On the one hand was madness, on the other someone's death.

The door was shut, but not locked. Entering, she didn't

want to look at the altar, but she had no choice. As she expected, there was no one there. She didn't know whether she was pleased or sad.

"Hello," she called. "Is there anyone here?" Her voice echoed through the rafters, sepulchral.

No one answered.

Walking down the aisle, she saw the vase had been replaced, although now there were no flowers in it. At the door to the rectory, she paused before knocking. Madness or death...

She knocked.

No one answered.

Turning the handle, she found the door was unlocked and she stepped through, feeling nervous as she walked through the rooms, looking for any sign of the vicar, but the house was empty.

Walking back into the church, she approached the altar and crouched down to inspect the floor where she thought she had seen the body. In the joints between the planks of wood, she thought she saw minute red streaks etched into the grain which might have been dried blood, but she couldn't be sure; at least not sure enough to wager between madness and death with any certainty.

Out of the corner of her eye, she saw the devilish coffee stain watching her and she shivered.

Shaking her head, she walked outside, thankful of the fresh air. She found the church air too dry and the atmosphere too claustrophobic. Or perhaps that was just her imagination, too?

***

As she approached the derelict farmhouse, the trees crowded around her, as though forming a screen from the world. Wary of the fall she had suffered during her last visit here, she cautiously approached the front door. Peering into the dark interior, she saw that although there didn't appear to be as many, the carcasses were still hanging from the ceiling like morbid decorations.

"I'm here for the next lesson," she said, feeling slightly foolish.

No one answered.

Stepping inside, she tentatively brushed a rabbit carcass out of the way, setting the macabre Newton's cradle in motion.

"Hello! Anybody here?"

"*Sit down*," a voice commanded, causing her to jump.

"Where are you?"

"*Sit.*"

Chase sat. Where was he? She looked around, trying to discern where the voice originated.

"You shouldn't have come."

"But you asked..."

"To the village," the Raggedy man interrupted, preempting her.

"Yes, but I did."

"Always the fool."

"Pardon?" She wasn't sure she had heard him correctly. Where was he? Movement in the next room caught her eye, a shadow among shadows, almost imperceptible.

"There's a disease. Can't you smell it? The winds of change are blowing, and it's a storm that can't be stopped."

"Storm, that's who brought me here. A competition, run by Storm Enterprises." Was there a connection?

The Raggedy man laughed, a chilling, hollow sound. "No, I brought you here."

"You? What do you mean?"

"I'm the magic man." He chuckled.

Chase started to stand up.

"*I said sit*," the Raggedy man hissed.

A shadow danced in the next room, as though prepared to take flight. She sat back down. There was something about the voice, but she couldn't quite put her finger on it.

"It's an apt word."

"What is?" She frowned.

"Storm. The vicar tried to weather the storm, but it

158

destroyed him."

"Is he really dead?" She swallowed, not knowing whether she really wanted to know the answer. Madness or death?

"Is who dead?"

"The vicar."

He hesitated. "Ah, yes, I remember the vicar. Is he dead?"

"That's what I'm asking you! Who killed him?"

"Who did? We did. They did. *I* did."

Chase flinched. The words reminded her of a sentence in the diary.

The Raggedy man laughed. "And so endeth today's lesson."

"Wait, you can't just leave it like that." She stood up and walked toward the next room. A shadow moved. Flitted away. Was gone.

Chase clenched her fists and ran after the shadow. A door opened and closed with a bang. Running through to the next room, she found she was too late. The Raggedy man had flown away. Shaking her head, she noticed animal bones scattered like runes on the floor by the camping stove, and she realised that the Raggedy man was eating the animals he had hung up to cure. She felt a momentary pang of disgust and her nausea returned.

Running outside, she retched, but was unable to be physically sick. Stomach acids still burnt her throat and she spat out a small amount of bile.

Overhead, a black bird circled and swooped, another witch searching for her head.

Chase hurried away from the old farmhouse. Who could she trust? Questions without answers, like a crossword without clues.

All around her the trees harboured flickering shadows, and Chase tried to keep her gaze on the path, tried to ignore the feeling that she was being followed. She wondered if it was the Raggedy man, or perhaps someone else, someone worse?

When she reached High Top Cottage, she quickly

unlocked the door and slipped inside, troubled to see another note on the mat. She hesitated before picking it up, now associating them with bad omens. Perhaps she should just burn it.

Curiosity got the better of her and she opened it with shaking hands.

It was from Adam, regretting he had missed her and thanking her for a wonderful night. He also asked her to meet him in the Slaughtered Dog at seven o'clock for a drink.

Unsure what to do, she decided to lie down and sleep on it, hoping answers would come in her dreams...

But all she had were nightmares.

Chapter 17

Ratty and Izzy had been kept locked up in the dark room. Izzy cried constantly. A man brought them food and water, nothing special, just ham sandwiches. They hadn't even been allowed out to use the toilet, having to face the indignity of using a bucket in the corner, both of them turning away when the other used it. The smell in the room was understandably rank, although the man who brought the food, also emptied the bucket and sprayed the air with something claiming to be the smell of summer meadows! He also provided fresh cleaning water, so at least they could have a wash.

Ratty thought they were being treated no better than animals. Worse even. From the sealed room, they had no indication whether it was night or day. Time was meaningless, a concept for those chained to a celestial timetable.

When Ratty tried to speak to the man, he got no response. It was as if Izzy and himself didn't exist, as if they were invisible.

He still couldn't believe his mother had signed him over to a bogus welfare company. What had she been thinking? He knew she was under a lot of strain, what with his father, but to do this...

Izzy sat up and spoke, bringing him out of his rumination.

"Do you really think they'll let us go?"

Ratty nodded. "Of course they will." He hoped Izzy couldn't tell he didn't believe it himself.

"I got the impression these people are above the law."

"No one's above the law."

Izzy took the cigarette packet from her pocket, looked inside and scrunched it up. She threw it on the floor. "I could do with a cigarette."

Even though Ratty didn't smoke, he knew how she felt. Cigarettes were a crutch, just like religion - he wondered whether it was too late to start praying?

As he contemplated their predicament, Ratty put his hands in his pockets, surprised to feel the penknife. He had forgotten it was there and no one had bothered searching them. Taking it out, he looked at it, turning it over in his fingers. Standing up, he approached the door and felt around the edge. There was a metal plate about six inches square to the left of the door and using the knife's screwdriver, he began to undo the retaining screws, more through boredom and frustration than with real purpose. It gave him a sense of doing something.

"What are you doing?" Izzy walked over and peered over his shoulder.

"Just trying to find a way out of here."

"You can't do that!" Alarm flashed across her face.

"Well, I don't know about you, but I don't want to stay here."

Izzy grabbed his hand. "Stop it. You'll only make things worse."

Shrugging her off, Ratty continued to turn the screws. "How can they get any worse?"

"These people are dangerous."

"I thrive on danger." He gave a half-hearted grin.

"Don't be stupid."

"Stupid is my middle name."

"You don't have to tell me." She shook her head and sat back down on the bed. "Well, I'm not having anything to do with it."

Ratty shrugged and turned his concentration back to the task of turning the screws. There were eight of them in all, and when seven of them had been removed, the plate swung clear of the hole to reveal a series of plastic air pipes worming through the wall like intestines. Ratty frowned, deep in concentration. He didn't know a lot about pneumatics, just that compressed air was used to push pistons. He recalled the sound of escaping air when the door opened and closed, and a vague idea took seed in his mind.

Grabbing one of the pipes he pulled on it; the pipe didn't move. From somewhere in the hole came the faraway sound of escaping air, like a snake hissing a warning. Without heeding it, he pulled on another pipe but it was also too tight to move. Exhaling an anxious sigh, he looked at the pipes, looked at the knife in his hand and then began stabbing the sharp point into the plastic pipes. Angry air hissed out, spitting condensation into his eyes like venom. But he didn't stop.

When all of the pipes were punctured, he approached the door, placed his hands on the flat surface and pushed. The door slid to the side and Ratty almost fell down in shock. He hadn't really expected it to work. Cautiously he peered out into the fog.

"Are you coming?" he asked, looking back at Izzy.

Izzy shook her head.

He felt as if his heart was breaking. "Okay, I'll go and get help then." He walked out of the room and into the fog. Before he had walked five feet away a hand grabbed his shoulder and he jumped, suppressing a scream.

"Okay, you win," Izzy said, her lower lip trembling.

Ratty let out a sigh of relief and smiled to himself. He wouldn't really have left her there on her own. "Come on then," he said, marching into the fog.

***

Chase woke with a start. Monsters had pursued her out of her sleep. She trembled, gooseflesh mottling her arms. Looking at her watch, she saw it was six o'clock; she couldn't believe she had slept so long. Still full of doubt, she decided to meet Adam at the pub. At least then she could surreptitiously question him about the vicar and about Paradise to see if he knew more than he was letting on.

As she put her make-up on, she heard a distant scream. Rushing to the window, she looked outside, watching for any sign of movement. But there was nothing to see. She wondered whether she had imagined it, or perhaps in her insecure state, had mistaken the call of a bird for something more sinister.

Checking all the windows and doors were secure, she slipped a serrated kitchen knife into her shoulder bag and left the house. She doubted she would use the knife to hurt someone, but knowing it was there made her feel more secure.

This time she had opted for a more conservative manner of dress: jeans, jumper and her green parka.

Walking down the lane, her gaze darted from the hedgerows to the trees to the houses, alert for any sign of movement. Clutching her shoulder bag more tightly, she felt comforted by the knowledge of its contents.

The sign outside the Slaughtered Dog swung to and fro, squealing for want of oil. The sound grated on Chase and she entered the dingy pub with her nerves set on edge.

The dark interior still held its secrets; the hint of people sat huddled in unlit corners. She couldn't believe a place could be so dark and dismal; she wished she had a torch, if only to prove that the only monsters were in her imagination.

George was in his usual place behind the bar. He eyed Chase with his usual disdain and walked down to serve her.

"Yes?" George grunted.

"Orange juice, please."

George bent down and took a bottle from the fridge beneath the optics.

"And how are you then, George?" she asked, trying to get more than a monosyllabic response from him.

George grunted in reply.

"And how's your leg?"

While pouring the orange juice into a glass, George looked up, spilling some of the drink across the counter. Chase saw a momentary flash of colour heighten his cheeks and a glint of madness in his eyes. The moment passed and he pushed the drink across the counter.

"One twenty," he grunted.

Chase rummaged in her bag for her purse, feeling the cold edge of steel brush against her hand before she paid for the drink.

"Is Adam here?" she asked, still trying to get a semblance of a conversation going.

George shook his head and walked back to his stool.

Shaking her head, Chase turned and looked for somewhere to sit when she spotted the young girl who had run away the last time she'd seen her. She was sitting by herself at a table, staring at the floor. Unsure whether to approach her, Chase remembered the book in her bag. Taking it out, she approached the girl, using the book as an excuse.

"Hello again." Chase smiled disarmingly.

The girl didn't acknowledge her.

"Are you on your own?"

As though hearing her for the first time, the girl looked up. A combination of exhaustion and fear was written across her face. She was dressed in the same clothes as the last time Chase had seen her, and there was a slight unwashed smell about her.

"You left your book behind!" She handed the book over, but the girl just looked at it morosely.

Chase put it on the table. "My name's Chase."

The girl started crying. She shook her head. "The world's gone mad."

"I beg your pardon?" Chase sat down next to her.

"I'll be next."

"Next what?" Chase frowned. She felt as though she was engaged in a cryptic conversation to which she didn't have the key.

"I don't want to change."

"Change?" She wondered whether she had heard right.

"We all change. I can feel it happening."

"What do you mean?" She heard footsteps behind her and turned to see George carrying a plate toward them. He slammed it down on the table along with a knife and fork, glaring at Chase as he did so.

"Your meal," he said to the girl before turning and walking away.

Chase smelt it before she saw it. Looking down at the plate, she frowned, unable to believe what she saw.

Still steaming in the middle of the plate was a turd. That can't be hygienic, she stupidly thought, still not quite able to believe what she was looking at.

The girl picked up the knife and fork and cut into the excrement, sliding a portion onto the tines of the fork and lifting it to her mouth.

"*Stop, don't eat that.*" Chase knocked the fork out of the girl's hand. She felt disgusted and sick just looking at it.

The girl looked from the plate to Chase, from Chase to the plate. Her hand was still hovering in the air, now without the fork. Comprehension seemed to drift across her face. "I'm going to be sick." Knocking over her stool, she ran for the door, her hand over her mouth.

Chase followed her, absently noticing George scratching his bottom and then sniffing his fingers as he walked back behind the bar, oblivious to the small commotion.

Outside, the girl threw up. As though it was catching, Chase followed suit.

"It's happening," the girl said when she had recovered.

"What? What's going on?" Chase sat down next to her.

"I don't know. But everyone's... changing."

"Changing! How?"

"I don't know." She started crying.

Chase put her arm around the girl's shoulder, causing her to flinch, but she didn't shrug her away which Chase thought was a step in the right direction.

"What's your name?"

"Mandy... yes, that's it, Mandy..."

Chase remembered the diary and then thought of George. "And when did all this start? No, don't tell me, after the fog descended."

Mandy nodded. "I think so. I don't really remember."

Chase frowned. She still wasn't sure what was going on, but she knew she was in serious trouble.

166

"I hope I haven't kept you waiting?" Adam said, walking down the lane, smiling. He was wearing black jeans and a gray shirt that was unbuttoned, revealing a white T-shirt underneath.

Chase looked up but didn't smile back. Above her head, the pub sign squealed as though in pain.

"What's wrong?" Adam asked.

"Apart from George trying to feed Mandy excrement, what could be wrong?" The sarcasm was as thick as molasses.

"Are you serious?"

"Do I look as though I'm joking?"

"You must have made a mistake. Come on, let's go inside and sort it out."

Chase stood up. "Come on Mandy. I'm not going back in and leaving you out here."

Submissively, Mandy followed them back into the pub. Chase walked straight to the table they had been seated at.

The plate was gone.

Chase looked around, confused.

"So where is it?" Adam shook his head, unable to disguise his humour. "I'm sorry, Chase, don't you realise how stupid it sounds?"

Chase clenched her fists, took a deep breath and walked to the bar. "George, where's that plate gone?" She pointed at the table.

George eyed her warily from his perch, like a vulture watching a prospective meal, waiting for it to succumb.

"You don't serve shit in here, do you George?" Adam said, laughing.

George gave a toothy, humourless grin.

"Although it sometimes tastes a bit like shit." He held his hands up in a placating manner. "Only joking. The food in here is excellent."

Looking across at Mandy, Chase saw her shake her head and frown, as though warning Chase not to pursue the matter further.

"You see. I don't know what's got into you, Chase. Let

me buy you girls a drink and we'll sit down. A pint of bitter, orange juice, and, Mandy, what would you like?"

But Mandy had gone. The door swung shut like a coffin lid in her wake. Chase made to go after her but Adam grabbed her shoulder.

"Let her go," he said quietly. "Her parents died recently. I don't think she's got over the shock yet. I think she just needs some time to grieve."

"Died! How?"

"Oh, it was a car crash."

Chase frowned. A car crash! Since moving to Paradise, the only vehicles she had seen were rusting carapaces left unused in some of the drives. "Here? How long ago?"

"No, they lived away from here, somewhere. I don't know where. It happened a few months ago. Terrible business."

***

"So Mandy lives here on her own?"

Adam nodded, but before she could question him further, George suddenly reappeared with the drinks and Adam busied himself paying.

For some reason, she felt that he was lying and she shivered.

168

Chapter 18

Conversation in the pub was stilted. Occasionally someone in the shadows would cough. A chair would scrape and someone would approach the bar before scurrying back to their dark retreat, drink in hand.

Chase didn't really know what to say. She had so many questions, but she didn't know whether Adam would tell her the truth. And if he did, how would she know?

"I'm still waiting for you to come and see me at the surgery," he said, sipping on his bitter.

"Oh, yes. I just keep forgetting."

Adam tutted. "You really have got to organize yourself. We need to check how the baby's doing. Besides, it would also give me an excuse to see you again."

Chase nodded. She still couldn't believe she was pregnant. It felt as if she was swimming through a murky pool - nothing was clear anymore. Where once there had been understanding and routine, now there was confusion and uncertainty. Her world had flipped on its side, twisted, inverted, somersaulted, rolled over and played dead without her knowing it. Now she was in a world inhabited by strange people. Sanity was replaced with insanity. Nothing was what it seemed. The only certainty she had was that she was going to get to the bottom of it. Unless it killed her, she thought, shivering at the morbid afterthought.

"Have you seen the vicar again?" Chase asked. "I called in at the church, but he wasn't there."

Adam swirled the contents of the glass. "It's funny you should ask that."

Chase found nothing remotely funny about it.

"You see, he's gone missing."

"Gone missing!" Her heart lurched and her breath hitched in her throat.

"Yes. Now before you start, I don't believe he's dead, like you said. But I never actually saw him when I said I did. You see, I just didn't want to upset you, not with the baby and all."

"So where is he then?"

"That's it. I just don't know!"

"Then why don't you believe he's dead?"

"Because he's not."

"So now you're calling me a liar."

"No, not at all."

"But I saw the body."

"Then where was it?" He sipped his drink. "You saw for yourself, there was no evidence of anything like you said. We don't breed killers around here." He laughed without humour.

Was he telling the truth? Chase didn't know anymore. She wanted to believe him, if only to take away the festering memory of a man with a slit throat. Where were the police when you needed them?

Madness or death? The question returned and the answer was as elusive as ever.

She didn't want to be mad. And she really didn't think she was. She knew what she had seen... didn't she? Or had she stepped onto the roller coaster of delusion, where everything swept past in a swirling blur? Was her memory playing tricks? Was she going mad? She remembered reading somewhere that a mad man doesn't know when he's going mad, so because she thought she was, did that mean she wasn't? And if she was, why?

She began to feel dizzy.

"Chase, are you okay? You've gone very pale."

"I think I'm just a bit hot. Can we go outside?"

"Sure."

Picking up the book that Mandy had forgotten to take, she walked toward the door with George watching her. He licked his lips with a reptilian flick of his tongue and she shivered as she recalled the snake eating the frog.

***

Mandy was scared. Very scared. Petrified even. She didn't understand what was going on - why people were changing. Why *she* was changing? In her case, it wasn't a physical change like some people had experienced when their ailments miraculously healed or went away. Those people had flocked to the church, offering praise and thanks to the Lord for the miracle. The vicar had been overwhelmed by the increased attendance, and the collecting bowl was handed out at every opportunity so people could show their thanks for the marvel.

But as the congregation swelled, the vicar's sermons had become darker in tone. She hadn't attended herself, but her parents had, before they...

She shut the thought out. Put it in a box. Locked it. Sealed it. Then threw it into an unused corner of her mind where she could forget about it.

The village grapevine whispered that the vicar was drinking to excess, which was why his sermons had become dark and strange, but Mandy wasn't so sure that was the reason. Although she never entered the church, she had, out of curiosity, once stood in the graveyard, underneath the stained glass window and listened as he preached from Revelation. He also liked to preach from the Old Testament, about the tree of knowledge and how thou shalt not eat from it. Although she was sure some of the things he preached about were not even in the bible: people who live in glass houses will invariably get cut; if you choose to sit on the fence, shit happens (she wasn't *actually* sure he did say shit, but it sounded like he said shit); damnation sits on the shoulder of greed; Humpty Dumpty was pushed (people had actually laughed at that one); bad things happen.

She knew that one was true, though.

Although she hadn't thought it at the time, she had later come to realise there was a sort of code among the sermons, a message, a warning... and when she felt the change, she

171

knew the warning had come too late.

It had started with her memory. First she forgot where she put things. Then she forgot what the things were that she couldn't find. Then it was names. People she had known all nineteen years of her life became strangers. Then came the absence of time when she couldn't recall where she had been or what she had done. Then there was her cat, Candle Wax. She had called him that because as a kitten he'd always been dripping on the carpet. But he was gone now.

She still saw him sometimes, padding across the carpet and purring as he rubbed against her leg, his tail erect and pointing up at her like an accusation. Other times she never saw him for days or weeks at a time, or if she did, she couldn't remember. Was he really dead? And if he was, had she killed him?

The reason she wasn't so sure whether he was dead or not, was because sometimes she saw her parents too, in the lane, in a field, in a room, and yet they *were* dead, weren't they? Hadn't she watched them die? Hadn't she been the cause of their death?

No, that was wrong. She hadn't been the cause, not directly anyway.

It was about a month after the fog descended, perhaps longer, perhaps shorter; it was before the change; the time was irrelevant...

It was raining heavily and the road was slicker than Brylcream. Mandy watched the water running down the lane, an impromptu river through Paradise. Her mother was in the kitchen, baking bread with the army rations that had been delivered to the village shop. Money no longer changed hands for food supplies - the government subsidised them, calling it emergency aid. Mandy thought aid only went to third world countries and areas damaged by natural disaster: earthquake, flood and the like. She never thought of Paradise as being a charity case, dependant on handouts.

Her father, unable to get to work in the city forty miles away was going stir-crazy. He sat around the house, trying to find something to do with his time. He tried gardening, but

172

everything he touched wilted and died, so he abandoned that idea (much to his wife's relief) and took to walking around the village. He was an intelligent man who worked in finance, and even though in the circumstances, he would have been able to work from home, all communication had ceased. First the phone lines went dead, and then there was never a signal available for the mobile phone. He had tried getting answers out of Nigel Moon, but he was as evasive and taciturn as an eel.

And then there was the fog.

Omnipresent.

Cloying.

Insidious.

It blanketed the area around the village like a shield, a nebulous barrier. At first people had tried to get through, but the fog had proved too thick; its stranglehold too absolute. Those who did try found they were disallowed from further attempts by security guards posted in the fog - apparently for the villagers' safety! Escape was futile. Mandy's dad said how it reminded him of the old television series, The Prisoner with Patrick McGoohan.

On that rainy day, he came home from one of his walks, drenched to the skin but wearing a determined expression. His usual affable demeanour was gone and he ran a hand through his dark hair, flicking water from his fingers.

"Karen, Mandy, get your things," he said, dripping water over the carpet.

"What's the matter, dear?" Karen asked. "Look at the state of you. You'll catch your death. And look at the carpet." She ran a hand across her forehead, leaving a slight dusting of flour on her face. Her hair was going gray, but she disguised it beneath auburn dye.

"Look, forget the bloody carpet," he said, walking into the kitchen and grabbing his wife by the arm. "We're going."

"Going where?"

"Anywhere away from here, that's bloody where." He hesitated. "We'll find a hotel until this fog has gone."

"Richard, what's got into you?"

"I'm fed up with being fucked around, now come on, we're getting out of the village. Mandy, get whatever you can carry and get in the car."

Mandy frowned. "But we were told we couldn't leave!" It wasn't like her father to lose his temper or swear.

"Fuck what they said."

"*Richard*, do you have to use that language." Karen frowned.

"Sorry, but get a bloody move on. Come on, shake yourselves."

Mandy went upstairs and threw a few belongings in a hold all. When she came back downstairs, her dad was impatiently goading her mother into action.

"I don't see what the rush is." Karen looked at Mandy as if for support.

"No, I'm with dad." Mandy grabbed her dad's hand and squeezed.

"Coming or staying," Richard said.

"Well, you're not leaving me here on my own! Just let me get my make-up."

"Forget the make-up, let's just go."

Karen sighed in acquiescence.

Richard led them to the car. It hadn't been driven for over a month, but it started first time. "German engineering," Richard said, gunning the accelerator and speeding precariously out of the drive, almost running Ms Woods, the shopkeeper over.

Looking through the rear window, Mandy was sure she saw old Ms Woods stick two fingers up at them, but as they sped around the corner, Mandy didn't think anymore of it, putting it down to her imagination.

Driving past the church, the fog lay before them, a sea of mist undulating like a phantom jellyfish. Licking his lips, Richard slowed the car down and edged into the fog.

Mandy watched it envelop them like a shroud. Richard put the headlights on, but the light glared off the fog, cutting visibility even more, so he turned them back off. The car crawled along at a snails pace and Richard craned his head like a tortoise to navigate, turning the windscreen wipers on to clear the condensation. With visibility down to a few feet, the car momentarily left the road, juddering over ruts on the grass verge. Richard quickly turned the wheel, trying to bring the car back onto the tarmac. The wheels slipped, trying to get a purchase in the mud.

"Shit," Richard muttered.

Mandy thought she saw movement in the fog, a ghostly apparition that hovered beside the window, peering in with bug-like eyes.

And then it was gone.

Cupping her hands against the window, she tried to penetrate the mist, but it was no good, she couldn't see anything bar her own reflection.

"Damn, it's thick," Richard muttered.

"Perhaps we should turn round," Karen said.

"*No*," Mandy hissed. Her dad smiled at her in the rear-view mirror.

"That's the spirit." He nodded his head, lips pursed.

Karen shook her head. "But it's too... we can't see where we're going."

"We'll be all right. Trust me."

"*Candle Wax*," Mandy screeched. "We've left Candle Wax behind."

"He'll be all right," Richard said.

"No, you've got to go back. I can't leave him."

"She's right Richard. We've got to go back."

"No, we're going on."

"Dad, *please*, we've got to go back."

She saw her dad looking at her in the mirror. This time he wasn't smiling.

Mandy heard a shout and peering through the mist, she saw they were approaching a roadblock. The barrier was down, and there were men stood in front of it, but instead of slowing down, her father put his foot on the accelerator. Karen screamed as the men dived out of the way. The car careered through the barrier; wood splintered like bone.

175

And then the shot rang out, puncturing the air.

Richard jerked the wheel in surprise. Hazy figures drifted through the mist, circling.

"*Dad, they've got guns,*" Mandy squealed.

Richard floored the accelerator. The wheels spun, sending the car zigzagging across the road like a pinball.

Mandy and her mother screamed.

The tyres found a purchase and the car shot forward, sending them blindly into the fog. A shot rang out and Mandy felt glass slice her cheek as the side window exploded.

"*Dad!*"

"Fuckin' hell," Richard said.

"*Richard!*"

Mandy never knew whether her mother's last word was an admonishment or a cry for help because the next bullet shattered her mother's window, entered her head and exited through the windscreen in a shower of blood, bone and grey matter.

"*Fuck,*" Richard wailed, slamming the brakes on.

"*Don't stop,*" Mandy screamed, causing her dad to put his foot back on the accelerator.

The car shot forward; a shot rang out, the rear tyre exploded and the car left the road, slamming into a tree. The impact launched Mandy out of her seat, her head smashing into the headrest and delivering her into the blackness of oblivion...

When she came round, Mandy was at home, in bed. Candle Wax was curled at her feet. The cat stretched, yawned and padded toward her. She stroked him, her head still fuzzy. The remnants of a bad dream still gripped her and she ran a hand down her face, feeling bandages instead of skin.

She screamed.

The nightmare had been real.

Bad things happen.

The memory was now vague. She had tried to recall the

events of that day, but as more time passed, the harder it got. After the accident (which is what *they* called it, *they* being Nigel Moon and his stooges) the doctor, Adam White ministered to her, bringing her food, and she recovered within a couple of days. Although she was sure the force of the collision must have cracked her skull, she didn't need any drugs. She was surprised there wasn't even a scar on her face, although the one in her mind remained, albeit faded.

Walking up the drive to her house, she tried to recall what she had just been thinking about, but for the life of her, she couldn't remember.

As she put the key in the front door and turned it, Candle Wax darted out of a bush and brushed against her leg, meowing. Mandy smiled and reached down to stroke the cat, but her hand passed through empty air and she stood up, frowning and unable to remember why she had bent down in the first place!

Chapter 19

Not long after Mandy departed, Chase made her excuses and left Adam to finish his drink. But not before she had asked him where Mandy lived; it was still light and she was concerned about her and she wanted to check she was all right.

Adam had given her directions to a large house at the end of a winding drive. The front of the house was covered by wisteria, the purple hanging flowers swaying in the breeze. There was an integral garage next to the front door - the garage door was open but there was no car and Chase considered the supposed crash, wondering whether it would be too rude or distressing to ask Mandy about it?

A curtain shrouding the large bay window twitched when she rang the bell; a hollow resonance could be heard in the bowels of the house. Chase waited patiently, but no one answered. She rang the bell again.

"Who's there?"

Chase recognised Mandy's voice. "It's me, Chase."

"Chase... Chase who?"

"Chase Black. We were just in the pub, remember? You forgot your book." She held up the copy of Paradise Lost and heard bolts being slid across and latches being turned before the door opened slightly. Mandy peered through the crack, the fingers of one hand curling around the edge of the door like a white crab.

"Chase. Yes, I think I remember." She opened the door, frowning before she scuttled back into the hallway so Chase could enter.

Chase held out the book and Mandy looked at it as though she didn't know what it was. Disconcerted, Chase placed the book next to a telephone. "Does it work?" she asked, indicating the phone.

"Sometimes I hear things on it."

"Do you mind if I try?"

Mandy shook her head and Chase picked the receiver up and put it to her ear. The line was dead and she suddenly noticed that the flex had been ripped from the wall. "You hear things on here!" Chase indicated the flex.

Mandy nodded. "Sometimes."

Putting the receiver back in the cradle, Chase looked at Mandy and shook her head. "I just wanted to check you were okay, that's all."

"Thank you... I'm... I'm scared." A tear rolled down her cheek.

A compassionate urge came over Chase and she walked toward Mandy and put her arms around her. Mandy rested her head in the crook of Chase's shoulder and wept, her body heaving as she fought to catch her breath between sobs.

"Don't worry," Chase said, ignoring the unwashed smell as she stroked Mandy's head. "Everything's going to be OK." Although she tried to sound convincing, Chase knew her words of encouragement sounded hollow.

When Mandy stopped crying, Chase said, "Feeling better?"

"A bit. Thank you for being so nice."

"Think nothing of it." She didn't think this was the right moment to ask about Mandy's parents. "Well, I've got to go now, there's someone I need to see."

Terror was written all over Mandy's face. "Please, don't leave me on my own."

Chase was going to offer countless reasons why Mandy couldn't come with her, but when she looked at Mandy's fearful expression, she said, "I won't leave you. Come on." Her reasons were also slightly selfish because she didn't want to be on her own, either! Taking Mandy by the hand, they walked out of the house.

Leading the way to the dilapidated farmhouse, Chase was determined to find out what was really going on; that was if the Raggedy man actually knew anything at all? She wondered whether he was just fooling her? But she wasn't

179

going to take any shit this time. If she wanted conundrums, she'd buy a puzzle book. She wanted straight answers and she wasn't going to settle for anything less.

Clouds painted the sky shades of gray and they walked beneath the trees surrounding the farmhouse without speaking. Occasionally, she had the feeling that someone was following them, but when she spun round, there was no one there; phantoms of the mind. She thought about what Mandy had said, about people changing. Things certainly weren't normal around Paradise. There was Belinda, Ms Woods, Patricia, the man with the knife at the reception, George, the Raggedy man. None of them could be called normal.

Reaching the farmhouse, she barged straight through the front door. Storming toward the back room, she dodged the carcasses like a boxer avoiding punches. Noticing Mandy's wide-eyed alarm at the sight of the dead animals, she tightened her grip on her hand. Although her eyes had not yet adapted to the lack of light, she heard a door slamming.

"*Come back here,*" she shouted, making Mandy jump as she tugged her through the door to the back room. But it was too late, the Raggedy man had gone. Running to the back door, she opened it and quickly scanned the area, but she couldn't see anyone.

Slamming the door shut, she kicked the broken remains of a cup across the room, venting her frustration. It hit the floor with a hollow thud and Chase frowned. Leading Mandy to where the cup had hit the floor she stamped her foot on the wooden boards, causing a hollow echo. Letting go of Mandy's hand she crouched down and ran her fingers across the floor until she felt a loose section. Finding a hole where a knot had been, she slid her finger through and pried open the trapdoor to the basement. Letting the hatch clatter to the floor it sounded like a door being slammed. Chase gave a knowing grin and peered down into the darkness.

"Come on, I know you're down there," she said. "Come up where I can see you." She saw movement in the darkness, a shadow. "I need more answers."

The shadow flitted away from the opening.

"Don't make me come down there. I've had about all I can take, and you won't like it if I get angry."

"I know," a voice replied, drifting up from the darkness.

"Get up here, *now*," she commanded.

The shadow fluttered back into the pale light of the hatch and began to climb the steps. She couldn't make out any features as the figures face was wrapped by a dirty looking piece of dark material that left only the eyes visible. Mandy took a step back, alarmed.

"It's okay," Chase said, "he won't do anything." She hoped that was true.

The Raggedy man was wearing a long, dark coat down to his ankles that billowed out like wings as he stepped into the room.

"Now, tell me what's going on, or God help me, I'll..."

"Who are you?" The Raggedy man cocked his head, quizzical.

Chase frowned. That voice. Familiar, and yet...

"You know who I am," she said. "You asked me to come here."

"I... did?"

"More to the point, who are *you*?"

"I'm no one."

"Look, cut the bull and take that rag off your head so I can see your face."

"I remember you. I brought you here." He shook his head and took a step back, as if about to flee. "I'm the magic man, and I want you to go."

Chase was one step ahead of him. Just as he made to turn and run, she cut across to her left. With a swift movement, she stretched out her foot and the Raggedy man tripped, sprawling across the floor and inadvertently knocking the hatch shut. Before he had time to gain his feet, Chase jumped on his back, pinning him down. As he struggled, she reached down and pulled the material from his face.

Although gaunt, pale and dirty, the face was instantly recognisable and Chase scuttled away from him, her mouth open in disbelief and her heart hammering.

"Mat," she whispered.

Chapter 20

Chase couldn't believe what she was seeing. Although his features were haunted, his eyes sunken and his hair greasy and longer than when she had last seen him, there was no mistaking the bedraggled figure lying on the floor: it was her disappearing boyfriend. Tears welled in Chase's eyes.

"Mat?" He said the name as though it was a foreign word. "Mat, it's me, Chase."

"Chase!"

"Why are you doing this to me? Where have you been? What are you doing here?" She couldn't understand what was going on.

"You've come for the next lesson," Mat said in a deep timbre. It was not a question. He stood up and bowed his head.

"Mat, look at me. Don't you recognise me?" Chase gained her feet and stepped toward him.

Mat took a step back. "*Don't,*" he hissed.

"Mat, for God's sake, it's me. Talk to me. Please... Tell me what's going on."

"Chase..." Recognition flashed across his pained features, and then it was gone.

"*I'm going mad here,*" Chase screamed. "Tell me what's going on. *Please.*"

Mat put his head in his hands. "I... I can't remember."

"Try."

"Remembering... it hurts."

"Remembering what?"

"Remembering it all."

"I can't take much more of this." Tears rolled down her cheeks. "Why did you leave me? I need to know why. What are you doing here?"

"Leave! They... they made me."

"They?"

"Full moon, half moon, the cow jumped over the moon."

"Mat, talk to me." Chase didn't understand what he was saying. Did he mean Nigel Moon had made him leave her? Why was he talking in rhymes?

"The vicar. How's the vicar?" he asked, suddenly cognisant.

"I think he's dead." It sounded ridiculous, and she was still secretly hoping that it wasn't true.

"Dead." He shook his head. "He knew."

"Knew what?"

"The truth."

Chase shook her head. She didn't think she could take much more.

"Are you all right," Mandy asked, putting a hand on Chase's shoulder.

Chase didn't miss the irony of Mandy comforting her. "I don't know what's going on anymore." She cradled her stomach and looked back at Mat. "I'm pregnant. We're going to have a baby."

"Dead. The vicar, dead?" He shook his head.

"Do you understand? I'm pregnant."

He looked at her, his eyes narrowed as he realised what she had said. "Pregnant! You can't."

"Can't?"

"Can't have the monster."

"Monster!" Chase frowned. "It's our baby." It was not the response she expected. What was wrong with him? What was he doing here?

Mat stepped toward her. "You can't have it." His face was bathed in shadows, his eyes gleaming with a feral glint.

Chase backed away, suddenly scared. "Mat, what are you doing?"

"They brought me here... it's my fault they found you... it's all my fault." He took another step.

"Mat, please. Look at me. Mat, I love you."

The word struck Mat like a body blow and he stopped

advancing. "Love... I remember." He staggered on the spot.

"Yes, remember."

"The first sin," he mumbled. "I committed the first sin."

"Something about food?"

"The food. Yes. I... I was working away..."

Mat's occupation as an electrician had often involved him working away from home. Chase had always missed him when he wasn't there, but they telephoned each other every day. He had even sent her love letters, decorated with hearts, flowers and fairies. He was quite an artist and she had saved all of his letters in a box, taking them out and reading them whenever she missed him.

It was only now, after hearing him say he was working away, that she remembered before he disappeared, he had been working somewhere here in Staffordshire. She had not thought about it before and it could have been a coincidence, although now she doubted it.

"What about the food?" Chase asked.

"It's tainted... yes, tainted."

"What's he on about?" Mandy asked, frowning.

"I don't really know." Chase rubbed her forehead. "There's something about the food here."

"The food!" Mandy shook her head. "What's wrong with it?"

Mat grinned like a lunatic. "Tainted."

Chase bit her lip, thinking. "We've got to get out of here and get help. Mandy, do you know how we can get out of the village?"

Mandy shivered as though recalling a bad memory. "There's no way out."

"There's got to be a way out. There's got to be."

"I'm afraid not, Miss Black."

The voice scared Chase to the core and she spun around to see Moon standing in the doorway.

"Don't you realise that it's dangerous to go wandering about, Miss Black? If I didn't make sure that someone kept an eye on you, anything could happen. Matthew. How nice to see you again." Moon gave a toothy grin like a shark. "I

184

wondered where you'd got to."

Mat backed away and a figure appeared in the doorway behind him, pressing a gun into the small of his back.

Chase furiously turned on Moon, about to demand answers when Jane stumbled through the door behind him. She was still dressed in the same clothes Chase had last seen her in, but now they were ripped in places, the flimsy top torn across one breast. Chase didn't know whether she could believe her eyes.

"Jane, is it really you?"

Jane nodded. "It's me, sugar." Her face was bruised and one of her eyes was slightly swollen.

"Where..." Before she could get her question out, Jane staggered further into the room, followed by Drake holding a pistol at her head.

"Don't you just love reunions?" Drake grinned.

"What the hell is going on?" Chase demanded.

"I don't think you're in any position to be asking questions, Miss Black," Moon sneered. "All you need to know is that we're looking after your friend, as a sort of safety measure if you like."

"Safety measure for what?" Chase spat.

"To ensure you don't try anything foolish. Now that we know you're pregnant, it's imperative you come to term."

"How did you find out...?" Adam. It had to have been Adam. That bastard had sold her out. But why? Why the hell was it so important to them?

"We didn't have any idea..." Moon shook his head, wistfully. "You can't imagine how glad I was to hear the news. It takes the experiment to the next stage ahead of time, but..." He shrugged.

"What damn experiment? What the hell are you up to?" Chase snarled.

"Now we don't want you getting all worked up. It's not good for the baby. Now, I just want you to go home. Forget about all this and just enjoy your new house."

"*Forget.* How the *hell* do you expect me to forget, you fuckin' son-of-a-bitch?"

He pointed at Jane. "Because if you don't, then..."

Drake ran a finger across Jane's throat and laughed.

Jane visibly shivered. "These people don't mess around." A tear rolled down her cheek.

"But people will be missing us by now," Chase said.

"People don't miss what isn't lost," Moon replied. "They mourn."

The implication of what Moon said made Chase shiver. "And what about Mat and Mandy. Do they have to *forget* too?"

"They will forget, in time. Memory loss is an unfortunate side-effect of our experiment, but we're working on it."

"The first sin," Mat mumbled.

"Take them outside and give them a sedative." Moon pointed at Mat and Mandy. "And be *gentle* with them." At Moon's orders, three burly soldiers with rifles slung over their shoulders entered the room

"No, don't shoot," Mandy wailed, stumbling away. "Dad, they're shooting at us. Dad..."

One of the soldiers carefully took hold of Mandy and led her out of the room. The other two soldiers took hold of Mat.

"Chase. I remember." Mat's eyes filled with tears. "It's all my fault." Before he could say anymore, the soldiers led him away.

"Now, Miss Black, I hope I can rely on you not to cause any trouble!"

"You won't get away with this."

"Have, can and will. I'm sorry to shatter any illusions you may have, but where Paradise is concerned, I am God."

"People will find out what you've done. You can't hide whatever the hell you're doing here for ever."

"Your naiveté amuses me." Moon shook his head, smiling. "What do you know about The Tuskegee Syphilis study in nineteen thirty-two?

Chase shook her head. "What the hell are you on about?"

"Two hundred black men diagnosed with syphilis were never told so they could be used as guinea pigs to follow the progression and symptoms of the disease."

"That's sick," Jane said from the doorway where Drake stood impassively with the gun against her head.

"It's the advancement of science, my dear," Moon said. "Project Paperclip in nineteen forty-five?"

Chase shook her head.

"Paperclip, the recruitment of Nazi scientists by the CIA and various other offices who gave them immunity and new identities so they could work on secret government projects.

"Nineteen fifty-three, project MKULTRA, where mind control drugs were used on unwitting human subjects? What about nineteen fifty when the U.S. Navy sprayed a cloud of bacteria from ships over San Francisco to test the extent of infection? No, well what about nineteen seventy-eight. Adverts went out specifically asking for promiscuous homosexual men for an experimental Hepatitis B vaccine trial, conducted by the CDC in New York, Los Angeles and San Francisco. Nineteen eighty-one, the first case of aids was confirmed in gay men. Where? Go on have a guess. Yes, New York, Los Angeles and San Francisco. Coincidence?

"People get away with things all the time. You just don't know it. Plausible deniability. At this very moment hospitals change the word experiments to investigations, or observations and no one bats an eyelid, but do you really know what they're doing? Of course not, because powerful people don't want you to know."

Chase shook her head, appalled at the extent of human corruption in the name of science. "And what's your *investigation* called?"

Moon smiled like a proud parent. "Project Evolution - the creation of a super food to combat illness and disease, leading to the prolonging of life, the alleviation of suffering and a healthy bank balance."

"Well it hasn't helped anyone so far. It's more like *evil*ution. People won't let you get away with it."

Moon stroked his chin. He had a wistful, faraway look in his eyes. "Do you know how much this is worth? We're talking billions, perhaps trillions here. No one will stop me."

187

"So really it's all about money."

Moon laughed. "It's always about money. The key to what makes people tick was discovered through the Genome project. They had all the answers, but they didn't know how to decipher them until I came along. After finding the genetic sequence for diseases, we set about creating enzymes to correct them." He smiled smugly.

"So why am I here?"

"Well your boyfriend was right. It is his fault you're here. He was one of several contractors foolishly brought in to set up the compound. I had insisted we use only reputable firms with the security clearance for such work, but our backers like to cut corners and save money where they can." He gave a shake of his head. "Well your *friend* was working on the food stores. We didn't realise any was missing until it was too late. The fool had eaten some of our early test batches - because he was hungry. Can you believe it?" Moon said, incredulously. "We had to take time out to find the idiot by doing medical tests on all the personnel; then we had to find out whom he'd had," he licked his lips, "*intimate* contact with. He compromised our field tests because he was hungry." Moon shook his head again in disbelief. "But fortunately we found him before any real damage could be done. And then we found you! We did hold Matthew, testing revolutionary food batches on him, but he got free." He scowled at Drake. "We knew he was around here somewhere, but we didn't know where until you led us to him."

"Well if it's such a super food, what's the problem? Why did you have to bring Mat back here?"

Moon shrugged. "Because as with all experiments, it has had teething problems and we have to contain the test subjects for the moment in a secure environment."

"Teething problems? You mean like the memory loss and the madness?"

"Among other things. It just needs tweaking, and then when we have sorted it out..." He smiled.

"Tweaking! You're mad," Jane spat.

188

"Madness is a state of mind." Moon grinned. "We will even cure that."

Chase shook her head, appalled. "And what about people like Belinda and Patricia, are they just part of the teething problems?"

Moon frowned. "Unfortunately, yes. There seems to be a rogue regressive element to the food. Cognitive function is impaired, but we *will* sort it out. It just takes time."

"And what if you *can't* sort it out? What happens to the people in Paradise then? What happens to Jane, Mat and me?"

Moon didn't reply, but his silence spoke volumes.

Chapter 21

As Ratty and Izzy approached the building in which Nigel Moon had interrogated them, the fog seemed less dense.

"Why are we going this way?" Izzy asked. "We need to head the other way." Her voice trembled almost as much as her body.

"Because I need to know what's going on." Although he felt responsible for her, Ratty was determined to find out the truth.

"But that's stupid. Let's just get out of here and tell someone that *something's* going on."

"What, and have them bring us back here. You're a drug addict, remember. Why should they believe anything you tell them? We need some proof because we don't know what's going on."

"I'm not a bloody drug addict!" She looked hurt by the accusation.

"Well, when we get the proof that something's going on, perhaps they'll believe you."

Izzy kicked at the floor, venting her anger and frustration. "Well, let's find something and then get the hell out of here."

Remembering there was a man on reception, Ratty headed around the side of the building. He tried to peer through the various windows, standing up just enough to look into the room without being seen if anyone should happen to be inside, but the glass was all blacked out.

Half way along the building, he spotted a partially open window. It was only about eight inches in height compared to about thirty inches in diameter, but with a squeeze, he knew he could get through. Standing on tiptoe, he peered into the room, relieved to see no one was inside.

"Wait here," he said to Izzy.

"No chance," she spat back. "Where you go, I go."

Ratty considered this for a moment before nodding his head. She was right. He didn't want to lose her again. "Okay, but you go first so I can help you up. And be quiet." Forming a stirrup with his interlaced fingers, he helped Izzy squeeze through the window before struggling through behind her.

The room was about fifteen feet square and stocked with tins of white labelled food. The only identification on the tins was the contents: baked beans, spaghetti, soup and so forth, stencilled in black. Some of the tins were in cardboard cartons, others were piled on shelves, but they were all kept in order. The only other marking on the cans was a batch number.

"This must be a storeroom." He picked up one of the cans and shook it.

"Don't do that," Izzy said as though she half expected it to explode.

Ratty grinned and put it back on the shelf.

There was only one door to the room and Ratty crept toward it and carefully turned the handle. Opening the door a fraction, he peered out into a deserted corridor. One of the neon tubes on the ceiling flickered, casting baleful light that was more orange than white.

"Come on," he whispered.

"Are you mad?"

"Well, we can't find out what's going on staying in here." He felt as scared as Izzy looked, but he tried to hide it behind bravado as he crept out of the room.

As Izzy followed him into the corridor, Ratty felt his heart pounding with an explosive mixture of fear and excitement. Adrenaline raced through his veins, a fuse ready to ignite him into action.

His eyes and ears were alert for the smallest sound, the slightest movement. He sensed Izzy behind him, felt her warm breath on his neck as she tried to control her breathing.

Some of the doors lining the corridor were labelled: STOREROOM, MEDICAL STORE, LABORATORY, EXAMINATION ROOM, and MORGUE. Most of the

191

rooms were only accessible with a swipe card, such as the laboratory and the medical store. One of the only ones that wasn't was the morgue.

Ratty pressed his ear against the door to check whether there was anyone inside (at least anyone that was alive), before turning the handle and pushing the door open a fraction.

"We can't go in there," Izzy wailed.

"Why?"

"Because... because it's a morgue!"

"And?"

"Well, you know..."

"Well if there's anyone in there, they're not likely to complain are they."

"That's sick." Izzy pulled a lemon-sucking grimace.

"Sorry. But there might be something in here that can tell us what's going on."

"Hopefully not."

Ratty shrugged his shoulders. "Well, we won't know if we don't look."

Izzy conceded with a shake of her head and Ratty slipped inside. Izzy followed, letting the door swing shut behind her, the resultant bang echoing around the room.

Ratty winced. He waited, tensed in case anyone heard the noise and came to investigate.

"Sorry," Izzy silently mouthed.

Shaking his head and satisfied no one was coming, Ratty looked around. The room was longer rather than wider, with one wall covered with small square doors. Walking the length of the room, Ratty approached one of the doors. There was a handle on each door and he grabbed the nearest one and pulled.

"Now what are you doing?" Izzy grabbed his hand, but it was too late.

The door opened to reveal a square hole with a metal tray. A zipped body bag was just visible on the tray. Shaking Izzy off, Ratty pulled it out on squeaking runners.

"Ratty, what the *hell* are you doing?"

192

Ignoring her, he unzipped the bag and parted the plastic covering. "*Jesus*, come and look at this."

Izzy shook her head.

"Look, come on."

Izzy still shook her head.

"He won't bite, come and look."

Exhaling in frustration, Izzy took a tentative step forward and quickly glanced at the contents of the bag before turning away, ashen faced.

"It's a vicar, see his dog collar."

"Congratulations." Izzy held her hand over her mouth as though she was going to be sick.

"Someone's cut his throat!"

Izzy coughed, clutching her stomach, and Ratty zipped the bag back up and slid the tray back into the hole before closing the door.

He approached another door and opened it before Izzy could protest. Pulling out the tray, he opened the body bag to reveal an old man. His features were waxy and bloodless; opening the bag further, he saw the man's body had been extensively operated on. Where the man's organs should be, there was now just a hollow cavity. Ratty quickly shoved the tray back into the wall without zipping the bag shut. The sight had made him feel slightly queasy and the tips of his fingers tingled.

He didn't want to open any more doors. He had got the general idea. Even if he didn't know what it proved, it was proof that *something* was going on, but he wasn't about to sling a dead body over his shoulder, even if he could lift it. He wanted something smaller.

"Come on, let's get out of here," he said.

Izzy let out a sigh. "At last."

Checking the coast was clear, they stepped out of the room and continued along the corridor. The floor had a type of rubber coating and Ratty winced whenever his footsteps produced a mouse-like squeak.

At the end of the corridor they came to a T-junction. "Which way?" Izzy nervously looked along both corridors.

Ratty didn't know. He could see Izzy looking at him, needing guidance. "Left." He tried to sound more sure than he felt.

They passed more doors which needed a swipe card to enter until they came to a door with a simple handle. A sign on the door said, VIDEO RECORDS. Pressing his ear against the door, Ratty satisfied himself there was no one inside and he turned the handle, pushing the door open to peer inside at shelves of videocassettes.

As though offering a warning, he heard footsteps squeaking along the floor and he dragged Izzy into the room, shutting the door just as a figure turned the corner. Both of them leaned against the door, holding their breath. The footsteps passed without stopping, the squeak receding into the distance.

Both of them let out a loud sigh of relief.

"We should get out of here," Izzy said when she had calmed down enough to speak.

"Not yet. Let's see what we can find in here."

They were in a large room, the walls of which were covered in videocassettes. There were also aisles of cassettes filling the room and a television and video player in the far corner. Ratty pulled out one of the tapes. It was dated and titled: *The Slaughtered Dog.* Another series was titled: *Church*, and dated accordingly. Others seemed to just have numbers on them.

Pulling out one of The Slaughtered Dog tapes, he took it to the video player and inserted it. Turning on the television, he saw a high angled shot taken from inside the pub. It seemed as though the cameras were motion activated as every shot contained movement.

"What *are* all these tapes for?" Izzy asked.

"I don't really know. It looks as though they were filming the people in the village."

"Why would they want to do that?"

"That's what we've got to find out."

Ejecting the video, a thought occurred to Ratty and he walked down the aisles and brought back cassettes marked

Church, which he began to play.

Some of them showed the vicar preaching to an empty church, others showed a few people in attendance, but they seemed distracted, rapping their fingers on the pews. On one tape he saw Chase asking the vicar questions and getting frustrated by his replies before they disappeared outside.

"That was the girl who's moved into my granddad's house," Ratty said. He still couldn't believe it. She couldn't have won the house in a competition. It didn't make any sense.

On another cassette, Ratty watched the vicar talking to a figure with their back to the camera. They seemed to be in a heated discussion and the vicar was trying to placate the other person, grabbing them by the shoulders and shaking them before turning away and kneeling before the altar where he started to pray. Ratty watched as the figure pulled out a knife. A funny feeling danced in the pit of his stomach as the tape whirred on, and he watched wide-eyed as the figure grabbed the vicar by the head and slashed the knife across his throat.

"Oh my God," Izzy shrieked, covering her face with her hands.

Clutching the wound, the vicar fell forward on his knees. The attacker raised the knife to plunge it into the vicar's back, but then stopped; disturbed by a distraction at the side of the church the figure scurried into the shadowy pews.

Ratty watched Chase appear on the screen, furtively creeping along the wall before she tried to get the vicar's attention. Panic swelled in his chest as he watched Chase. She was in the church with a killer, and yet she didn't know it. He felt like a macabre voyeur as he watched her approach the vicar and touch his shoulder, causing him to slump to the floor. Then she was running for the door, the figure chasing her.

As the camera angle didn't show the main door, Ratty couldn't see what was happening out of shot. Recorded after he met Chase, he wondered whether she was dead too?

Watching the video was surreal, and he was angry that he

couldn't help. He wanted to know if Chase was alive. As he continued watching, the figure came back into view and looked up at the camera as though knowing it was there. The face on the television was haunted, lost and distressed. Ratty had never seen a real killer before, and as the killer fled, he hoped never to see one again.

Because the cameras were motion activated, the next shot happened without a pause and showed figures in white suits enter the church, remove the body and quickly clean the mess. A digital clock on the tape showed the time elapsed in real-time was about fifteen minutes before the next arrival, which was a man who quickly scanned the area and then left. Ratty felt a sense of relief as the man returned, dragging Chase behind him. So she wasn't dead, but she looked scared, very scared.

The killer had obviously disappeared, but to all intents and purposes, so had the vicar's body.

"Ratty, have you finished yet? We're going to get caught if we hang around here any longer."

Ratty nodded. "I've seen enough." Ejecting the tape, he slipped it under his T-shirt and tucked it in to stop the tape falling out. He didn't know what it meant, but it was evidence of something.

He left the room feeling uneasy.

The corridor was empty and Ratty and Izzy made there way along it like furtive rats, ears twitching at the slightest sound. Leading the way back to the storeroom, Ratty's heart was racing. He knew he was pushing his luck hanging around, but he still needed answers.

Ratty heard the voices before he saw them and he peered around the corner, quickly withdrawing his head when he saw Moon and Drake walking toward him.

Izzy tugged his shoulder. "*Come on, let's get out of here*," she whispered.

Ratty held his hand up. "*One minute.*"

Izzy pursed her lips. "*Now.*" She looked as though she could have punched him.

"Why did we have to step in like that?" Drake asked.

196

"Because she was getting too suspicious. I always find it's better to get things out in the open. Let them know how powerless they are, and they'll become acquiescent. She'll be a bit angry for a while, but now she knows we've got her friend *and* her boyfriend, she won't try anything. She's a clever girl."

"I'm not so sure. It's taking too much of a risk. We should have just left things as they were."

"Crush the spirit and you kill the motivation, Mr. Drake. I think her spirit is well and truly crushed, don't you. Besides, now we know she's pregnant... well, that's a whole new ballgame. We want to make sure nothing happens to interfere with the birth of this baby."

Ratty heard the squeaking footsteps stop.

"*Nothing*, do you understand me, Drake? That's why I've decided to bring her into the complex. I'll admit things are getting a bit out of hand in the village. In fact, I'm beginning to think we should concentrate all our efforts on Miss Black and that we should send a disposal team in to take care of the problem."

They started walking again and Moon continued talking. "Do you realise how important this baby could be? It could hold the key. If my calculations are correct, it will be the first child born with perfect immunity from disease. I think that's where we've been going wrong. From little acorns, Mr. Drake, from little acorns. We have lots to do. I want you to ensure Miss Black is monitored around the clock."

Ratty heard a door open and close, cutting the conversation off.

"Did you hear that," Ratty whispered.

"Yes, but I didn't understand it."

"Well Miss Black, that's Chase. I remembered her name as soon as Moon said it. They're saying she's pregnant, and for some reason the baby's going to be immune from disease." He shook his head. Things had gone from strange to downright bizarre. "It also sounds as though they're holding some friends of hers to make her do what they want."

"Yes, but what was that about sending in a disposal team?"

"It sounds as though whatever they're doing has gone pear shaped and they want to get rid of the evidence."

"Which is?"

"Paradise!"

Chapter 22

No matter how hard she tried, Chase couldn't get the tears to come. She wanted to cry, wanted to cry for Mat, for Jane, for Mandy, for everyone affected by Moon's evil project, but she couldn't. She had gone beyond tears, to a place of cold numbness. Her face was stony, devoid of expression, a granite block waiting to be given a facial cast. Moon had detained Mat and Jane, leaving Chase to return to the cottage. The threat of what he would do to her friends was her prison.

Even though the house was cold, she didn't feel it and although night had fallen, she didn't switch a light on, letting the darkness surround her as if it would hide her from the horror. Apart from the occasional blink of her eyes, she didn't move and the only sound was the regular cadence of her breathing, slow and steady.

Thoughts raced through her head, carrying her on an emotional roller coaster. She couldn't believe Mat was here, in Paradise, and that Jane was being held as a prisoner. It was too unbelievable to take in.

What Moon had said about people getting away with things echoed through her thoughts. She knew he was right. What reason did he have to lie? But she still couldn't believe things like this went on, where human life was used as an unwitting pawn in experiments. She couldn't believe someone could be so callous to another human being.

One thing was for sure, she wasn't going to eat any more of the tinned food.

Although she knew she should have remonstrated more, the men with guns had scared her. They looked too menacing. Pulling the trigger would be another notch in their belt.

She knew mentally berating herself achieved nothing, but what else could she do?

A furtive knock at the door brought Chase out of her reverie, but she didn't move to answer it. She turned her head to look toward the hallway. The knock came again, more insistent, the hollow sound echoing along the hall. Fear prickled Chase like a rash. She would never have believed such an innocent sound could instil so much dread, but after what she had been through, nothing was innocent anymore. She wouldn't be surprised if it was the devil himself knocking at the door asking her to sign her soul away, but he would be too late because Moon had got there first!

The knock came again. Whoever was outside obviously wasn't going to go away. Standing up, Chase crept toward the window and peered out, but she couldn't see anyone.

Flowers swayed in the nocturnal breeze, keeping time with the malodorous night-time melody of rustling leaves.

After a couple of seconds, Chase backed away from the window and the knock came again, louder, heavier, longer, as though whoever was outside was trying to break the door down. She ran back to the window, pressing her face against the glass in an attempt to see the front door, but it was no good. The angle was too acute, allowing whoever was out there to remain out of sight.

Panicked, Chase instinctively picked up her shoulder bag and ran toward the back of the house. Another loud knock at the door caused her to risk a backward glance, but she didn't stop. She opened the back door and ran outside, hoping to put as much distance between herself and whoever was at the front of the house. Fear fuelled her flight as she ran up the cobbled path, and out through a small gate at the top of the garden. There wasn't a proper road at the back of the house, just a worn path between hedgerows leading to a copse on the top of the hill. As she ran, the trees seemed to close in around her, living barriers that formed a wooden jail. Nocturnal sounds pervaded the area, the hoot of an owl, the sibilant rustle of leaves, the flutter of dark wings; feral creatures that passed through the undergrowth, the darkness their domain.

The path ended abruptly, and she brushed through the feather-like fronds of ferns, which gave the copse a wild and untamed primordial aspect. A fallen tree lay like a dragon across the ground, it's bark transformed into scales by the bewitching darkness. The ground became uneven, formed into dips and hollows where animal burrows were visible like dark eye sockets in the earth. Movement caught her eye as a large animal with a ghostly black and white striped head scurried through the ferns. She didn't know what it was - didn't *want* to know what it was. She momentarily wondered whether there were snakes slithering through the undergrowth, which made her run faster.

Something scurried up a tree, disturbing leaves in its wake.

Something flitted past her face, winging its way into the night.

The gloom embraced a phantasmagoria of sights and sounds. A chimerical domain inhabited by hunters and prey. Too tired to run any more, Chase doubled over and clutched her stomach as she fought to catch her breath. At the moment she was the prey. She didn't know whether it was because she was pregnant, but she felt an overpowering determination to stop running and stand up for herself, a mother's instinct to protect her unborn baby.

When she had got her breath back, she looked up to find that she was standing in a depression surrounded by trees. Walking out of the hollow, she looked down on the village. The fog was visible in the distance like dragon's breath, a gray smoky residue that encircled the village. Although it appeared the fog went on forever, she could see lights in the distance, twinkling like stars in a luminescent sea. It was hard to judge how far away the lights were, but she guessed they were about six miles, (although they may as well have been fifty miles away for all the good they were).

Looking down at the village, she could just make out the houses through the trees. Almost all of them were in darkness. What lights were lit seemed to be moving, sweeping in arcs like lighthouse beams, but she didn't feel they conveyed warmth and safety. Shadows danced away from the lights like vampires trying to avoid the sun. Some of the beams converged and flashed toward her, forcing her to duck down. She instinctively felt whoever was down there, was searching for her. In the distance, someone shouted an unintelligible order.

A shot rang out, puncturing the night and a flare shot into the air, illuminating the night sky with an incandescent light that slowly descended on a small parachute which swayed in the breeze.

Cautiously, Chase crawled back down into the hollow, out of sight. When she felt it was safe to stand up, she ran toward the far side of the hill, dodging trees, and began to descend. The flare illuminated her path, but she hoped the searchers were all on the other side of the hill. As she dashed through the undergrowth, branches whipped her face and hawthorn bushes scratched her hands, but she ignored the pain.

She didn't spot the rusted barbed wire fence that was hidden in the undergrowth until it was too late, and she tripped on the wire, sprawling painfully onto the ground. Picking herself up, she winced as pain lanced up her leg from her ankle. Bending down to look at the injury, she saw blood oozing through her ripped jeans; she had a nasty gash across her shin.

The sound of animated voices from back up the hill forced Chase on, but each step caused her to grimace when she put weight on her ankle. She silently cursed as she tried to hop on her uninjured leg, using branches to steady herself.

Overhead, the flare petered out, the darkness returning with a vengeance after the bright light. It took a few minutes before her night vision returned, by which time the voices had got closer and louder. Lights flashed between the trees behind her as torches scanned the area. She thought she heard someone shout 'blood', but if she was leaving them a macabre Hansel and Gretal trail, there was little she could do about it as she didn't have anything to staunch the flow with.

Struggling on, she staggered, tripped and hopped down the hill. Whenever she could, she used branches like monkey bars to try and take the weight off her ankle, using her good leg like a pogo stick to launch herself to the next handhold.

She was making more noise than she wanted as branches bowed beneath her weight, the leaves rustling in protest.

The light beams flickered through the trees, making the leaves appear to dance. Nocturnal animals scurried away, causing ferns to sway as they moved through the undergrowth, adding to the confusion as Chase thought the hunters had got in front of her.

As the trees began to thin, she recognised the derelict farmhouse that Mat had been hiding in and she headed toward it. Moved by the breeze, the front door squealed and she hobbled inside, heading straight for the back room. The hatch to the cellar was still shut from when she had tripped Mat over and she hopped toward it. Beams of light played across the walls as her pursuers broke from the trees, shining their torches across the building. Hurriedly, Chase opened the hatch and hobbled down the steps, closing the hatch behind her so that she was in total darkness. She prayed that her pursuers would not know about the cellar, and that they wouldn't spot the hatch. It was only by chance she had found it. If she hadn't heard the dull echo of the broken cup as it hit the floor, she would have been none the wiser to the cellar's existence, and Mat would still be free. She felt a momentary pang of guilt that she had unwittingly got him recaptured. She didn't know how long he had been hiding down here, but from the smell, it was quite a while.

Footsteps echoed overhead and Chase held her breath. Torchlight played through cracks in the floorboards, illuminating clouds of dust that fell from the ceiling above.

"Anything?" a deep male voice asked.

"No."

"Well, keep looking. Drake wants the girl taken back to the compound. She can't have just disappeared. Find her, because if I'm in the shit, then you men are drowning in it. Do you understand?"

"*Yes sir*," a chorus of voices replied.

Chase fearfully listened to the men traipsing through the house, overturning cupboards and kicking down doors. The search seemed to go on for ages before the men left. By this time, Chase's eyes had become accustomed to the lack of light and she could see that she was in a room that appeared to run the length of the house. She could only see so far into the room, the far end a black abyss, but from what she could see, the room appeared to have been used to store preserves. Jars lined the shelves. A lot of them had been opened, the contents devoured, but there were still a lot of full ones: strawberry jam from 1970 to 1982, pickled onions from 1969 to 1982, gooseberry jam from 1978 to 1980, honey from 1972 to 1976. As she perused the shelves, Chase realised just how hungry she was and her stomach growled. When had she last eaten? She was so hungry she would eat anything, as long as it wasn't in a white-labelled can. Taking down a jar of pickled onions and a jar of strawberry jam, she opened them both and dipped the onions in the jam before eating them. The combination tasted delicious and she devoured half a jar of each before she was full, contentedly licking the sweet and sour residue from her fingers.

In a corner of the room there was a makeshift bed and Chase hobbled toward it. There was a small photograph next to the bed, and Chase picked it up, holding it so that she could see it more clearly. Tears filled her eyes. It was a worn photograph of Mat and herself, taken in a photo booth outside Birmingham train station. She remembered having the photo taken. It was when Mat had taken her out shopping for her birthday. Chase was pulling a surprised expression because after discovering she wasn't wearing a bra, Mat had grabbed her boob as the flash went off. He was smirking like the cat that had got the cream. She smiled thinking about it. Holding her hand up, she looked at the ring he'd bought her that day, turning it with her thumb like a prayer bead.

She was surprised he still had the picture, even more surprised to find it here. Did that mean he still cared for her? Did he use the photograph like a map, finding a way back to sanity, an anchor connecting him to the real world?

Lying down on the makeshift bed, she held the photograph to her chest and cried herself to sleep.

Chapter 23

When Mandy woke up, she was lying on the living room floor. She felt sore and there was a large bruise on her arm that made her wince when she touched it. She had no idea how it had got there. The last thing she remembered was... what? She couldn't remember.

A knock at the door brought her to her feet and she stepped into the hallway and peered out of the glass panels that ran up the side of the door. Adam White was standing outside and Mandy smiled. She liked the doctor.

"Mandy, I was starting to worry about you," Adam said as she opened the door. "You were meant to be at the surgery over an hour ago for your appointment."

"Was I?" She looked down sheepishly.

"Not to worry. I'm here now. Do you mind if I come in?"

Mandy stepped back from the door and Adam entered the house, following her through to the living room. He was carrying a leather bag that he put down on the living room table.

"You see how I spoil you with these home visits," Adam said, smiling warmly.

Mandy blushed.

"Now I just need to do a few routine checks. If you can just put this thermometer underneath your tongue." He opened his bag and took a thermometer out before placing it in her mouth. "And I'll just take your pulse." He took hold of her wrist and frowned. "Where did you get this bruise?"

Mandy shrugged.

Nodding his head, Adam continued taking her pulse while consulting his watch. "That's fine. Now let me take that thermometer out. There we go. Let me see, thirty-seven degrees, perfect." Next he checked her blood pressure. "And how are you feeling? Any problems lately? Have you had any sickness, diarrhoea, upset stomach?"

Mandy shrugged. "Well..."

Adam patiently looked at her.

"Well, I still keep forgetting things."

"Such as?"

"Anything. Everything. I can't remember." She started crying.

"That's all right, take your time." He deflated the sphygmomanometer. "One twenty over eighty. Textbook perfect," he said, taking the cuff off her arm. "Now I'll just take a blood sample and then why don't you tell me about these forgetful episodes you're experiencing, and perhaps we can work out where you got that bruise."

Mandy winced as Adam drew her blood.

"Mandy, are you OK?"

Mandy nodded and watched Candle Wax pad silently across the carpet. "Yes, I'm fine," she whispered, smiling at the cat.

***

It was gloomy when Chase woke and she was momentarily disorientated until she remembered that she was in the cellar of the derelict farmhouse. The photograph was still clutched to her chest, a bit more crumpled than it was before. Flattening it as best she could, she slipped it into her bag before tucking into a gooseberry jam and pickled onion breakfast. It was only when she had finished eating that she realised her ankle was no longer hurting. She was thankful for that, it would make it easier to flee.

Wan light filtered into the cellar through cracks in the floorboards and she could now see her surroundings slightly better. The far end of the cellar was still in darkness. Apart from the food supplies, the cellar seemed to be fairly barren. Water dripped down one of the walls and from the pans stationed at the foot of the wall, it looked as though Mat had collected the water to drink. Cobwebs proliferated in the rafters supporting the floor above, although from the amount of dust trapped in the webs, she doubted there were any spiders in residence. She couldn't believe Mat had been living in these dismal surrounds; couldn't believe she had found him here.

Venturing toward the dark recess at the back of the cellar, she found an old wooden bureau against the wall covered by a few old newspapers that had gone mouldy. There was a ragged coat and a pair of walking boots hanging from a rusty nail on the wall. Ignoring the mouldy looking coat, she took the boots down to inspect them. The laces broke straight away as she tested them, and although the boots were slightly too big for her, they were in good condition and better for the terrain than the trainers she was wearing. Taking the laces out of her shoes, she re-laced the walking boots, tapped them on the floor to make sure there were no creepy crawlies in them and put them on.

Gingerly pulling open one of the bureau drawers, she found a few rusty old nails. Closing the drawer, she opened the next one down to find a can of oil and a few hard rags wrapped around a rusty hammer. Shaking her head, she opened another drawer. Inside she found a rotten old map that disintegrated when she picked it up, an old calor gas stove, a few tent pegs and a length of fishing line with a few hooks. There was also a tobacco tin. Taking it out, she pried open the lid, the scent of old tobacco still evident. Inside there was a small penknife and a circular compass. She surmised that whoever previously lived in the house must have been a keen camper. Checking the compass, she pocketed it. Opening the penknife, she ran her finger along the blade. It was still sharp and she put the penknife and the fishing tackle in the tin before putting them in her bag.

She waited a while before venturing out of the cellar, listening for movement in the house above. When she was satisfied the men had gone, she carefully pushed open the trapdoor, peering out at a room more ramshackle than the one she remembered. Bits of broken furniture littered the floor and the doors had been smashed.

Closing the trapdoor, she cautiously stepped through the

debris to the front room and approached the front door where she peered outside, her eyes alert for any movement. Confident there was no one around, she started to walk back toward the hill. She could have followed the lane, but she thought it was too risky. But she needed to find Mat. She couldn't leave him. Not now she knew the truth, and she hoped if they had released Mandy, she might be able to help her.

Chase knew she was risking her life, but without Mat, she knew she didn't have a life. When he had disappeared, she had been devastated. Her world didn't just deteriorate, it collapsed. It was only because of Jane that she managed to hold herself together. Jane had been there for her, now she had to be there for Jane, too. It was her fault Jane was in this mess. Too many people had suffered because of her. Besides, it would be no good escaping on her own, because who's to say anyone would believe her story? She knew Moon must have powerful allies. If they could make a village disappear, what was one person? No, she had to get her friends out first so that they could corroborate her story. There would be strength in numbers. People would have to believe them, wouldn't they?

Even though coming down the hill she'd had a bad ankle, it was harder walking back up. She stopped halfway up to catch her breath and to rub her thighs, which had started to ache. The boots she had put on handled the precarious ground better than her trainers had, but they were heavier than her previous footwear, which added to the exertion.

Like a portent, dark clouds were gathering in the sky and she shivered.

At the top of the hill, she made her way to the hollow, crawling up the bank to peer out over the village. Everything seemed quiet but she proceeded with caution, scrambling over the top and darting between bushes and tree trunks. The ground was muddy and slippy in places, but the grip on the boots helped keep her upright. She decided to circumnavigate High Top Cottage in case someone was waiting in hiding for her, and she kept to the gardens and fields behind the hedge that lined the lane. She kept herself low, trying to hide as much as possible behind foliage. As she ducked behind a large red rhododendron bush at the bottom of a garden, a spot of rain hit her cheek and she cursed.

"Who's that?" a voice demanded.

Startled, Chase almost fell over as Belinda appeared from around the side of the rhododendron, a pair of menacing secateurs in one hand and deadheaded flowers in the other. She was wearing a floral print dress and Wellington boots; her grey hair was tied up in a ragged bun that looked like a spider on her head.

"What are you doing in my garden?" Belinda asked, waving the secateurs in the air.

Chase heard a wind chime ringing in the distance, but it did little to soothe her with it sonorous tones as she tried to think what to say. She nervously eyed the secateurs. "I, erm..."

"Oh, it's you." Belinda glared down at Chase. "What are you doing hiding in my garden?"

"Oh, I... I came for those cakes." Chase didn't know what to say and she didn't want to antagonise Belinda, not when she had secateurs in her hand.

"Cakes?"

"Yes, you invited me for tea and cakes."

Belinda frowned. "I don't remember that."

"Well, if it's inconvenient..."

"No, no, if I invited you for tea and cakes, then tea and cakes you'll have. But you won't find them down the bottom of my garden, you silly girl."

Shaking her head at her misfortune, Chase followed Belinda up the garden toward the house. She didn't want to refuse in case Belinda *changed.*

"Wipe your feet before you come in," Belinda said, not heeding her own advice and leaving a muddy trail across the kitchen floor.

Chase wiped her feet on a mat and tried to avoid Belinda's muddy route when she entered. The large kitchen was warm and inviting. Saucepans hanging from hooks in the low-beamed ceiling knocked gently together as a breeze blew through the open door. Hanging among the pans were dried herbs that emitted a pleasant aroma.

"Well, sit down, sit down," Belinda said, putting the secateurs and the deadheaded flowers on the table in the middle of the room.

Chase sat as Belinda went to the sink and filled a kettle with water.

As the wind picked up, a window banged somewhere in the house. Chase bit her lip as she watched Belinda take a large tin of cakes out of a cupboard, arranging them on a plate before putting them on the table. How could she refuse to eat them without angering Belinda?

"Help yourself." Belinda put a small plate on the table and stared down at Chase with her arms folded across her chest.

"If you don't mind, I'll wait for my tea." Chase said, trying to buy herself a bit of time. No way was she going to eat anything this mad woman had made, especially not when she knew that the ingredients were genetically modified.

Belinda shrugged and turned to the kettle, which had come to the boil and switched itself off. While Belinda wasn't looking, Chase took two of the cakes and quickly broke some crumbs onto the plate before dropping the cakes in her bag.

When Belinda turned back with two cups of tea, Chase licked her lips and ran the back of her hand across her mouth. "Very nice."

"I thought you were going to wait for your tea?"

"They looked too nice to wait." Chase smiled, hoping that Belinda believed her.

Belinda put the drinks on the table and fetched a bowl of sugar. Somewhere in the house, the window banged again.

"You'd better shut that window if you don't want it to break." Chase picked up her drink, letting it warm her hands.

Belinda sat down.

"I think the wind's picking up."

Taking a sip of her tea, Belinda eyed Chase from above the rim of the cup.

"If the window breaks, it could be expensive."

Begrudgingly, Belinda nodded her head and stood up. When she left the room, Chase quickly poured her drink down the sink and sat back down.

She heard the window slam shut, and a moment later, Belinda appeared at the door. As she looked at the floor, her face slowly flushed with colour.

"Mud!" Belinda frowned and looked at the floor. "Where's all that mud come from?"

"It was on your boots."

As if she hadn't realised Chase was there, Belinda looked up from the mess on the floor and glared at her. "You've walked mud into my house. Do I walk mud into your house? No respect. That's the trouble today..."

"No, it wasn't me, you did it. Look at your boots!"

"Muddy bugger. Who are you anyway? And what are you doing in my kitchen?"

Chase stood up and pushed the chair back. The wooden legs squeaked across the tiled floor.

Belinda stepped into the kitchen and picked up the secateurs. "Muddy bitch. Mess my floor. I'll show you." She lunged across the table, snipping the blades inches from Chase's nose.

Chase stumbled back. "I didn't do anything," she protested.

"Didn't do anything. *Didn't do anything.* Look at my floor. Filthy. Muddy mud."

"You walked it into the kitchen, look." Chase lifted her foot up to show that her boot was clean. "There's no mud on my boot, see!"

"That's because it's all over my bloody floor. Muddy bugger. I'll show you." She charged around the table, knocking the deadheaded flowers to the floor.

Terrified, Chase fled for the door. She could hear Belinda running behind her, her footfalls loud on the tiles.

"Muddy bitch. I'll show you."

Outside it was raining heavy, distorting the view, as though it was all an illusion. Chase ran across the patio with Belinda screaming at her heel. Across the garden and she was at the gate leading to the lane. The latch was stiff, but it moved and Chase flung the gate open and ran out of the garden, slamming the gate shut behind her to try and slow Belinda up. The rain lashed down, drenching her, but that was the least of her worries as she heard the gate bang open behind her.

"*I'll teach you,*" Belinda screeched. "Breaking into my house and muddying the floor."

Running down the lane, Chase forgot all about keeping out of sight. Not knowing where else to go, she kept to her original plan and headed for Mandy's house. Even though she was an old woman, Belinda kept up with her, screaming obscenities as Chase ran up Mandy's drive.

Just before she reached the house, the front door swung open and Mandy appeared. Adam stepped out behind her.

"Chase, what...?" Adam began.

"It's Belinda..." Chase could hardly breathe. "She's gone mad. She wants to kill me, she..."

Before Chase had time to finish her sentence, Belinda appeared in the drive, snipping the secateurs like a crabs pincers. She ran up the drive, her bedraggled hair plastered to her face by the rain. Her floral print dress was soaked, sticking to her like a second skin but it was her face that alarmed Chase. There was a mad glint in her eyes and tendons stuck out on her neck like taut steel wires. For a brief moment it looked as though her features were changing, a subtle realignment of the flesh that made her look like a monster.

"The change," Mandy said, her voice shaking.

A gunshot punctured the air and from the corner of her eye, Chase saw a flash of light. Belinda's features contorted from madness to shock as the bullet entered her chest and she clutched the wound, lifting away her sodden dress and slipping her finger through the bullet hole in the material as though wondering what it was.

212

Mandy wailed.

"*My dress*," Belinda screeched. "My *bloody* dress." The mad glint returned to her eyes and she rapidly opened and closed the secateurs, *snip, snip, snip*, metal on metal, like huge incisors gnashing together before she lunged at Chase.

Another shot rang out, hitting Belinda in the shoulder and spinning her round like a dervish. The exit hole was larger than the entry hole and Chase could see glistening shards of bone. Turning back to face the house, Belinda raised her head with protracted slowness, her teeth bared in a feral snarl until the next shot entered her skull. There was no watermelon-like explosion as Chase might have expected, just a neat little hole in her cheek. She fell to the floor, still snipping the secateurs as her body twitched.

The ringing in Chase's ears was deafening. She turned, shocked to see Adam with a pistol in his hand. "You, I... I don't understand." With the ringing in her ears, she could hardly hear herself speak.

"Sorry, Chase." Adam shrugged apologetically.

Chase spat in his face. "Sorry! You bastard. I trusted you."

"You still can."

Mandy was slumped in the doorway, her head in her hands.

Chase backed away, shaking her head. "How could I ever trust you after what you've just done? Aren't doctors supposed to *save* lives, not take them?"

Adam shook his head. "I did it to save you."

"Bollocks."

"Chase, you've got to believe me."

Shaking her head, Chase backed further away.

"Look, you're right. I do know what's going on, but it's not what you think. This experiment is for the benefit of mankind. Imagine it. A world without disease. How could I refuse to be a part of that after Nigel explained it to me?"

"What about ethics. What about the villagers you've been experimenting on. What choice did they have?"

"You're right. We went about it the wrong way. It wasn't

meant to be like this." He shook his head. "Things have been going wrong. You've got to believe me, Chase. I didn't know this would happen, but we'll sort it out, given time."

"And what about Belinda? What about all the others who've died?"

"I know what you're thinking, believe me, I regret it."

"Do you really! How much are they paying you?"

Adam vehemently shook his head. "This isn't about money."

"It's *always* about money."

"Not for me."

"And what makes you so special?"

"Look, come into the house and I'll explain everything. You've got to trust me."

"I haven't got much choice when you've got a gun pointed at me."

Lowering the gun, Adam put it in his bag. "There, I've put it away. Please, you've got to listen to me. Please."

Chase wiped rainwater from her face. Her head was spinning. She didn't know what to do.

Suddenly a hand grabbed her leg. Startled, she looked down to see Belinda staring up at her with a contemptuous scowl. Her bloody fingers tightened their grip and Chase tried to shake her off, but Belinda had too tight a hold on her.

"*Muddy mud,*" Belinda spluttered through blood soaked lips, a bubble of blood bursting from her mouth and splattering her chin. Chase kicked her in the chest and yanked herself free.

On the driveway, Belinda coughed once and blood dribbled from her mouth as she died.

"Chase, are you okay?" Adam stepped toward her, his face showing concern.

"What do you think," she snarled.

"Look, come into the house out of the rain."

Dejected and too tired to protest, Chase walked into the house and helped Mandy to her feet. Adam shut the door behind them.

"We can't leave Belinda lying out there like that."

"That's the least of your worries," Adam said, locking the door.

214

Chapter 24

After exiting the building, Ratty and Izzy returned to the fog. With no visible points of reference, they could be going round in circles. Shapes would appear, vague and indistinct before the fog devoured them. An alarm had started ringing in the distance, muffled and tuneless as though it was being strangled. Ratty surmised that their escape had been discovered.

Coming across one of the pipes that wormed through the fog, they used it to navigate a path. Izzy had a tight grip on his hand, tight enough that her nails dug into his flesh, but he didn't complain.

The going was made slightly easier because the fog was actually thinning, allowing them to see more than a few feet in front. Ratty considered that they might be coming to the outer limits of its confines and he increased their pace, anxious to get out when suddenly the pipe erupted in a geyser of smoke.

Izzy squealed, let go of Ratty's hand and stumbled over in shock.

Ratty stood opened mouthed, staring at the clouds of fog billowing into the air.

"What's going on?" Izzy yelled.

Helping her to her feet, Ratty shook his head. He almost laughed. "The fog's manmade!" Even if the implications terrified him, it explained why it never dispersed.

Izzy scowled. He could hardly believe it himself. He put a hand in the gushing cloud; surprised by how cold it was, he quickly withdrew it.

He reasoned that the pipes were vented at various places and when the fog thinned enough, something activated the vents and emitted clouds of artificial fog to continue the illusion.

"Come on," Ratty said, following the pipe until they came to a nondescript, squat building. He could hear a generator chugging away inside and the sibilant hiss of compressed air as valves opened and closed. Cautiously, he checked around the building before trying the door, which was unlocked. Finding a switch inside the doorway, he flicked it on, flooding the room with light, revealing large, steaming tanks.

"I think we'll be OK in here."

"Famous last words." Izzy ran a hand through her hair and shook her head. "What's happening here? How on earth did we get in this mess?"

Ratty didn't have any answers. "Look, let's get some rest, try and get some sleep," he suggested.

"Sleep! I don't think I'll ever sleep again."

But she did.

It was Ratty who couldn't.

The hissing machinery kept him awake, but at least the squat building was warm and dry. He huddled in a corner with Izzy, the compressed air playing a tuneless recital as valves opened and closed. At times, his stomach seemed to join in with its own musical accompaniment. He was hungry, but there was nothing he could do about it; and besides, he had more pressing issues to deal with.

Just because he couldn't sleep, didn't mean he couldn't let Izzy. Besides, he liked cuddling her as she slept; the rhythmic cadence of her breathing had a comforting influence.

When Izzy eventually woke a few hours later, Ratty examined the machinery more closely.

"I think this must be used to make the fog," he said. "If we can damage this machinery enough, then I think we could stop it working." He knew there must be lots of fog generators around the village, but he hoped that by breaking at least one of them, it would disperse enough of the fog to allow them to see where they were going.

"It looks too dangerous to me." Izzy examined a pipe and jumped as compressed air hissed out at her.

"We've got to do something," Ratty said, checking the generator. "If I just turn it off, they'll come and turn it back on. That's why I've got to break it."

"And what if there's a back up generator somewhere that kicks in?"

Ratty hadn't considered that. He frowned. "Well, we'll just have to hope there isn't."

"I don't know. I think we should just take the videotape you've got and carry on following the pipe. We don't want to make them angry."

"*Angry*. I want to make them more than angry, I want to make them pay for what they've done." He remembered his granddad. He wouldn't have bothered about making them angry. He didn't get awarded medals commending his bravery for nothing. And Ratty was damn sure he wasn't going to worry about making the enemy angry either. What was it his granddad used to say, 'when you've lost your temper, you've lost the battle'. Ratty wanted to make Moon and his companions very angry. Very angry indeed.

The generator was about eight feet square and water was leaking into a pan from a pipe at the back. Other pipes went from the generator to a large tank surrounded by metal cylinders about five feet high and a foot in diameter. Ratty decided his best course of action was to break the generator. Breaking something else could prove too dangerous. Taking the knife out of his pocket, he unscrewed a faceplate on the generator to reveal a circuit board before fetching the pan of water from around the back.

"Stand back," he said before he threw the water over the electrics. There was a loud bang and sparks shot out; smoke curled lazily into the air and the generator fell silent. Air still wheezed through the pipes, but it was getting quieter, like a snake too tired to hiss.

Hoping that a main trip switch had been thrown somewhere and that none of the wires were now live, Ratty reached inside and tugged out wires, circuit boards and various other components. Dropping the bits on the floor, he ground his heel into them so they were well and truly broken.

"I'd like to see them put that back together again." He nodded his head as he inspected his handiwork. "Now let's get out of here, before they come to see what's wrong." He grabbed Izzy's hand and led the way outside where it had started to rain. He didn't know how long it would take for the fog to disperse, but he planned to try and speed up the process by blocking up as many vents on the main pipe as he could. If the vents interlinked with other generators, then he knew breaking one generator wouldn't be enough.

They followed what appeared to be the main pipe, stopping to stuff earth, grass, branches and anything else they could find into each vent they found. After walking for about an hour, Ratty was sure the fog was thinning slightly. But perhaps it was wishful thinking. He didn't know how many vents they had blocked; it seemed like hundreds.

Then without warning the pipe disappeared beneath the ground like a huge worm and they floundered on in the fog; souls lost in damnation.

He knew it had been too much to hope that the pipe would lead them out.

Although he was sure the fog was dissipating, shapes were still silhouetted in bas-relief; trees stood like cardboard cutouts in a bleak landscape where everything appeared dead. It was like being in a nether world, halfway between heaven and hell. The rain didn't help. It made the atmosphere cold and miserable and Ratty was deliberating on his circumstances when he suddenly stepped out of the fog into a clear vista.

Ratty was stunned. They were out. He turned and looked back at the undulating bank of fog, his mouth open in disbelief.

"We've done it." He punched his hand in the air, unable to believe their luck.

Izzy shook her head and pointed behind him. "Yes, Einstein, you've done it all right. We're in the village!"

Ratty looked where Izzy was pointing and through the hazy rain he saw the church in the distance, and beyond that, the houses of Paradise leading up the hill.

"I don't believe it." He felt the strength drain out of his body and his shoulders slumped.

Izzy punched him hard on the shoulder. "You bloody stupid idiot. Of all the..." She shook her head in disbelief and punched him again. "I told you we should have gone the other way. I told you I thought we were going the wrong way. Didn't I tell you?"

"What do you want, a medal." Ratty grabbed her wrists to stop her hitting him.

"Now what are we going to do? I'm soaked wet through."

At that moment a shot rang out, the sound muffled by the rain. Another two shots followed the first one.

"What's that?" Izzy asked.

"I don't know, but I'm not waiting around to find out." He released his grip on her wrists. "Look, stay here if you want, but I'm going back into the fog to find out what's going on."

"Are you mad?"

"Quite possibly, but I'm not angry."

"And what's that supposed to mean?"

"It means I haven't lost the battle."

***

Chase backed away from Adam, her teeth clenched. "What do you mean, that's the least of my worries?" She looked at the locked door, panic etched across her face.

Adam raised his hands in a placating manner. "Moon's men are searching for you, that's all."

She eyed him suspiciously. "Why? What does he want with me?"

"You're pregnant. He wants you where he can keep an eye on you and do tests."

"Like a lab rat, you mean?"

"Something like that."

"No, that sounds exactly like what you're saying. So when are you going to tell him where I am? I mean, it was you who told him I was pregnant!"

Adam looked sheepish. "I'm not. I told you, you can trust me, and I mean it. Come on let's get Mandy through into the lounge. You need to dry yourself."

Although she didn't trust him, Chase helped him carry Mandy down the hall and into the lounge where they lay her on the settee. Mandy was mumbling incoherently to herself. Chase could hardly make it out, but she thought she was talking to someone called Candle Wax!

"If you go upstairs, I'm sure you'll find some of Mandy's dry clothes. I doubt she would mind you wearing them and you're about the same size."

Chase had to admit she was soaking wet and that she felt uncomfortable and the thought of being dry was favourable to catching pneumonia, but she didn't trust Adam. She thought that as soon as she left the room, he would somehow contact Moon to tell him she was here.

As though he sensed her apprehension and distrust, Adam said, "I'm not going to do anything. Don't worry, if I was going to do something to you, I would still have the gun in my hand!"

Chase conceded that he was right and she walked out of the room and went upstairs to find some clothes.

When she came back down wearing green combat trousers and a black jumper, Adam was checking on Mandy. "Is she okay?" Chase asked.

Adam looked Chase up and down. "Yes, she's just in a narcoleptic state. I think it was brought on by shock. Seeing Belinda... killed like that." He shook his head and sighed. "I didn't have any alternative. You've got to believe me. She would have killed you."

"And what about the vicar? Is he dead too?"

Adam nodded imperceptibly.

"Then you did lie to me?"

"I had to. I couldn't tell you the truth."

"No, but you could tell Moon I was pregnant."

Adam sighed. "That's my job. I thought I was doing the right thing."

220

Chase was exhausted and she sat down on the plush settee. The room was richly furnished, although it looked slightly unkempt. There was also a mouldy smell in the air, as though the room hadn't been cleaned in a long while. Ornaments dotted the mantelpiece above a mock coal fire powered by gas. She recognised pieces of Ditchfield and Murano glassware placed either side of an ornate carriage clock. There was also a samurai sword hanging on one wall, the scabbard and grip of which appeared to be carved from bone. In fact, the more Chase looked around, the more items of value she spotted. There was a porcelain harlequin figure on a walnut side table by the window and Venetian wine glasses in a display cabinet along another wall. There was also a vast library of antiquated leather bound books in a bookcase that reached to the ceiling.

"So now why don't you tell me the truth," Chase said when she had finished admiring the room. "Why don't you tell me why you aren't in it for the money."

Adam linked his fingers and stared at the floor. "Have you ever seen someone you love die? I have. I was married once. Her name was Nicola." He took a wallet out of his pocket and produced a photograph from it that he passed to Chase. Tears moistened his eyes.

She looked at the picture of a dark haired girl with vivacious eyes and a jaunty smile before passing it back.

"We were married for six years," Adam continued, taking the photograph from Chase and looking at it. "After the first year of our marriage, she was diagnosed with Huntington's disease." He shook his head. "I had to watch as she slowly deteriorated. At first she started forgetting things. Then came the change in her personality. She became antisocial, having outbursts of temper. It broke my heart when she suffered involuntary movements, difficulty speaking and swallowing, weight loss, depression." He shook his head. "We tried everything, but there's no medical cure. There are experiments with stem cells being injected directly into the brain, but it isn't yet an effective treatment, so it wasn't an option."

"And you think what you're doing in Paradise is? These people don't even have the option."

Adam continued, unfazed. "She took five years to die. *Five years.* Out of the six years we'd been married, she was slowly dying for five of them." He held his head in his hands. When he had composed himself, he looked up and his eyes sparkled with tears.

"When Nigel Moon came to me with the idea of combating illness of every sort, I thought it would be my chance to help, like a lasting legacy to Nicola. I didn't want other people to suffer like she had. Of course I was sceptical, but Moon was so convincing. If you've watched someone you love die, you'd know how inadequate you feel. How helpless. And then here was someone saying *I* could make a difference. All I had to do was monitor the test subjects. Deep down I knew it wasn't right not telling people they were being experimented on, but all I saw was an end to the suffering. You have to believe me. I didn't want it to be like this."

Even though Chase didn't want to believe him, she did. She wanted to have someone to blame, but she didn't feel that someone was Adam and she found herself feeling sorry for him.

"Using molecular biology they located diseases and traits at precise points within a known chemical structure. Then products introduce genetic material into the body to replace faulty or missing genetic material, thereby treating or curing a disease or abnormal condition. At first the results were encouraging. Well, more than encouraging really. People who had suffered years of sickness were improving. Blood pressures improved. Cardiovascular health improved. It was a minor miracle. Arthritic patients could grip things for the first time in years without a twinge of pain. But then things started going wrong. I didn't have a lot to do with the test results as Moon's main research team dealt with them, but I'd noticed people were becoming forgetful. And then there was the violence. That's why I've got the gun. I asked Moon for it when I felt my safety was in jeopardy. I only wanted it as a sort of last resort. I never thought I'd use it. But I was still convinced the work was going to succeed. I still am."

"Then you're a *fool*," Chase spat. "How many more people do you have to kill before you realise? Doctors are supposed to save lives, not take them. I thought that was what you took the Hippocratic oath for, to observe medical ethics. Or should that be the hypocritical oath? What went wrong?"

"Nicola," Adam whispered. "I did it for Nicola."

"You're just using her as an excuse. Would she want you *killing* people in her memory, for gods sake?"

Adam didn't answer.

"So why the change of mind. Why haven't you told Moon where I am?"

Rubbing his face with his hands, Adam shook his head. "The whole idea behind the project was to alter food so that it could cure people of any illness they might have. It would also stop people getting ill. This just improves on nature, improving the evolution process. But now... I don't know what to think."

"So what went wrong?" Chase asked

"Well, from what I've heard, it looks as though the human system contains too many pollutants. The experiment didn't take into account the amount of chemicals we unwittingly ingest. Fluoride in the water, formaldehyde that leeches out of the plastic containers into the milk, oestrogen in the water system, pesticides, additives, e-numbers, and they're only the ones we eat. There are others that are absorbed by the skin or carried on the air. We take in a chemical cocktail every day without realising. This cocktail has reacted unfavourably with the food enzymes, and as it's the enzymes that determine the function of a cell, the intended chemical reaction is being inhibited or it's interacting with the wrong cells. Unfortunately, this has resulted in a form of functional psychosis."

"You mean they're going mad!"

"Yes."

Chase let out a sighed whistle and shook her head. "I

223

don't believe people could be stupid enough to mess with our food." She suddenly remembered Belinda's face and how her features appeared to change. "And is there anything else? Is the food doing something more physical?"

Adam looked down at his hands. "There might be something else going on, but it's hard to tell. I think that the food might be causing mutations. Evolution is all about mutating, so to be more precise, it's taking us to the next stage of evolution before we're ready... But it might not be our natural stage..."

"Holy shit."

"Well, Moon now seems to think that you hold the key. That your child will be born with perfect immunity to disease and that they'll be able to obtain the ultimate insulin from it. He hopes that this will also stop the mutations, letting the body reach a happy medium."

Chase protectively grabbed her stomach. "You mean they want to cut my baby up to use it as a pharmacy!"

"Well, not exactly like that..."

"That's what you're saying."

"I don't know what I'm saying anymore, but I like you Chase. And I don't want to see anything happen to you."

"So what am I going to do? Moon will find me wherever I am."

"We'll find a way. Trust me."

What choice do I have, she thought, staring out of the window and watching the rain fall like Gods tears on a blighted land.

224

Chapter 25

Ratty could hear voices in the fog, muffled and indistinct. Grabbing Izzy's hand, he dragged her into a hedge. He knew it wouldn't hide them from anyone wearing the goggles, but it was better than standing out in the open, waiting to get caught.

"I knew this was a bad idea," Izzy protested.

Ratty glared at her and covered her mouth with his hand. "*Shsss*," he hissed.

He didn't know whether it was his imagination, or whether he had been walking around in it for too long and got used to it, but the fog definitely appeared to have dissipated slightly and there were no new emissions from the vents. They had circled the village, and rather than using the lane where they were more likely to come across wandering patrols, they had walked behind a hedge that ran parallel to the lane.

As the voices drew closer, Ratty tensed, his muscles bunched like taut springs. Making sure Izzy and himself were as prone to the floor as they could get, he peered through the hedge, but at first he couldn't see anything. The hedge was prickly and sharp and the more branches he tried to move out of the way, the more it scratched him. He silently cursed. Then he saw them, drifting like ghosts through the fog: men dressed in white fatigues.

One of the men suddenly stopped and turned toward Ratty, and he felt a spasm of fear knot his stomach. Then the fog drifted thick and impervious over the scene, and when it eventually dispersed, the men had gone, vanished into the fog.

Ratty let out a sigh of relief. "Come on, let's go," he said, standing up.

"Who *was* that? Was it them?"

He knew she was referring to the hunters or soldiers or whatever they were, but he didn't want to scare her by telling her the truth. "I don't know. Come on, let's go."

"Are you mad. We can't carry on."

"Would you rather stay here?"

Izzy scowled at him. "If I didn't like you -" She abruptly stopped talking, her cheeks flushed.

Ratty pulled a quizzical expression. "If you didn't what?"

"Nothing. Just forget I said anything."

"If you didn't like me, is that what you said?"

"I didn't say anything. Now can we get a move on because I'm cold, wet and miserable?"

Ratty grinned and kissed her on the cheek.

"What was that for?" she said, wiping the spot where he had kissed her.

"Because I like you too." He couldn't believe what he had just done.

Izzy shook her head and snorted. "Come on Romeo, why don't you get me out of here."

Still grinning, Ratty took Izzy's hand and they continued walking through the field, following the hedge.

After about twenty minutes, they came to the fence surrounding the compound and they followed it round. Ratty assumed that it must be a boundary fence, erected to either keep people out or in!

In the distance, he could hear the humming sound of a generator and using it as a beacon, they headed toward it.

When they reached the source of the sound, they had to quickly duck behind the building where it originated as there were people wandering between other facilities, their appearance indistinct in the fog, like ghosts, trapped between the past and the present. When the coast was clear, Ratty checked the door to the generator room. This one was locked so they skirted around the building, looking for another way in.

High up the side of the building, there was a ladder, but it was too far up to reach as it needed another section to enable anyone to climb it. Further on, pipes emanated from the side of the building. Ratty surmised these were more pipes used to distribute the fog. They had a metal fan of spikes stopping anyone climbing up them. He found it ironic they had decided to take so many precautions when the building was blanketed by fog and surrounded by a fence and guards; but then again, Izzy and himself had got in, so perhaps it wasn't so ironic!

With no visible way inside, Ratty dejectedly led the way back to the front of the building where they crouched out of sight around the corner from the front door.

"So now can we go?" Izzy asked.

Ratty ground his teeth. It was looking as though Izzy was right. Perhaps they shouldn't have come back here. Perhaps they should have just tried to find a way out of the fog, but he couldn't admit he was wrong.

Just then he heard the door open; he was apprehensive about looking around the corner but he knew this was the only chance he might have.

Carefully, he peered around the corner to see a figure disappearing into the fog and before he lost his nerve, he dashed out and slipped his hand between the door and the frame before it shut. He held his breath, hoping there was no one inside as he opened the door and called Izzy. She stepped from around the corner, looking dishevelled and scared as he pulled her inside the building, letting the door shut behind them.

His heart was beating fast. Casting a cautionary glance around the room to check there was no one around, Ratty made his way to the generator. He didn't want to waste any more time. He had stuck a stick in a wasps' nest, now it was time to wiggle it about.

Without any hesitation, he cut wires and pipes, much to Izzy's alarm.

The generator chugged to a halt, steaming and hissing in protest. Ratty punched the air and gave a silent whoop of joy. Strike two. He didn't know how much effect his sabotage would have, but it was better than doing nothing.

Izzy looked at him with undisguised panic. He knew she

thought he was being foolish, but it made him feel better to break things, and hopefully, as a result, the fog would disperse.

Before he had time to speak to her, an alarm started ringing and Ratty's expression momentarily mirrored Izzy's. He should have known the generator would be alarmed for a situation such as this. The last one he broke was most probably alarmed too, but they had been too far away to hear it. From somewhere outside he heard shouting, and before Izzy had a chance to protest, he pulled her toward the door and they exited the building before anyone came to investigate. Ducking around the corner, he led the way along the side of the building. At the far end, they hurried into the fog. Ratty's only aim now was to get as far away from the building as he could.

***

"So what are we going to do?" Chase asked.

Adam shook his head. "I really don't know."

Having recovered from her faint, Mandy sat beside Adam. She still appeared a bit woozy, and she had difficulty remembering exactly what had happened, which Chase envied. She could still see Belinda's face as the bullets struck home, supersonic termites that ate into flesh and bone. No matter how mad or deranged Belinda had become, Chase didn't believe she'd deserved to die. She had not been responsible for her actions - Nigel Moon had. If anyone deserved to die, it was him. He had used people as guinea pigs and turned a whole village into one huge experiment. And somewhere down the line, someone had let him. Someone, somewhere had allowed this to happen. Whether it was sanctioned behind the organised chaos of governmental departments or whether the authority came from a higher, shadowy echelon, she didn't know, but someone had to be held responsible. Somebody, somewhere wielded the power to make things disappear, to sweep them beneath a covert carpet, now she just needed to lift the rug and let people see

228

what had been hidden.

"Do you know if there's a way out of the village?" Chase asked, leaning forward and staring at Adam.

"All I know is that there's a fence around the village, the only road is blocked and there are soldiers patrolling in the mist."

"Well they're not doing a very good job if a teenage boy can get in," she said, thinking of Ratty. "Perhaps after so long they've become complacent." The thought instilled her with hope.

Adam shrugged. "I don't know what to say."

"Say that you'll help me."

"You know I will."

Just then Chase heard a vehicle approaching. The sound was more noticeable because there was no traffic in Paradise. This also made it more menacing. "Can you hear that?" She stood up, alert and tense.

Mandy looked scared, staring around the room as though searching for a way out.

The noise increased, sounding like a primordial beast as the engine revved.

"It's only a car." Adam raised his palms and shrugged as though wondering what all the fuss was about.

"Only a car! And when was the last time you heard a car in the village?"

"I don't know. I suppose it's when the deliveries are made to the shop, or when Moon's men come into the village."

"They must have heard the shots and come to investigate."

The noise of the engine was now right outside the house. Mandy was still on the settee, curled up in a ball.

"We've got to get out of here," Chase said, sounding calmer than she felt.

"It's too late. They're here." Adam clutched his face in his hands and shook his head.

Chase grabbed his hands away from his face. "We've got to go. *Now*."

"It's no good. We can't go anywhere without Moon knowing about it."

"Well we've got to try. Mandy, come on, we're getting out of here." She grabbed Mandy and pulled her to her feet. "If you don't want to come, fine." She looked down at Adam. "But we're out of here." She started toward the rear of the house.

"Hold on, wait for me," Adam called after her.

Chase felt relieved he was coming with them. She felt there was safety in numbers, and although she didn't like it, Adam was armed.

At the back of the house, Chase hurtled through the kitchen and fled through the back door. She pulled Mandy down the garden, almost tripping on unkempt weeds that had forced their way through cracks in the path. A rusted gate at the bottom of the garden led to a narrow lane and she tugged it open, snapping weeds that had entwined the rusted gate to the post like a natural padlock.

Unsure which way to go, Chase headed further away from the house, wanting to put some distance between themselves and whoever was in the vehicle. She thought she heard shouts to their rear, but the rain and wind dampened and dispelled any sound so that she wasn't sure whether it was just her imagination, the wind through the trees, or the rain spattering off the leaves?

Mandy followed at her side like a well trained dog and Adam brought up the rear, casting fearful glances over his shoulder. As they rounded a bend, two figures appeared blocking the lane ahead, their features indistinct as they hunched themselves against the deluge. Chase hesitated, unsure whether the figures were soldiers, out to capture them.

"It's okay," Adam said, as though he sensed Chase's uncertainty, "it's only the pub landlord, George and a young man who lives a couple of doors down from the pub, Eric Stone."

Chase wasn't relieved, but she continued along the lane. As she approached George and Eric, Chase noticed the two men look up, their faces distorted by rivulets of water so that their flesh appeared to be melting (or was it changing?). Dismissing the thought, she suddenly recognised Eric as the man she had seen at her reception in Paradise. The man with the knife.

"George, Eric," Adam said, acknowledging the two men.

Chase noticed that Eric's brow was furrowed into a menacing glare, his close-set, piggy eyes staring out from fleshy sockets. He had a stocky build, his arms folded across his barrel chest. Long hair was plastered to his face and his thick lips were pushed out in a contemptuous sneer.

At his side, George wore a sinister, lopsided grin, his crooked teeth protruding like fangs from behind his thin lips.

"Excuse me," Adam said, indicating that he wanted to get past.

Neither George nor Eric moved.

Adam stepped forward, trying to pass between the men. He placed a hand on George's elbow to gently nudge him aside. George looked from Adam's hand to his face and growled, a low, phlegmy, menacing sound that rumbled from the back of his throat.

"George, we really need to get past."

George's growl turned into a snarl and his lopsided grin transformed into a viscous grimace.

"George, are you all right?"

"Of course he's not all right," Chase spat. "Just look at him. Come on, let's go back the other way." She felt an intense knot of fear twist her insides as she turned to go back the way they'd come.

"They've got the *change*," Mandy whimpered.

"Adam, come on." Chase turned back toward Adam and saw that George had got hold of him by the wrists.

"Let me go, George," Adam said, his tone of voice rising an octave or two as he tried to pull free.

"*Pushed me*," George spat, his eyes glinting with madness. "*Pushed me*." He vigorously shook Adam, causing him to stumble back into Eric who winced as Adam stepped on his foot.

"*Fucker*," Eric snarled, reaching out and grabbing Adam around the throat with his two, large meaty hands that looked more like claws.

Adam gurgled, his face going red.

"Let him go." Chase's voice trembled. She didn't know what to do. She knew that she should help, but the physical appearance of George and Eric held her back. She could see the change in their features, could see the physical manifestation as their body chemistry changed, and it terrified her.

"Mandy, get away from here," Chase said, suddenly realising that Mandy was one of them, *tainted*, and susceptible to the change, and in effect, just as dangerous.

Mandy looked at Chase with wide, fearful eyes.

"Mandy, please, just back away and I'll try and help Adam."

But Mandy didn't move. She was rooted to the spot, her jaw beginning to clench while her eyes narrowed into defensive slits.

Adam's face had gone almost purple. He thrashed around within George and Eric's grasp like a fish on a hook. Spittle flew from his lips and he tried desperately to kick out.

Beyond fear, Chase ran to help him. She grabbed Eric's hands and tried to prise his fingers apart, but his grip was too tight. Frantic, she slipped her bag from her shoulder and took out the kitchen knife she had dropped in there when she was going to meet Adam in the pub - when had that been? It seemed like a lifetime ago.

Without thinking about what she was doing, Chase slashed out at Eric's hand, slicing a vicious cut across his knuckles. Eric hardly acknowledged the cut and Chase slashed out again, almost severing one of Eric's fingers. Releasing his grip on Adam, he glared at Chase. Freed from the choking hold, Adam toppled backwards, coughing violently. Still holding onto his wrists, George toppled with him, landing heavily on top of Adam.

As Eric moved toward Chase, she held the knife up like a crucifix, a talisman, hoping that the sight of it would stop

Eric from advancing - but it didn't. He was overcome by the change. Nothing scared him.

Backing further away, she waved the knife like an ineffectual wand, hoping to dispel the monster. But of course it didn't work. Eric Stone was oblivious to the knife. With a sudden burst of speed that took her completely by surprise, Eric was on her, his teeth gnashing inches from her face, a thin drool of saliva hanging from his lip as he forced her to the floor, pinning her arms down and causing her to drop the knife.

Chase screamed.

It happened so quickly; Chase was momentarily paralysed by shock. One minute, Eric Stone was about to bite a chunk out of her face, and the next minute Mandy attacked him like a vicious tornado, a whirl of teeth, hands and feet.

Taken by surprise, Eric fell off Chase, and Mandy - or whatever she had become - seized the upper hand by leaping astride his back and clutching at his face. It was like watching a bizarre, hideous rodeo show as Eric bucked and jerked while Mandy held on to his face. It seemed to go on for ages, but in reality it was only a few seconds before her finger sank into his eye. Almost immediately, Eric slumped to the floor and Mandy rolled off him, breathing in short, controlled bursts as she looked across at Chase, her anger manifest.

Chase wanted to be sick. She felt the bile rising, the familiar caustic burn of acid in her throat.

She knew that she should run, but where to? Nowhere was safe in Paradise.

Mandy started toward her, her teeth bared in a feral snarl.

Chase was paralysed by fear.

Adam was swearing and shouting for help.

The rain lashed down.

The wind blew.

And help arrived.

Chapter 26

"For Christ's sake, don't just stand there, help me," Adam wailed as George tried to bite his ear off.

Drake stood over Adam and George with a supercilious smile on his lips. Three armed men stood either side of him, their faces devoid of expression. Two other men grabbed Mandy, while another man administered an injection to her arm, causing her to slump unconscious to the floor, her features relaxing, returning to normal.

"Now why would I want to help a snivelling runt like you?" Drake sneered.

"Fuckin'... get him... off me." Adam could hardly speak, his words coming between bursts of exertion as he fought to restrain George.

"You don't deserve any help. *You* were meant to be on our side." Drake glared at Adam with open dislike. "You were only meant to study the bitch, not try and fuckin' help her escape."

"I'm sorry... but get this fucker... off me... and then... we'll talk about... it!" Adam's face contorted with pain as George tried to pull his ear off.

Drake sighed and shook his head. "What if I told you Moon had given me instructions to kill you."

Chase didn't know whether Adam's eyes went wide in pain or fear.

"He... he wouldn't. I'm too... fuck it Drake, get this madman off me."

Drake stroked his chin. "The precious doctor asking for *my* help. I always knew this day would come. What was it you first called me, a hired shit-kicker that you didn't want in the village in case I..." he made imaginary speech brackets in the air with two fingers on each hand, "... *interfered* with the experiment." He grinned. "And now you're asking me to get directly involved. You can't have it both ways doc."

Chase wanted to help Adam, but she knew Drake and his men would stop her, but she had to do something. "Why don't you cut the bullshit and just help him," she snarled. She thought about the gun in Adam's bag, but one of the guards had picked it up.

Drake turned to glare at Chase. "And why don't you shut the fuck up unless you want me to cut something other than bullshit." He seemed to think about something for a moment. "Then again, I could always treat you to my meat injection like I treated your friend, what's her name, Jane." He gave a lecherous grin.

"What sort of monster are you," Chase spat.

Drake laughed. "I think the only monster around here's growing inside you."

Chase reflexively gripped her stomach.

"If it wasn't for the money, I wouldn't have anything to do with these Frankenstein experiments, but at least I'm not going to give birth to some genetic fuckin' freak."

"That's enough," Nigel Moon boomed, appearing behind Drake, his face reddened with anger. "You men," he pointed at the soldiers, "administer a sedative to George and help Adam to his feet."

One of the soldiers grabbed George while another stabbed a hypodermic needle into his arm. The sedative took effect almost immediately and George's eyes rolled up and he slumped to the floor. Refusing the soldiers' offer of assistance to stand, Adam gained his feet and brushed himself down.

"Thank you, Nigel," Adam said.

"Don't thank me just yet. Did you really think I would just let you go?"

Adam stared down at his feet like a scolded child. "I... I don't know what I was thinking. Everything happened so fast. Nigel, I'm so sorry. You know how much this experiment means to me."

Drake snorted derisively.

Moon gave Drake a withering glare before turning back

235

to Adam. "Then why betray me? I thought out of all the people who would understand... of all the people I could trust..." Moon shook his head. "I asked you to befriend Miss Black; gain her trust, not run off with her!"

"I admit it, I was scared. I know I shouldn't have been, but... I'm the one living in the village. You don't know what it's been like."

"You're just a pussy." Drake spat on the ground.

"Mr. Drake, I will handle this, if you don't mind."

"He's still a pussy." Drake turned away and ordered one of his men to call up a transport vehicle.

Moon turned back to Adam. "You're wrong, Adam, I do understand. We've all been under a great deal of strain, but how can I ever trust you again now?"

"Because I give you my word."

"Adam, don't listen to him. You know this is wrong," Chase said. "Don't let him bully you into grovelling."

"No, Nigel's right. I've been a fool. I wanted to be a part of this because I saw how much benefit it would be to people. We would create a Utopia. A place without illness." He shook his head. "I've let Nigel down, I've let myself down, but more than that, I've let Nicola down."

"You've let her down more by actually being a part of this." She couldn't understand why he had renounced all that he had said in Mandy's house. "You said you'd help me."

"And I will. By making sure you give birth to your child, I'll be helping everyone."

Moon nodded his head. "You know it'll be a long road back to my trust, don't you Adam. But I hope you get there, I *really* do."

"Don't worry Nigel. I don't know what came over me."

Moon sucked air through his teeth. "I hope so. I would hate to *lose* you."

Chase noticed Adam flinch at the word 'lose', as though it held more meaning than just letting him go from his position. "Is this what Nicola would have wanted?"

Adam ignored her.

"Perhaps it's better that she did die then. At least now

you can lie to yourself that this is what she would have wanted."

Adam glared at her. "You've got no idea what it's like for me. You don't know anything about me..."

"That's obvious."

"And you certainly don't know anything about Nicola. You don't know what she was like."

"If this is what she would have wanted, then I'm glad, but deep down, I think you know you're only lying to yourself. You're just using her as a scapegoat, an excuse to justify what you're doing."

"You wouldn't understand."

Chase shook her head. "I don't know who I feel more sorry for, Nicola or you."

Adam clenched his fists.

"Now that's enough," Moon said, intervening. "Guards, escort these two back to the base."

Two men stepped forward and grabbed Adam and Chase by the arms.

"Nigel, you don't need to do this." Adam struggled against his captor. "I thought we'd sorted things out."

"Do you take me for a fool, Adam. It'll take more than a few declarations of remorse on your part before I trust you again. This isn't a case of saying three Hail Mary's and finding absolution."

"But Nigel..."

"*But* nothing. Now unless you want to try my patience, I would suggest that you do as you're told."

"This is your fault," Adam snarled, turning on Chase.

Moon held his hand up, signalling the men to wait.

"Why don't you grow up," Chase retorted. "You should be adult enough to take responsibility for your own actions rather than blaming everyone else."

"Touché. Game set and match." Moon smiled. "She is uncommonly perceptive, wouldn't you say."

Adam clenched his fists.

"I can see that although Chase was not a part of the equation, things have a way of working out for the best."

Moon chuckled. "If it wasn't for life's little accidents, Alexander Fleming would never have discovered penicillin and Louis Pasteur would never have discovered vaccinations. Chase Black will undoubtedly get a mention in history as - if you'll excuse the pun - having had one of the greatest little accidents of all time. Although of course the greatest accolade will be bestowed upon myself."

"People will never praise a killer," Chase spat.

Moon gave a heartless laugh. "Unlike a soldier, trained to kill and being hailed a hero for doing so in battle, you mean. People are so fickle."

"That's different, and you know it."

"Why? They kill. You see my dear girl, the means justifies the end if it furthers the advancement of human life. A soldier kills to ultimately save lives. In my field, people sometimes die, yes, but their deaths lead to greater knowledge. Does the recovering cancer sufferer want to know how many people have died so that they may ultimately live? No. But through the deaths and suffering, cures have been discovered. I offer cures for *all* cancers, for *all* disease. Isn't that worth a few sacrifices along the way?"

"Tell that to the victims."

Moon shook his head. "You are not looking at the whole picture."

"No, I'm looking at the *whole* picture all right. You've consigned a *whole* village to untold suffering. *Nothing* is ever worth that."

"If you could go back in time and kill Adolf Hitler, would you?"

"What's that got to do with anything?"

"Humour me. He caused mass genocide, killed thousands, millions even. If you had the chance, would you go back and stop him before he started? Would the taking of one life be worth it to save millions?"

Chase scowled. "That's different."

"Is it? Or is it that you could justify taking one life? Well where do you stop? Pol Pot had thousands killed in a radical restructuring of Cambodia. Do you stop him too? Or do you

238

go further back in time and stop Christopher Columbus discovering a country that was never lost! The Native Americans were wiped out as a result of his sojourn. How about Attila The Hun? Caesar? Where would it all end? How many would you have to kill to save the many?" Moon smiled. "I hope you see my point. You would kill if it meant saving lives. What we're doing now is sacrificing the few to save the many."

"But these people haven't done anything wrong. They're not mass killers."

"That's purely incidental, but you get my meaning." He waved his hands in the air as if swatting a fly.

"Well to answer your question, no, I couldn't go back in time and kill Hitler. I couldn't kill anyone. Unlike *you*, I haven't got it in me to be so inhumane."

Moon nodded his head. "I see." He smiled to himself. "Take them away." He motioned to the guards before he turned and headed toward a Land Rover that had pulled up at the end of the lane.

Adam gave Chase another withering glare as they were led away.

"And to think I thought you were a nice person." She shook her head.

Adam frowned. "I am. Can't you see this is ground breaking work?"

"Then why did you have your doubts? For a brief moment, you must have seen it for what it was?"

"And what's that?"

"It's just another disease. In finding the cure to other diseases and illnesses, you've opened a Pandora's box and just created a new disease."

"You don't know anything," Adam snarled.

"I know enough to know that people should have a choice, and that they shouldn't be unwittingly experimented on."

"Even when the results can outweigh the risks?"

"Why don't you ask Belinda that? Oh, I forgot, you can't. You killed her. Is that the result you're on about?" She shook her head in disgust before the guard boosted her into the back of a canvas-covered troop carrier. For a moment she thought she saw a look of remorse on Adam's face, but then it was gone, replaced with a steely-eyed determination as he was forced into the truck.

She couldn't believe he had changed so much. To think she had even kissed him. But it had all been a sham. He was just meant to pacify her for Moon's experiment.

As the truck moved through the village, Adam looked down at his feet and refused to look up, even when Chase tried to engage him in conversation. The two guards rode silent shotgun, their guns drawn, fingers tensed on hair triggers.

Through a flap in the back of the truck, Chase could see they had entered the fog, the truck driver navigating an unerring path through the mist. She absently wondered how he could see, but then she realised they must have special devices that allowed them to see where they were going. The ride was bumpy and the truck emitted clouds of diesel smoke, causing her to wonder how a soldier survived the ride, never mind the battle! The truck stopped once and Chase heard the driver talking to someone before a soldier peered over the tailgate into the back of the truck. Chase could see that the soldier had some form of goggles pulled up onto the top of his head. Letting the flap drop back, he shouted something incoherent to the driver and the vehicle started moving again.

After about ten minutes, the truck stopped again. One of the guards dropped the tailgate and the canvas cover was thrown back so they could exit. Without being prompted, Chase dropped to the ground.

They were in a clearing, surrounded by low buildings and she looked around, wondering how the hell she had got herself into this mess. The fog was evident, but patchy, and an alarm was ringing with a forlorn, lost sound that reverberated between the buildings. People were dashing around, seemingly oblivious to the truck and its occupants. Perhaps Moon's men had overstretched themselves? More

240

and more things were occurring which made her think they had become complacent. The experiment was falling apart around them. With the alarm ringing, and the panic and confusion, she thought it must resemble Jericho before the walls fell, the alarm representing the trumpet that sounded the death knell.

She only hoped she didn't fall with it.

Chapter 27

Nigel Moon sat in his office surrounded by research papers. He could feel the start of a headache, and he wished someone would turn that damn alarm off. His life's work was hanging in the balance, and he was damned if he was going to give it up without a fight.

Drake stood before him wearing an impervious mask of indifference. "What do I pay you for?" Moon asked, keeping his tone of voice calmer than he felt.

"Security."

"Security." Moon nodded. "Now can you kindly explain to me how two small children have escaped? And it's not as if this is the first time it's happened is it!" He was referring to Mat.

"Because we never anticipated taking prisoners, we don't have a proper holding cell."

"And that's your excuse. For God's sake man, are you incompetent as well as stupid?" Moon was pleased to see a nervous tick afflict Drake's left eye. For all his bravado and macho bullshit, he knew Drake would toe the line. He was being paid too well to rock the boat - and Moon's powerful aura defied anyone to challenge him.

"It won't happen again."

"It shouldn't have happened in the first place." He narrowed his eyes and scowled. "And have you found the cause of that blasted alarm?"

Drake coughed to clear his throat. "Someone's sabotaged the generator."

"I already know that, now tell me something I *don't* know."

Drake looked up at the ceiling, his Adam's apple bobbing as he swallowed. "No, I mean a second generator."

Moon stood up so quickly that Drake took an inadvertent

step back. "*Another* generator. *Where?*"

"In the compound."

Moon swept a pile of documents off the desk. "I'm surrounded by fools and amateurs," he bellowed, his cheeks flushed. "As if I haven't got enough problems to deal with. Is it them?"

"Them?" Drake frowned.

"The children."

Drake shrugged.

"Give me strength. I expect you to deal with the problem at once. *And* I want those generator's back up and running, immediately."

"Well, there's a problem with that."

"Why doesn't that surprise me?" Moon closed his eyes. "And what is this problem?"

"The main circuits are fried. We've got to get replacements, and it'll take a few days."

"No, it'll take a few hours, do I make myself clear."

Drake opened his mouth to speak, but Moon interrupted him.

"Think very carefully before you reply, Mr. Drake."

Drake swallowed. "I'll get on to it right away."

Moon opened his eyes and smiled. "Make sure you do. And I think we can kill the alarm now, don't you. Also, find those children before they do any more damage. Use the dogs."

Drake visibly shivered.

"Do you have a problem with that?"

Drake shook his head.

"Well, get on with it then." He watched Drake leave the room before sitting back down. If it wasn't one thing, it was another. He was too close to his objective to have it interrupted by a couple of kids. He had to admit that things hadn't been going according to plan, but now Chase had changed all that. He hoped she was the key he had been searching for. No, she *was* the key he had been searching for, otherwise it was all in vain. That's why it was now so important that she came to term.

There were always bleeding hearts that would condemn his work, saying that he was playing at being God. But didn't they realise he wasn't playing, he *was* a God. He had the power to alter life.

The preliminary enzyme tests on lab rats and monkeys had been encouraging enough to go ahead with the human field trials. The top brass had not offered any objections. Most of them were old and they knew that if the experiment was successful, it would work in their favour. They all wanted their health and youth back, but if the shit hit the fan, they would deny all knowledge of the program. That was their way: disassociation. There had been a couple of dissenting voices, but they had been silenced, permanently.

The animal tests had been abandoned after the human trials began, and the first plant crops had been left to grow wild. They would have to be destroyed eventually, but that could wait. The new crops were growing in a sterile facility in a secret location. With accelerated growth, they didn't have to wait years to harvest the results.

The alarm suddenly stopped ringing and Moon exhaled a sigh of relief. Now that he had Chase, it was time to start winding down the operation in Paradise. He had enough data and on the whole, the results had been encouraging. He knew that, to an extent, his food worked. It just needed the creases ironing out. Although Mat now showed symptoms of psychotic behaviour, he hadn't been as badly affected when he impregnated Chase. That had all changed now though, after Moon had used him as a guinea pig for another unsuccessful batch, which he thought, might have reversed the problem. As there were normally two genes controlling a trait, one from each parent, Moon hoped that Chase's baby would inherit the stronger traits. The result in the child would depend on whether the gene was recessive or dominant, and Moon hoped that Mat's previous mild, psychotic trait was going to be inhibited by Chase's genes. It was a fifty-fifty gamble. If it was successful, she wouldn't give birth to a baby, she would give birth to a pharmacy. Moon smiled. Everything would be all right. He could feel it.

Leaning back, he interlinked his fingers behind his head, closed his eyes and enjoyed the silence.

***

Ratty's only plan of action now was to get out of the fog and get home. But which way? It all looked the same. He was sure that they had already passed certain trees, but he didn't mention it. Besides, he could be mistaken. Didn't all trees look the same? But they didn't all look like witches on broomsticks like the lightning scarred one they were leaning against. He had already seen it once; he remembered being momentarily scared by its peculiar shape as it loomed out of the mist.

As Ratty stood contemplating a course of action, a low growl emanated from the fog. His eyes went wide, alert. The sound was peculiar. Panic coursed through his veins as the sound grew menacingly closer.

"What's that?" Izzy asked, her body tensed as the growls got closer and louder.

Ratty couldn't answer because he didn't know. As the fog eddied and swirled, it took him a moment to spot anything. Then he saw them, coming out of a depression, four figures and three dogs straining at the leash.

"Quick, come on." He grabbed Izzy's hand and dragged her in the opposite direction, running for all they were worth. But the men and their dogs were getting closer, the dogs growls growing steadily louder. But there was something about the growls that didn't sound quite right.

Dodging around a tree, Ratty accidentally caught his foot on a distended root and stumbled, letting go of Izzy's hand as he fell into a mulch of leaves. And then the growls were in his face, and for the first time in his life, Ratty wet himself. He could smell rotting flesh and he looked up into the salivating maw of a disfigured beast. Although it was definitely canine, probably Doberman pinscher, it was also something more. Its muzzle was impossibly elongated. Ratty couldn't quite place it, but as the dog opened its maw to

245

snarl, he was reminded of a crocodile. Rows of teeth disappeared down its throat, which made its growl more ragged. Whatever they had done to the dog, it was now an abomination, a genetic freak, engineered to be a terrifying killing machine. It was a case of purpose over aesthetics.

As the creature strained against the leash, it's powerfully muscled body quivered. The man holding it was having difficulty keeping it under control.

"I would suggest that you don't move."

Ratty recognised Drake's voice.

"Ratty, what's going on?" Izzy squealed.

"It's okay, Izzy. Don't worry, everything's going to be all right."

Drake laughed. "Take them away and get those blasted beasts under control."

Someone manhandled Ratty upright. He had trouble seeing Izzy clearly, but he could hear her crying and he couldn't help feeling that it was his fault she was crying. If he hadn't insisted on staying, perhaps they could have escaped; perhaps they could have convinced someone that *something* was going on. Now he would never know.

"I'll take the girl." Drake's voice was hollow, dispassionate.

Izzy screamed.

Ratty struggled against his captor. "If you lay one hand on her, I'll..."

"You'll what?" Drake snarled.

"I mean it," Ratty said, full of gusto.

"Get him out of here," Drake commanded.

Ratty kicked and fought but it was no good. The last thing he heard was Izzy screaming.

Chapter 28

As Chase and Adam were goaded toward a squat building that sat hunched against the fog, the alarm fell silent. One of the guards punched a series of numbers on a key pad and the door hissed open. Following a bright corridor, they were forced toward a door at the end, which one of the guards unlocked, pushing Chase and Adam through before shutting the door behind them with a metallic clang and locking it.

"Chase, is that you?"

"Jane, oh my god, Jane." Chase turned to see her friend and she rushed over and embraced her. "I'm so sorry," she mumbled. "This is all my fault." She was overwhelmed with relief that her friend was all right.

"What the hell's going on?" Jane asked, her bruised face full of confusion.

"We're in trouble, that's what's going on."

"I already realise that!"

Looking around, Chase saw they were in a small windowless room with a single dirty bulb emitting a cancerous yellow light. Having been taken in an earlier truck, Mandy was also in the room, sitting on a bunk bed. The sedative must have worn off because she was crying. There was a rank smell in the air from confined, unwashed bodies and she could see there was also someone else in the room, sat hunched in the corner, almost hidden behind the bunk beds.

"Mat." She hardly dared breathe in case he disappeared like smoke.

"Best leave him," Jane whispered. "He's not all there." She twirled a finger at the side of her head.

But she couldn't just leave him. Walking toward him, she hunkered down and laid a hand on his shoulder. Mat looked up, shook his head and then lowered it again.

"Mat, it's me, Chase. You know who I am. That's why you tried to warn me about what was going on. Talk to me, please."

"He's got the change..." Mandy said, looking up. "Just like me." She shook her head and started crying again.

"It's like being locked up with a couple of loons," Jane said.

"Mat, talk to me."

Mat batted her hand away. "I know who you are," he mumbled. "I wished you here."

Chase frowned. "I don't understand." Why was he doing this to her?

"I conjured you from a picture. I'm the magic man." He grinned.

Chase was confused. "You mean the photograph?" She took it out of her bag and handed it to him.

Mat snatched it from her. "I had almost convinced myself that you didn't exist, that you were a figment of my imagination, someone I had dreamed. And then you showed up. I conjured you here." He shook his head and looked up, his eyes moist with tears. "You don't know what it's been like for me. I knew there was no going back, I needed someone."

"Why didn't you just tell me what was going on. Why be so cryptic?"

"Perhaps *you're* not real." He reached out and pinched Chase on the arm, causing her to flinch. "If you're a dream, I don't want to scare you away. I don't want to wake. But I am awake, aren't I... and you're a part of my nightmare, a ghost from a past that I can't remember. I conjured you from a photograph, and now you're here, haunting me."

"Oh Mat, what have they done to you." Tears rolled down her cheeks. She turned to look at Adam who was still standing by the door. "Is this what you wanted? Take a good look. Is this the price you were willing to pay?"

Adam looked at the floor and didn't reply.

"It's okay Mat." She turned back to him. "I'll get you out of here."

248

"Haven't you realised yet?" Mandy shook her head and sobbed. "There is no escape, not for any of us."

"Don't give up. There's always a way out. There must be a cure. Adam, tell them."

Mandy laughed.

Adam shook his head. "They don't know exactly what's gone wrong yet, so how can they cure it?"

Mat grabbed Chase by the arm. "She's right. There is no escape, not for us, but you need to get out of here. You need to tell people what's happened so it can't happen again. They've fucked my head up so bad. Sometimes I don't even know who I am."

"I can't leave you here. I *won't* leave you here."

"It's out of your hands."

Chase refused to accept what he was saying. Her head was spinning. Everything was so confusing; none of it seemed real. She felt a hand on her shoulder and she looked up to see Jane.

"They're right, sugar."

"What's going to happen to us?" Mandy asked, her chest heaving between sobs.

"We *can't* just leave them," Chase vehemently said.

"What choice do we have," Jane replied. "You've seen what's happening to them. How do you think they'll act when they see a party political broadcast?"

"This isn't a joke." Chase was angry and annoyed with Jane.

"Don't you think I know that?" Tears filled her eyes.

Chase shook her head and put the palms of her hands to her temples. "I don't know what to think. I still can't believe what's happening."

Jane suddenly went pale.

"I... I've been eating the food they gave me." She looked at Mat and Mandy. "Am I going to become like them? Oh god, don't let me be like them."

Chase stood up and hugged her friend. "It'll be okay. Trust me."

"I do trust you, sugar. It's them I don't trust." She looked back at Mat and Mandy.

"Well, we've all got to trust each other."

"Does that include me, too?" Adam asked.

"That depends on you."

"I thought we were doing the right thing."

"And now?"

He momentarily looked at Mat and Mandy before lowering his head to stare at the floor. "I don't know."

"Well you'd better get off the fence. You're either with us or against us."

"Then I suppose I'm with you."

Chase eyed him suspiciously for anything that might indicate otherwise, but Adam didn't move. "Okay," she said, turning her back on him, "Now we need to plan how we're going to get out of this."

"Haven't you realised yet, we're damned." Mat looked up, his eyes dull and lifeless as though the spark of life had been extinguished. "We're the new lepers. Unclean."

"No, there's got to be something we can do. Moon must be able to undo what he's done." Chase wasn't going to admit defeat. She hadn't found Mat just to lose him again. She wasn't going to let him bury his head in the sand.

At that moment the sound of footsteps echoed outside and a key turned in the lock. The door opened and two small figures were shoved into the room.

"Ratty!" Chase instantly recognised the young boy, and she was relieved to see that he was all right. The other figure was a young girl. Drake stood in the doorway behind them, grinning arrogantly.

Ratty looked up and gave a half-hearted smile that suddenly melted into a fearful grimace. He backed away, protectively keeping the young girl behind him.

"That's who killed the vicar," he cried, pointing past Chase.

Chapter 29

Chase was confused. For some reason, Ratty was pointing behind her, into the room! She turned around. Standing behind her was Adam, who had moved away from the door, Jane, Mandy and Mat.

She turned back to Ratty. "What do you mean, that's who killed the vicar?"

"Him, he killed the vicar." Ratty was still pointing accusingly.

Chase turned around again. Him! She stared at Adam and Mat. At the time of the murder, she remembered running to the surgery and bursting in on Adam and Mandy.

"How did you manage to get back to the surgery so quickly, and why on earth did you kill the vicar?" She eyed Adam warily and backed away. She had already seen him kill once.

Adam held his hands up. "Hold on a minute, you don't think he means me do you? Tell her kid."

"No, not him, him." He pointed at Mat.

"You must have got it wrong." Chase couldn't believe what she was hearing.

Ratty pulled the videocassette from underneath his T-shirt. "I saw it all on this."

"I'll take that." Drake stepped into the room and grabbed the tape. "Didn't you men frisk them before you chucked them in here. What are you, fuckin' amateurs?" There was an embarrassed cough from out in the corridor. "Well you'd better check them now. God knows what else they could have on them."

Chase couldn't believe what she was hearing. She looked at Mat, shaking her head. "Is it true?"

Mat frowned. "Why is everyone looking at me? Who are all you people?"

"It's the change," Mandy wailed. She put her hands on her head and began rocking back and forth as a guard entered the room.

"You," the guard pointed at Mandy, "against the wall. And you, back away." He pointed a gun at Chase.

When Mandy didn't move, the guard shoved her, causing her to stumble and hit her head against the wall.

"I said against the wall," the guard repeated as Mandy rubbed her head.

Chase knew that it was too late.

"Quick, Jane, Ratty, and you," she pointed at the girl, "get out of here."

"No one's going anywhere," Drake drawled, blocking the exit.

"Let us out, you fool," Adam bawled, pushing past Jane. "Don't you realise what's happening."

"You're the fool, fuck face." Drake punched Adam in the stomach, causing him to double over in pain. "Now let my men do their job."

"Back away," the guard covering Mandy said, his voice rising slightly. "If you don't back off, I swear to God I'll shoot." The guard took a step back, his gun levelled on Mandy.

"Drake," Chase shouted, "Can't you see what's happening?"

"Shut it, whore."

"For God's sake, don't just stand there." As Chase spoke, Mandy advanced on the guard, her fingers flexing like claws.

"Drake, do something."

But before he could reply, Mandy flew at the guard and a shot rang out, deafeningly loud in the enclosed space. Chase could hear the sound reverberating in her head and Mandy was flung back, the wall suddenly painted with a bloody splatter effect.

"What the fuck's going on in there," Drake barked.

Chase watched in shock as Mandy's body slumped down the wall, a glistening slug trail of blood left down the brickwork. Jane was screaming, her hands covering her mouth, but the sound was muffled by the reverberating sound of gunfire.

"Don't look." Chase tried to shield Ratty and the girl from the sickening sight, but the blood trickling down the wall was too copious to hide.

"I warned her, I warned her," the guard gasped.

"Get a grip," Drake ordered. "Is she dead?"

"I don't know. They didn't tell me I'd have to kill someone."

"Well check her then, you idiot, and if she isn't dead, then make sure you finish the job."

The guard approached Mandy's slumped body, feeling her throat to check for a pulse when she suddenly reached out and grabbed his hand. The guard jumped in a mixture of shock and revulsion and he accidentally fired off another shot, the bullet whining around the room.

Before the guard had time to react, Mandy bit into his hand, shaking her head from side to side like a dog with a rag. The guard screamed and instinctively hit out to get her to release her grip, but that only seemed to aggravate her even more, like swatting a wasp.

"What the fuck's going on in there?" Drake snarled, stepping into the room. "Let me pass." He pushed Adam out of the way and stormed into the room.

Chase knew that she only had one chance to execute the plan that formed in her head. It was dangerous, but considering her options, what choice did she have? Moving quickly, she jumped on the guard that Mandy was biting and wrestled him for the gun. It wasn't easy to make the guard let go of his weapon, and he pulled the trigger again, almost deafening her as a bullet embedded itself in the wall, spraying the air with dust. His grip was tenacious, until Chase copied Mandy and bit his hand, causing him to let go of the weapon. She had no idea how to use it, but as the guard had just fired a shot off by accident, she knew the safety catch wasn't on. All she would have to do was pull the trigger. Slipping her finger around the trigger, she raised the barrel and pointed it at Drake who was forcing his way

253

toward her.

"Don't move." Even though she had never fired a gun in her life, Chase felt empowered by it. The weight, the feel, and the way it looked. It was almost sexual.

Drake came to a stop, shook his head and laughed. "Don't be stupid. Give me the gun."

The guard on the floor screamed again. The sound made Chase flinch, but she didn't lower the weapon that was surprisingly light for its size. She knew that it wasn't a handgun as it was too big, neither was it a rifle. It was midway between the two with a curved magazine and a handle beneath the snub barrel. There was a switch on the side, which could be flicked between three positions.

"Now be a good girl and take your finger off the trigger." Drake was no longer laughing.

"Don't give it him," Jane screamed, running to stand behind Chase.

"Shoot him," Adam shouted.

"Way to go," Ratty cheered.

Drake cast a withering glare at Adam before turning his attention back to Chase. He stepped toward her, his hands raised in a placating manner. "Now just make it easy on yourself and give me the damn gun."

"I said don't move." Her voice wavered almost as much as the gun barrel.

"Now you know you aren't going to shoot me, and so do they." He indicated the room's occupants.

As Drake took another step, Chase gritted her teeth and pulled the trigger. The room was filled with the hellish sound of the guns retort and a bullet flew past Drake, whining in protest as it missed its target and hit the wall. "Now, don't move again." She forced herself to remain calm even though the guns recoil had hurt her wrist.

Drake stood still, his eyes narrowed to slits. "That wasn't very clever," he whispered menacingly.

"Neither was moving," Chase retorted. "Now get the other guard in here. *Now.*"

For a moment, she didn't think Drake was going to

respond, then he turned and barked at the guard standing outside the door to come in. The guard tentatively peered around the door frame, his gun held tightly in his hand.

"That's it, in you come, don't be shy," Chase said as the young, acne scarred guard stepped into the room. "Now, you and Drake both drop your weapons. Easy, take it slow, otherwise..." She motioned her eyes toward the gun in her hands.

"You can't escape," Drake warned, slipping a pistol from a holster around his waist and dropping it on the floor. Adam scurried over and picked it up. When the guard dropped his machine gun, he picked that up too and pointed both barrels at Drake.

The guard on the floor was still crying in pain, forming a hellish musical accompaniment to the strange tableau as Mandy continued to clamp her teeth on his hand, her bloody fingers scratching at his face.

"Now apart from Drake and his men, everyone else get out of the room." They didn't need much encouragement. "You too, Adam."

Adam looked at her. "But what about Mandy?"

Chase looked down at the young girl. She had released her bite on the guard. He was now slumped against the wall, clutching his hand. Blood was pooling around Mandy's body. "Can you do anything for her?"

Adam shrugged and went over to her. He crouched down and inspected her wound. Chase could see Mandy was having difficulty breathing, her ragged breaths causing grotesque little bubbles of blood to burst from her lips. When Adam eventually stood up, he shook his head.

"Well, we're not leaving her in here." Making Drake and the uninjured guard sit on the floor, Chase made them sit on their own hands before she helped Adam to lift Mandy and carry her out of the room. Closing the door, she turned the key in the lock and threw it along the corridor. Mandy gurgled incoherently and coughed up blood. Her eyes were open, but the spark of madness had been extinguished.

"You won't get away with this," Drake snarled, his voice

255

menacing even from behind the door.

"Come on, let's get out of here," Chase said, ignoring Drake's threats. "Jane, can you help Adam carry Mandy."

Jane nodded.

"Why didn't you leave *him* locked in there?" Ratty said.

Chase looked at Mat. She had forgotten all about him during the fracas; now he looked lost and forlorn. Ratty was giving him a wide berth and protectively holding hands with the young girl who she realised must be Izzy, the girl he had mentioned back in High Top Cottage. But what was she to do? She couldn't believe Mat was a killer, but then she realised that the man standing before wasn't really Mat - he had changed, becoming something else entirely.

***

What was taking Drake so long? Nigel Moon impatiently tapped his fingers on the desk. He had been informed that Drake had recaptured the boy and girl, which with the help of the genetically modified dogs was only to be expected. The animals had been adapted using the traits of some of the world's most vicious animals. Their eyesight was on a par with an eagle, and like a shark, they could smell their prey from miles away. Ethical morals aside, they were perfect killing machines, although slightly unpredictable as one of the handler's discovered to his misfortune when he turned his back on one of them. He knew Drake was wary of the dogs, but he didn't pay him to be wary. He was paid to carry out orders, and he had been *ordered* to report to Moon, immediately. Moon didn't like to be kept waiting. He punched a button on the intercom. "Miss Coombs, where's Drake? I sent for him over half an hour ago."

"Yes sir. We're still trying to find him."

"Well try harder." He let the button go and shook his head. That man was trying his patience. If he weren't such a ruthless, dispassionate killer, Moon would have no time for him. As it was, Drake was good at what he did. He was a man without morals and normal compunctions. And as long as it didn't interfere with Moon's project, the man could fuck anything he wanted, young, old, alive or dead. His peccadilloes could be overlooked, but Moon would only tolerate so much when it came to the man's work ethics. If he wasn't on the job, he was off the payroll.

But above all else he was discreet. He would not breathe a word about his past, and Moon only knew as much as the dossiers disclosed. Drake would take his atrocities to the grave. He was also not the sort of man to write a book about his ordeals. Not that anyone would believe them. No one would believe that the government employed men like Drake to clean up their mistakes or to put civil unrest to bed by cutting the head off the chicken. Discreet but deadly summed him up.

A lot of the other guards around Paradise didn't even know what was really going on. They knew that they couldn't talk about what they saw or what they heard, and they were kept in the dark as to the project itself, so they couldn't tell anyone about it. Their job was to keep people out and to keep the residents in. Period. If they got too inquisitive, Drake would have a *quiet* word with them, which never failed to impress upon them that they could be silenced, permanently. Fear was a notable silencer.

Suddenly the intercom buzzed and Moon pressed the button to take the call. "Yes, have you found him?"

"Yes, sir. He's been detained."

"*Detained*, what the blasted hell does that mean?"

Miss Coombs coughed slightly. "Well the prisoners have escaped, and they seem to have locked Mr. Drake in the room they were being kept in."

Moon took a deep breath. His temples throbbed and he was out of the chair and out of the room, standing before the diminutive Miss Coombs before she could blink. He placed his hands on the edge of the desk to steady himself and said as calmly as he could, "Sound the alarm. They must not get away. Order the dogs to be released. And get someone to let Drake out."

Chapter 30

Ratty followed behind the group, holding tightly onto Izzy's hand. He kept a wary eye on Mat, still not sure why Chase hadn't locked him up with Drake. If he had killed once, what was stopping him doing it again? Even if he wasn't to blame, unable to recall the incident as he said, that didn't mean it hadn't happened. Besides, he seemed as mad as a hatter.

Mandy was fading fast and slowing them down considerably. Ratty couldn't believe someone could lose so much blood and yet still be alive. He absently wondered whether her prolonged demise was anything to do with the experiment.

Entering the fog, Chase produced a compass from her pocket that she said she had found in an old farmhouse, and they used it to follow a path due North.

As they proceeded, Ratty had the familiar feeling of being followed and once or twice he heard leaves rustle, but he couldn't see anything. The fog was just too thick.

That was when he heard the dogs in the distance.

"Oh shit," he said.

"What is it?" Although he couldn't see her, he recognised Chase's voice.

"The dogs," Izzy said for him, her voice full of panic.

"We should be okay with the guns," Chase responded.

"I wouldn't be too sure," Ratty said. "These aren't normal dogs. They're... different."

"Different?" Jane said.

"What he means is they're worse than any dog you can imagine. They look like alligators, or sharks or something like that," Izzy said.

Ratty could feel her shaking. "She's right. There's things going on here that aren't normal."

"You can say that again," Jane said.

"I've never seen any dogs." Adam looked confused.

"Try looking in the mirror," Jane replied.

"That's enough," Chase said. "We've got to get out of here, and we can't do that if we fight among ourselves. The enemy's out there, somewhere, now come on, let's go."

The dog's throaty growls were getting closer. "Hurry up," Ratty pleaded, trying to make them move faster - but they couldn't move fast, not with Mandy.

The fog drifted around them, an undulating spirit world, halfway between reality and dreamscape. Shapes loomed into focus - trees, branches, hedges - caught midway between the two worlds before the fog devoured them.

The undergrowth rustled. Ratty heard the click of teeth and felt Izzy tighten her grip on his hand. A growl filled the air and a shot rang out, puncturing the fog.

"Adam, you idiot, stop firing," Chase shouted. "You'll hit one of us."

"I'm trying to scare them away."

"Then why not just look at them," Jane said.

"At least I'm doing something."

"Come on, let's keep moving." Ratty didn't want to stand around any longer than was necessary, and if the others had seen the dogs, he was sure they'd agree.

Close by, something howled and as if on command, the pack attacked, dashing through the undergrowth in a rabid frenzy of gnashing teeth.

Someone screamed, "*Run*," but the instruction fell on deaf ears - they were all ready running, propelled by fear.

A shot rang out, followed by another, the bullets scything dangerously through the fog.

The ground was steadily rising and as they entered a copse, the fog started to thin. Ratty wished it hadn't as he saw the beasts. A nightmare incarnate. Their maws were filled with serrated daggers, while their heads were hairless and shark-like in shape. They had small pointed ears that were flat to their heads and their nostrils flared as they breathed.

Ratty counted four beasts.

One of the dogs had run in front, blocking the way and

Ratty quickly ducked as it launched itself on powerful, muscular legs, teeth snapping angrily at empty air as it sailed over his head and crashed into a tree trunk, infuriating it more. Another shot rang out and Ratty saw Adam aiming the gun, his hand shaking as he pulled the trigger again, the shot going wide of the mark and splintering a branch. He had the guards machine gun slung over his shoulder, having refused to give it up to anyone else, especially Mat, which Ratty was grateful for.

To allow himself to fire the gun with both hands, Adam had dropped Mandy, and as though they smelled the blood, the pack of dogs circled around her like a tornado, whipping up leaves in their wake. Adam loosed off a couple more shots, and whether by luck or skill, he hit one of the dogs in the flank. The animal howled and pitched over, but it didn't stop. It dragged itself on its front paws toward its quarry. It was relentless, but as it was moving considerably slower, Adam was able to fire another bullet into it, causing it to roll over and play dead.

While Adam concentrated on the animal he had shot, he didn't notice one of the remaining three slink up behind him and launch itself at his back.

"Look out," Ratty shouted.

But he was too late. The dog landed on top of Adam and knocked him to the ground, sending the pistol flying out of his hand. The animal's powerful jaw clamped down on his shoulder, causing Adam to scream and strike at the beast, but he couldn't get any force behind his punches.

"*Help*," he screamed, his arms flailing uselessly as he rolled on the floor.

Adam's screams seemed to incite the dogs more and the remaining two attacked.

Another shot rang out as Chase opened fire, cursing as she missed. Ratty watched her momentarily tilt the weapon, frown and then flick a switch on its side. When she next pulled the trigger, a stream of bullets arced through the air, the gun bucking in her hands. Two of the bullets hit one of the remaining dogs, smashing through its skull and spreading bone shards like mystic runes.

Jane gave an encouraging whoop of joy. "Go girl."

The remaining loose dog changed direction and bounded off into the foliage. Chase sent a hail of bullets in after it. Adam was still shouting and cursing and Ratty ran over and started kicking the dog that was attacking him as hard as he could, but his efforts seemed ineffectual. A deep snarl emanated from the dog's throat, but Ratty continued kicking it, joined by Chase until it eventually let go of Adam who writhed on the floor, his features scrunched up in agony.

The dog stood its ground, snarling, bloody saliva dripping from its maw. Chase raised the gun, and as if instinctual, the dog performed a standing leap, its powerful leg muscles powering it through the air and away into the trees.

Chase bent down. "Adam, are you okay?"

Between gasps of pain, Adam shook his head. "What do you think?" He sat up, his shoulder a bloody gash, the skin hanging in tattered strips like a grotesque zip had been pulled open to reveal the bone beneath.

"What the hell are they?" Jane asked, warily watching the trees.

From the foliage came the sound of growls and barks, although there was no way of pinpointing the source, as it seemed to be moving, circling.

"I think they're taking stock, biding their time before they attack again," Ratty said.

"Don't talk stupid. Whatever they are, we scared them away," Jane replied. "Or at least Annie Oakley here did." She grinned at Chase like a proud parent.

Ratty shook his head. "We can't scare them away. They aren't scared of anything. Can't you tell?"

"Then why did they run off?"

"Because they aren't stupid. They saw what guns could do, so they'll wait."

"That's ridiculous because that would mean they were intelligent." Jane gave a derisory laugh, "And apart from fetching sticks, dogs are *not* intelligent."

Shaking his head and ignoring the implied ridicule, Ratty

said, "Didn't you notice? They weren't exactly poodles!"

"Don't be stupid."

"No, I think he's right." Chase placed a hand on Ratty's shoulder. "I only wish I'd listened to what he'd said earlier." She smiled and kissed him on the cheek.

Ratty blushed slightly and he noticed Izzy scowling. Was she jealous? He couldn't believe it.

"Where's Mat?" Chase asked, her expression turning anxious.

Ratty looked around. "He was here, wasn't he?" He couldn't actually remember the last time he had seen him.

"And where's that pistol gone?" Jane asked, staring at the floor where Adam had dropped the gun.

Chase called his name, cupping her hands around her mouth, but there was no reply.

"I knew we should have locked him up," Ratty whispered as darkness crept in to steal the last of the daylight.

***

"So what's your excuse this time?" Moon asked as Drake stood arrogantly before him, unflinching and seemingly calm under Moon's close scrutiny.

"The men you've hired are worse than useless."

"So you're saying that it's my fault, is that it?"

"I'm saying that if you'd let me hire the team I wanted, then we wouldn't have these problems."

"And I thought you were a professional," Moon spat.

"Have they escaped yet?"

"No, but I'm not taking any chances. They are now armed and dangerous which is why I've let the dogs out. They *cannot* be allowed to get away."

"They won't. But I thought you wanted the girl alive? The dogs can't make that distinction."

"When it comes to the security of the project, I'm afraid she's as expendable as the rest of them. Like chess, you sometimes have to sacrifice pieces to win. We can always get more test subjects and carry on with what we've learnt here, but if the project is unveiled, then that's it. Our backers will leave us to carry the can, and I do not intend to carry anything. Do we understand each other?"

Drake nodded.

"Now gather up your merry band and good hunting."

Drake strode out of the room, and after a moment of contemplation, Moon pressed the button on the intercom. "Miss Coombs, I think it's time we prepared to shut up shop. Have my car ready will you, and put a call through to all the necessary parties. Tell them..."

"Yes," Miss Coombs prompted when Moon went silent.

"Tell them Project Evolution is a success." He let go of the intercom button and leaned back in his chair. Wars were not won by the weak and in the back of his mind, an idea was taking shape. He looked at the framed photograph of his wife on the desk and nodded his head. He had to be strong. God had created man on the sixth day; it was up to Moon to correct the faults.

Chase shouted until she was hoarse. Where the hell had Mat gone? She couldn't believe she had found him, only to lose him again so soon. She knew that because of the food, he was ill, changed, but she still hoped there was a cure, that Moon could correct whatever he had done. But deep down, she had her doubts. And even if he did have a cure, he wasn't likely to administer it to people he was now trying to kill. Why else would he have released the dogs!

Mandy had gone pale, the blood draining from her body and taking the colour with it. Adam was not much better. He kept shivering, though from shock or pain, Chase couldn't tell. Even though she was cold herself, she had taken her jumper off and wrapped it around Adam who mumbled incoherently. Jane ministered to Mandy, rubbing her in an attempt to warm her up.

Ratty and Izzy sat huddled together, sharing body warmth. Chase envied them their bond. She ran a hand over her belly. She had tried not to think too much about the baby she was carrying because the more she thought about it, the more distressed she became. Was Drake right? Was she carrying a monster? Would it be born deformed? And could she love it if it was? The questions she pondered only led to more questions, and she didn't have the answers. She had always intended to have a family one day, but not like this. But she knew there was another option. But could she take it? Could she have a termination? What if there was nothing wrong with the baby and she had got rid of it. Then she would be no better than a murderer, and hadn't she told Moon that she couldn't kill!

"We can't just sit here," Ratty piped up, bringing Chase out of her reverie.

As though in response, one of the mutated dogs howled from somewhere close by. The sound sent a chill down Chase's spine. She gripped the gun tightly, her knuckles going white.

"He's right, Chase," Jane said.

But what could they do? They had two wounded people to consider and it didn't look as though Mandy could go any further. Her life was ebbing away, the sands of time almost run dry. But Chase couldn't just leave her to die. Not like this. Not out here in the middle of nowhere on her own. Especially not after she had inadvertently saved Chase's life when Eric had attacked her in the lane. Chase knew Mandy had been under the influence of the change at the time, but she had still saved her. That counted for something more than being left to die on her own.

Adam was also a problem. Although he was in a sort of comatose state, he wouldn't let go of the machine-gun he had taken from the guard. He seemed to hold onto it with a religious zeal, as though it was the Holy Grail and no one else was allowed to touch it.

But Ratty and Jane were right. They couldn't stay here. With the advent of nightfall, noises were amplified and distorted, the dogs howls, barks, whines and growls given a hollow, soulless inflection as they circled their prey.

Chase knew that before they went anywhere, she had to get rid of the immediate threat.

"What are you doing?" Ratty asked as Chase opened the tobacco tin.

"Going fishing."

Chapter 31

As the moon came out from behind a cloud, the clearing was bathed in luminescence. A breeze tickled the surrounding foliage, causing rustling, papery laughter.

Chase stood in the centre of the clearing, scanning the shadows. She flinched at every sound. Every movement. Separating herself from the group, she had made herself more vulnerable and she had never felt so exposed in her life. Her heart did a little fandango as an owl hooted somewhere above her, its wings sweeping the night air with little *whumps*. Further overhead the lights of an aircraft gave a conspiratorial wink, the roar of the engines sounding like a distant roll of thunder. Chase gave a tremulous shudder as something brushed through the undergrowth, the foliage sighing in response. A twig snapped like a wishbone; but Chase only had one wish, and that was to be far away from the nightmare in which she was embroiled, perhaps on the aircraft overhead, flying to a tropical destination where she could laze on a beach. She tried to imagine being up there now, looking down on the fog-shrouded village as she flew toward her destination. Would it look like a cloud fell to earth, a gossamer sheet beneath which the land slept in eternal slumber? Or would it look like a malevolent cloud of gas, a poisonous blot on the landscape?

Without her jumper, she shivered. But it wasn't just because of the chill breeze. The things brushing through the undergrowth chilled her more than the climatic conditions. She knew they were stalking her, watching her, smelling her scent, tasting her on their tongues in anticipation of the kill - how she wished to be on that aircraft and not here, prey to the beast.

Although it seemed stupid, and undoubtedly was stupid, she had entered the clearing unarmed. She had credited the dogs with an unnatural intelligence, which meant that if they saw the gun, they wouldn't attack because they had learnt that the tube that spits fire takes them to the great doggy pound in the sky. And she wanted them to attack. So she patiently waited while they assessed her. While they circled, checked, sniffed and scanned.

Another bush rustled as something brushed through it, and a shadow danced on her periphery before clouds drifted over the moon, extinguishing the light and plunging her into darkness. She held her breath, ears straining for the slightest sound. Then she heard it and her heart missed a beat: the scurry of long nailed claws clicking through the undergrowth, a panting breath, the grating of teeth and the forlorn howl which signalled the attack.

The beasts were closing in fast. She could hear them, could imagine their fetid maws, the lines of teeth eager to crunch down on flesh and sinew before snapping bone. Although every instinct in her body told her to run for dear life, she had to hold her ground. Her limbs felt like jelly and the blood was pumping in her head.

A breeze caressed her cheek, or was it the beast's fetid breath? If it was the beast's breath, her plan had failed. In response to her thought, a howl of pain (or was it anger?) filled the air and Chase felt a glimmer of hope. As the wind blew the cloud from the face of the moon, light radiated down, illuminating the clearing and Chase let out a whoop of joy.

She had hardly dared hope that it would work, but it had. Less than three feet away one of the dogs was snarling and hopelessly gnashing its teeth as it strained to free itself from the trap Chase had set. By the light of the moon, the fishing line snares were just visible like a spider's web, but the dog had most likely been too full of killer lust to pay them much attention. Now it struggled and snapped at the line that had ensnared its leg. Already there was a trickle of blood coming from where the line dug into its flesh as the beast pulled it tighter. Knowing that the line was liable to break at any moment, Chase called out for Jane at the top of her voice.

She knew there was another dog out there somewhere, but she put that thought to the back of her mind.

Almost immediately, Jane burst into the clearing.

"Quick, shoot it," Chase screamed.

Taking a moment to assess the scene, Jane lifted the gun in her hand and pulled the trigger. The gun bucked like a bronco and three shots rang out. The snared dog fell silent in the wake of the peal of death.

"The other one's around here somewhere." Chase ran to stand by Jane who swept the barrel of the gun round the clearing. But deep down she knew that the other dog wouldn't fall into the trap, not after seeing the last of its pack outwitted. No, it would bide its time, but at least now there was only one of them left.

The odds were getting better, but she knew it wasn't just the dogs they had to worry about. The handlers and the guards would be out there somewhere, too.

***

Izzy shivered and Ratty hugged her tighter. At this distance, and distorted by the trees, Chase's whoop of joy sounded like a cry of pain and Jane had gone to help even before Chase called her name. After a moment they heard the sound of gunfire. Three shots which punctuated the night.

"Oh Ratty..." Tears streamed down Izzy's cheeks.

"It's OK. They'll be all right." But his tone of voice betrayed his own lack of confidence.

Sitting hunched against a tree, Adam flinched as the shots rang out, but he didn't look up. Lying next to Ratty and Izzy, Mandy moaned, blood trickling from her lips. Ratty didn't know what to do. If he was by himself, he could cope. But now with Chase and Jane gone, Adam being unresponsive, Mandy dying and Izzy scared witless, he felt as though he was responsible for the remaining little group. He was in charge. But he didn't know what to do. Which was why a wave of relief washed over him when he heard a rustling in the leaves.

"At last." He extricated himself from Izzy and stood up, grinning with relief. "I'd almost given up on you."

The grin dropped from his lips and his relief turned to panic as instead of Chase and Jane, it was a salivating mutated dog that stepped out of the bush.

***

It didn't take long for Moon to gather up his files. Most of the relevant ones were kept locked in his safe. These were the ones that contained the results of the experiment. He could have kept it all on compact disc, which would have made it less bulky, but he preferred to read and study from good old-fashioned paper. Computer screens were too harsh on his eyes and after a while they gave him a headache. Of course there were master copies kept on disc that the scientists in the lab had access to, but he preferred his reams of paper. But then some of the files he had didn't have master copies. He had the one and only paper copy.

Various departments handled the work, and Moon was the only person who had access to the results that he alone collated. This was made possible because not all of the work was carried out in the same place. Keeping the experiments separate meant that he was the only person to know what worked and what didn't. If one group was working on inherent diseases, and another group was working on the effects of toxicity on the immune system, only he could build up a picture of what the combined results or effects were. This meant that he was always on top. Indispensable. He knew the nefarious nature of his backers and what they could do. But without him, the results were useless because only he knew where the shadow groups were, and what they were working on. This was his ace up the sleeve, and when this was all over, it was what he hoped would keep him alive.

Taking a sip from the bottled water on his desk, Moon looked around the room to make sure that he hadn't forgotten anything when he noticed the photograph of his wife on the desk. He picked it up and smiled. She was a pretty woman, small of stature with high, defined cheekbones and sharp, clear blue eyes. Her wavy brown hair was left long, cascading over her shoulder and framing her face. When the experiment was a real success, he would feed her the food of the Gods, his Elixir, and they would turn back time. Until then he would make sure that she continued to eat only the organic food he farmed on his smallholding and drink only bottled mineral water. He didn't trust all of the chemical laden food or water that could be bought commercially. You just didn't know what you were eating!

With one final look around, Moon left the room, laden down with folders.

Out in the reception, he saw Miss Coombs gathering personal items from her desk and putting them in a cardboard box.

"Don't bother with those. Help me carry these." He held out the folders and Miss Coombs took some from the top of the pile. He knew that she wouldn't argue. It was hard to find good workers, but he'd come up trumps with Miss Coombs. She was reliable, discreet and diligent. He trusted her implicitly. They had been through a lot together in fifteen years, but she had never questioned her employer or his motives. In fact, over those years, Moon had seen more of Miss Coombs than he had of his wife, and his wife had not been too happy about this. But Moon had convinced her that theirs was a purely business relationship, and that no one could replace her in his heart. She was his fallen star, a little drop of heaven here on Earth. And she had believed him because she loved him.

"Did you make all of the necessary calls?" he asked as they made their way through the building.

"Yes, Nigel. So is it really finished?"

Knowing that she knew him well enough to see through a lie, Moon evaded the truth. "It's finished here."

Miss Coombs nodded but didn't ask any more. She was too discreet to pry for more information.

Out in the main reception the guard stood to attention but didn't salute. Most of the guards in the compound were ex-military, and while they still carried the bearing of military service, they didn't salute someone who had not been or was not in the forces, as though they had not earned that honour. That privilege was only bestowed on the few visiting generals and field marshals that occasionally came to inspect the project. The military were always hovering around on the periphery of Moon's work, looking for new weapons to add to their arsenal. Moon tolerated them, but it wasn't what he wanted. But he had made some concessions. The dogs were one of them. It was a case of not biting the hand that feeds, especially when the hand was powerful enough to crush his dreams. Most of the money that was put into projects such as Moon's had been tainted by military connections. Even the government didn't know the true extent of military projects. There were shadow operations, wheels within wheels and siphoned expenses that ran into billions of pounds that never showed up on any records. The government was just the public face of corruption, puppets for higher powers.

Outside it was dark and Moon was sure that he heard gunfire in the distance. He mentally shrugged it away and cast a look back at the building.

"*Fait accompli*," he whispered, turning and walking toward the waiting Land Rover.

Chapter 32

The dog growled, saliva dripping from its maw. Ratty took a step back and Izzy screamed.

"Shoot it," Ratty screamed at Adam.

But Adam didn't even look up. He mumbled something that Ratty didn't quite catch, although it might have been 'Nicola, forgive me'.

"Shoot the bloody thing," he cried again.

"Adam," Izzy screamed. "Shoot the bloody dog."

But Adam didn't move.

The dog took a growling step forward. Its eyes reflected the moon like twin pools of silver and its hackles were up. Ratty took another step back, almost losing his footing on a branch that snapped beneath his foot like bone. Then the dog stopped and sniffed the air, turning its head from side-to-side as though it could sense something. It stretched out its neck, its nostrils flared. But whatever it could smell didn't stop it from advancing.

Ratty looked across at Adam and the gun in his hands. Could he make it over to him before the dog leapt? And if he did, could he wrestle the gun from Adam and fire it successfully?

There was a rustling sound in the branches above but Ratty didn't look up. He couldn't take his eyes off the dog.

"Izzy, run."

But Izzy didn't move. He didn't know whether she was paralysed with fear, but he couldn't let the dog get to her. Perhaps he could lead it away. If he ran, perhaps it would follow him. But if it didn't it would attack Izzy and she would think that he had run out on her like a coward. He wasn't going to leave her. Not now. If he had to, he would lay down his life for her. And as the dog prepared to pounce, he thought that's what he was going to have to do.

With no time to lose, Ratty crouched down and picked up the branch he had stepped on. He jumped to his feet with two, sharp, jagged spears in his hands. Giving a scream that shocked both himself and the dog, he rushed forward, not noticing the rabbit hole into which his foot disappeared, causing him to stumble, his chin hitting the ground and chipping a tooth.

Without hesitating, the dog leapt at Ratty. It seemed to fly through the air in slow motion. Ratty rolled over; he could see its open jaw lined with teeth, its tongue far back in its throat like a bloated red slug, saliva dripping from its maw. He could see its sharp claws, clenched like a cats talons, its eyes glinting. He could even smell its fetid breath as it landed on top of him, knocking the wind from him, the salivating jaw inches from his face. Ratty closed his eyes, and his life didn't so much flash before him as flicker like a flame before he felt the dog's face on his. He steeled himself for the pain of those teeth biting into his flesh, but it never came and he felt something warm and sticky running down his hands. When he eventually opened his eyes he saw that the dog had been inadvertently impaled on the sticks he held. Blood was running down his hands and tears of relief filled his eyes. Rolling the dog off, he stood up, his legs shaking uncontrollably.

The next thing he felt were arms flung around his neck and Izzy sobbing into his ear.

"I'm OK." Izzy silenced him with a kiss. It was as though a bolt of electricity passed between them and Ratty felt more tears welling in his eyes. As their lips separated, he heard more rustling in the bushes and for one terrifying moment he thought it was another dog, but then Chase and Jane appeared, their bewildered faces taking in the scene.

"How did you kill it?" Chase stared down at the dog.

"Luck," Ratty replied.

Izzy squeezed him tighter and Ratty gave a little cough, but she wouldn't let go, and he was glad.

"Why didn't Adam shoot it?" Jane asked.

Ratty shrugged. "He's out of it. I don't know whether he

can understand what's going on."

Jane shook her head and spat on the floor as she gave Adam a disdainful look.

"It's not his fault," Chase said.

"He's a man isn't he, then it's his fault. It's always men that create the problems, sugar. He's a part of all this, and he can't even help when we need him."

"How's Mandy?" Chase asked.

With all the excitement he had forgotten all about her and he followed Chase to where she lay.

Bending down, Chase frowned and felt Mandy's wrist, then she felt her neck before putting her ear next to her mouth, listening and feeling for an exhalation before she stood up and shook her head with tears in her eyes.

"She's gone."

Izzy started crying and Ratty hugged her.

But they had no time to mourn as the sound of voices drifted through the trees.

"It must be the guards searching for us," Izzy squealed.

"Right, let's go," Chase said, gritting her teeth.

"We can't just leave her," Jane cried.

"And we can't take her with us."

"But it doesn't seem right."

"I know... I know." Tears rolled down her cheeks. "Don't you think I know? She helped save my life. All I can do for her now is make sure she didn't die in vain. Come on, help me get Adam up and let's get out of here."

***

Chase didn't like to leave Mandy's body lying out in the open, but there was nothing she could do. If they were to have any chance of escaping, they had to go now. She looked at the compass, bit her lip and helped Jane carry Adam through the trees and back down into the fog.

It had been a welcome relief to get out of the fog, but now it wrapped its cold embrace round them as though welcoming back a long lost friend. Chase hoped never to see fog again in her life. She hated it. It was cold. It was wet. It was insidious. It was bloody everywhere, but it also seemed to be thinner, as though it was dissipating. A wind had also risen which seemed to help scatter it.

"I think the fog's disappearing," Ratty said, voicing what Chase had thought. "Perhaps my sabotage is working at last?"

Behind them, Chase could hear voices, barking out orders. They obviously didn't think she and her companions were a real threat otherwise they would have been on silent manoeuvres. As it was they sounded like a bunch of kids on a fun day out. And perhaps they were having fun! Perhaps this was one big game to them.

Progress was slow, mainly due to Adam who hardly seemed capable of putting one foot in front of the other.

"Can't we just leave him?" Jane suggested.

"No, we can't."

Jane shook her head. "But we'd get out quicker without him. We could always send back help after we escape."

Chase shook her head. "If we leave him, they'll most probably kill him and he knows more about what's gone on here than we do. If we want people to believe us, we need him."

Jane still didn't seem to think leaving him was so bad, but Chase refused to listen to her. She didn't want to feel responsible for anyone else's death.

After a while they began to climb steadily uphill through long grass with the fog becoming less and less substantial, allowing Chase to easily spot a road. She led the others toward it and checked her compass when she heard an engine approaching and a vehicle sped out of the fog about five hundred feet away, heading straight for them, headlights blazing and cutting a swath through the night. It was closely followed by another vehicle.

"Quick, give me the gun." Dropping Adam by the side of the road, she took the gun from Jane and got them all to crouch down. "It's too late to run as they're bound to have spotted us. This is our last stand." Chase stood her ground,

274

levelling the barrel of the gun toward the lead vehicle. She held her breath as it skidded to a stop about fifty feet away. She could hear the engine ticking over, purring like a big cat before the driver floored the accelerator. With a squeal of tyres the vehicle headed straight at her and Chase pulled the trigger.

Nothing happened.

Forty feet away...

She looked at the gun, flicked the switch to another position and pulled the trigger again.

Nothing.

Twenty-five feet...

Gritting her teeth, she shook the gun, banged it but still nothing so she threw it at the vehicle before diving out of the way.

The gun clattered harmlessly off the bonnet and the vehicle skidded to a stop less than ten feet away. The headlights blazed, forcing her to shield her eyes from the glare and a door opened and an armed man stepped out, using the door as a shield. The other vehicle drew alongside him, the vehicles combined headlights pinning her to the spot and sending her long shadow running away behind her.

"Stand up so we can see you," the soldier shouted as another guard stepped out of the other vehicle.

Apart from Adam, everyone stood up.

"And you," the man said.

"He's in shock." Chase covered her eyes from the glare.

"He'll be in more than shock if he doesn't stand up. Now throw your weapons over there." He indicated a spot away from them.

"We haven't got any." Chase felt dejected at having come this far for nothing.

"Then what's that he's got, a pea shooter. Hey, you, toss the weapon away."

Adam didn't move.

Another door on the lead vehicle opened and although the lights were stinging her eyes, she was surprised to make out the figure of Nigel Moon. He walked around the side of the vehicle, much to the guard's annoyance. Moon shrugged aside the man's protestations and stepped out into the open where she could see him better.

"Adam, I would suggest that you relinquish your weapon before you get shot. I'm only saying this because you have been a great help to me, so I owe you that much. This is your last chance."

As though something had pricked him, Adam looked up. He had tears in his eyes as he caressed his wounded shoulder. Carefully, as though each movement caused him pain, he stood up and slowly unslung the gun and dropped it to the floor.

"Now that wasn't too hard, was it?" Moon smiled. He turned to the guard and nodded. "Now shoot them."

Chapter 33

A shot rang out and Chase flinched and closed her eyes. She didn't feel any pain. She didn't even feel the bullet hit. Opening her eyes, she realised with great relief that she hadn't been hit because it wasn't the guard who had fired the shot. He was looking away from her, across the field toward the fog.

"Where did that shot come from?" Moon asked. He stood like a rock, unmoved.

The guard shook his head and peered from around the door of the vehicle he had dived behind. "I don't know, but you should get back inside the vehicle, sir."

Moon narrowed his eyes and looked around.

"Sir, it's for your own safety."

"I'll be the judge of my own safety. Now find where that shot came from."

The guard motioned to the other vehicle and a door opened. Another guard jumped out to join the one still crouched behind the door, and then all three of them spread out and disappeared into the long grass.

Chase didn't know what was happening. She expected to be dead. Her confirmation that they were now expendable had been confirmed when Moon told the man to shoot them. Her heart was still hammering like a pneumatic drill and her fingers tingled; but if Moon's man hadn't fired the shot, then who had?

Across the field, she could vaguely make out the movement of long grass as the guards crawled through it.

Looking back toward Moon, she noticed a movement in the grass close to where he was standing, but it couldn't be one of the guards, because they were moving in the opposite direction. Confused, she watched the grass waving as though disturbed by a small breeze and she thought back to the snake. As Moon was watching the progress of his men, he failed to notice the movement and a figure suddenly leapt out and grabbed him around the throat, holding a gun to his head.

Chase couldn't believe it.

"Mat, is that you?"

At the sound of her voice, the three guards stopped and turned to look back, their guns pointed at Moon and Mat.

"You'll never get away with this," Moon spat.

"And neither will you," Mat hissed. "Now tell your men to throw their guns into the grass as far as they can."

Moon stood for a moment without saying or doing anything and then Mat prodded him in the head with the gun.

"Do it or die. I'm the magic man, and I can make you disappear if I want." Mat laughed

"If you kill me, you've got no bargaining power. Without a hostage, you're a dead man."

"I'm already dead, now tell them to throw the guns away."

Moon nodded. "Do as he says. But the first chance you get, kill him. Kill them all."

Chase started running toward Mat, tears of joy in her eyes. "Mat, I... I thought I'd lost you again." She couldn't believe he was here.

"All of you get in that vehicle and drive," Mat said, indicating the Land Rover the two guards had exited.

Jane quickly led Ratty and Izzy toward the vehicle. The engine was still running as they clambered inside. Chase made no move to join them and neither did Adam.

"I'm not going to lose you again," Chase said with tears blurring her vision.

"I'm giving you a chance to get away. I wished you here, now I'm wishing you gone. I'll hold them off until you get away. They won't do anything while I've got their boss." He frowned, as though fighting an internal dilemma. "Besides, I'm not safe to be around. I... I remember the vicar. I... I didn't mean..."

"That doesn't matter," Chase said. "I'll get you some

278

help."

"I think I killed him, but I can't remember why?" He choked back tears. "I'm not safe to be around."

"I can't leave you here." She took another step toward him. She wasn't bothered what he had done, because she knew that it wasn't Mat who had done it. Not the Mat that she knew anyway. She couldn't run out on him. She loved him.

"Chase, come on, we've got to go." Jane gunned the accelerator, sending a plume of smoke from the exhaust like a smoke signal.

"Not without Mat." She turned back to Mat and Moon. "I'm not losing you again. We can take Moon with us."

Mat shook his head. "They won't let him go with you." He indicated the guards. "This is my nightmare and he stays. Now go."

"Well, they won't do anything if he's with us."

"Your friend's right." Moon smiled. "The guards wouldn't let you drive out of here with me."

Chase noticed movement inside the vehicle Moon had stepped out of. "*Mat, look out, behind you*," she screamed, running toward him.

Mat spun round with Moon still in his grasp as a severe looking woman with her hair tied up stepped from the vehicle holding a pistol.

"As efficient as ever, Miss Coombs." Moon grinned. "Now shoot the woman."

"If you kill her, then your boss is a dead man," Mat glared at the woman.

"Continue, Miss Coombs. That's an order."

Miss Coombs levelled the gun at Chase and Mat screamed as he took the gun from Moon's head and turned it on Miss Coombs. He pulled the trigger before Miss Coombs could react and a bullet tore into her shoulder, spinning her like a top. This was all the opportunity Moon needed and as Miss Coombs distracted Mat, and the gun was no longer pointed at his head, he elbowed Mat in the stomach, causing him to double up in pain.

"Ever faithful Miss Coombs. Good employees like her are so hard to find these days."

Mat lay on the floor and Chase ran toward him. She could see that he was in pain, his face etched with creases as he fought to catch his breath.

"Chase," Jane shouted. "Come on, we've got to go."

Moon bent down and took the gun out of Mat's hand. He shook his head and pointed the pistol at Mat. "A valiant attempt, but it was always doomed to failure. Life's full of winners and losers, and you, my friend, are a loser."

Chase came to a stop a few away from Moon and Mat. She could see that as Mat recovered and got his breath back, he appeared different. His eyes had taken on a glassy sheen and his features had relaxed into a deadly, emotionless expression.

"Tick, tick, boom, the ticking bomb." Moon shook his head. "I'm so close to curing the problem. The answer's on the tip of my tongue, but it's too late for your friend." He shook his head again, as though in true remorse.

"How can you be so two-faced saying that you want to find a cure-all to help people, when so many people are having to die. You're just a hypocrite."

Moon studied Chase, the gun still pointed at Mat. "I thought that I had explained all that. It's a necessary evil."

"So why are you going to kill us?"

"Not you my dear, just them because I cannot leave anything behind which would implicate me. I still have plans to use you, but your friends are too much trouble to keep around. My time here is done and I've learnt as much as I can. I've got the seed of an idea about where I've gone wrong, now I just need to plant it and see what grows."

"You mean another experiment?"

"Life's an experiment, haven't you realised that. We've mutated since crawling out of the primordial swamp, and we'll continue to do so. That's the biggest experiment of all time."

"And what about the villagers?"

Moon shrugged. "A fire, an explosion, a plane crashing

onto the village, a toxic leak, there can be so many ways to explain their deaths. Toxic leak might be best as it would deter people from venturing here."

"But why?"

Moon pointed at Mat who was now slowly getting to his feet. "Because it's always best to put a wounded animal out of its misery rather than letting it suffer." He took a step back, away from Mat.

Chase frowned. Behind her, she heard voices and she turned to see Drake walking along the lane, closely followed by more men. She felt her courage slipping away.

Moon raised his gun and pointed it at Mat. "*Si vis pacem, para bellum.* If you want peace, prepare for war."

"*Noooo.*"

Chase heard the scream from behind her and she turned to see Adam levelling his gun at Moon.

"I can't let you do it, Nigel. Chase is right. The killing has to stop." Adam pulled the trigger and three shots rang out.

Diving to the floor, Chase felt the heat of the bullets as they hissed past her ear. Looking up, she saw Moon jump for cover; Mat flew back as one of the bullets accidentally hit him. His face momentarily regained its normal aspect, registering shock and surprise.

"*Nooo.*" Adam charged at Moon, the trigger pressed and more bullets scything the air, ricocheting off the Land Rover Moon had run toward. One of the tyres exploded, bits of rubber flying through the air like bats.

Chase heard more gunfire from her rear. Drake and his men had opened fire, their bullets kicking up little plumes of dust around her prone body. Suddenly a vehicle intervened, creating a barrier between Drake and Chase.

"Come on, sugar, time to scoot." Jane leaned across and held open the door.

Chase looked up at Jane as one of the Land Rovers windows exploded. Glass diamonds poured over her and Jane ducked and cursed.

Picking herself up, Chase dived through the open door

and Jane floored the accelerator. The wheels spun, flipping the rear end of the vehicle across the road. In the rear, Ratty and Izzy cowered on the floor.

"We've got to help Mat and Adam," Chase said, ducking as more bullets rained on the vehicle with a sound like hailstones.

"There's no time." Jane regained control of the vehicle and levelled it.

"Damn it, I'm not leaving them." Chase reached over and grabbed the steering wheel, turning it so that they headed back toward Moon's vehicle. As the Land Rover left the road, the front wheels hit a bump and the wheels left the ground, the vehicle momentarily airborne. As they landed with a bang, Chase hit her head on the roof and bright sparks of light flashed before her eyes.

Through the windscreen she could see Moon levelling his gun at them and smiling.

***

Ducking behind the door of the Land Rover, Nigel Moon was glad that Adam was not a very good shot. Besides, it looked as though the damn fool had saved him the job of shooting Mat.

Peering around the door, he saw Drake and his men open fire before the other Land Rover screeched to a halt beside Chase, obscuring Drake behind it. But they wouldn't escape. This was their Alamo, their last stand.

The thought empowered Moon and he stood up, raised his gun and began to open fire at the Land Rover. The pistol kicked in his hand, but he brought it to heel like a well-trained dog, making sure that his shots were not wasted.

But the Land Rover was speeding away from him and he cursed until it suddenly spun round, turning in a wide arc as it left the road, hitting a bump and making a short, ungainly flight. As it hit the floor, the front wheels were sent aloft once more and when it settled, it was heading straight for him.

Moon smiled and levelled his gun at the vehicle. It was going to be like shooting fish in a barrel.

He tensed his finger on the trigger and held his breath. But then he felt the breath knocked out of him as someone rammed him from behind and he fell in a heap on the floor. Trying to catch his breath, he felt sharp teeth bite into his arm and jagged nails scratching at his face. Twisting, he tried to stand, but he was pinned down. Looking up, he saw Mat's savage features glaring back at him.

"Why can't you just die," Moon wheezed, trying to manoeuvre the gun around to fire a shot. Behind him he could hear the approaching Land Rover, the wheels coming to a stop beside his head. With a final surge of power, he twisted the gun round and pulled the trigger until it was spent.

Mat jerked like a fish.

***

"*Mat*." Chase jumped out of the Land Rover and crouched down next to him, tears rolling down her cheeks. He was still breathing, although his breaths were short and ragged.

"Mat, don't leave me."

Mat opened his eyes. There was no sign of the change in his face, just pain. "Chase, is..." he coughed. "Is that you?"

"Yes, hold on, I'll get you help."

Mat shook his head. "You're really here... It's not a dream, a nightmare... I'm... I'm sorry..." he coughed up blood, closed his eyes and his chest deflated as his last breath was exhaled.

Chase screamed and shook his shoulders, but it was no good. He was gone.

"Very touching, now come with me," Moon said.

"Fuck you," Chase spat.

"Chase, move it." Jane gunned the engine.

With a final look at Mat, Chase dived for the open door of the Land Rover and Jane floored the accelerator. But she didn't get all the way in as Moon grabbed her legs, holding her back. She had a tentative grip on the seat, but she could feel her fingers slipping and she screamed. Ratty grabbed her wrists, trying to help her in as the Land Rover moved away, Moon hanging on to her like a bizarre water-skier trailing in her wake.

"Drake, don't let her get away. I want her alive," Moon boomed.

Bullets tore into the vehicle and Chase managed to free one of her legs. With a vindictive look back at Moon, she kicked him hard in the face, feeling the satisfying crunch of his nose as her heel connected. Moon let go immediately, falling to the floor with his hands covering his face as he rolled through the grass.

"Adam..." Chase pulled herself into a sitting position and looked through the shattered rear window. She could just see him firing back at Drake and his men, but it was no good. He was outnumbered and outclassed. Bullets tore into him, lethal kisses of death that took his life. As he pirouetted in the air, Chase thought she saw him smile, and she knew that he had found his redemption.

As Jane sped away from the scene, Chase felt empty. She could hear gunfire from their rear, but they were now too far away for it to be effective. She clutched at her belly as the fog drifted around the vehicle.

"I can't see very well." Jane leaned forward and peered through the windscreen.

"Try these." Ratty passed her a pair of funny looking goggles from the back seat. Chase dimly remembered that she had seen someone wearing them when Adam and she were in the back of the truck.

Jane slipped them on and fiddled with them for a moment before she smiled. "Well aren't we just over the rainbow. Let's just follow the yellow brick road and see if we can't just get ourselves home." She grabbed Chase's knee and gave it an encouraging squeeze.

Chase closed her eyes. She felt exhausted. But she didn't think she would ever be able to sleep again.

It took about twenty minutes of cautious driving before they came out of the fog. Chase twisted in her seat, watching it close like curtains in their wake. She had expected to see vehicles following them, but as Moon's Land Rover had an exploded tyre and any other vehicles were most likely too far away, nothing appeared.

Apart from Ratty who gave directions to civilisation and the nearest police station, none of them spoke much during the flight to freedom. It was as though they were all trying to come to terms with what had happened. Chase was certainly trying, although it all seemed too unreal, too unbelievable. She had taken a roller coaster ride into madness and horror, but when would it end? Her stomach felt as though she was still on the vertiginous descent and she felt sick.

Winding down the window, she leaned her head out, feeling a rush of cold air that left her breathless. The sun was peeking over the horizon, an orange ball of flame that seemed to set the sky on fire. To all intents and purposes, it looked like the end of the world.

Chapter 34

Four months later.

The bedsit was cold. Chase sat wrapped in a blanket, shivering. Since escaping from Paradise, she had always felt cold, mainly due to the nightmares she suffered. Partly due to wondering whether it had all been real. She often wondered whether she was going mad. They had tried hard enough to convince her that she was.

After they had driven out of the fog, Ratty had directed them to the nearest police station where they had tried to persuade a bemused desk sergeant of their ordeal. He'd smiled patiently at them while they told their story, then they had to repeat it again in an interview room, separately.

It was an infuriating experience. Chase had tried to make the police drive her back to the village straight away so that she could show them what was going on, but they were only interested in why Chase and Jane were in the company of two children reported as missing? She had tried to explain that they weren't missing, that they'd been kidnapped. That only made things worse as the police then wanted to know why Chase had kidnapped them! This line of questioning seemed to go on for hours. And when it did stop, they placed her in a holding cell until the next day. She had banged on the door for a while, but a drunk in the next cell was having a seizure and they told her to shut up and stop making a racket while they attended more serious matters. Chase had felt humiliated and angry.

After Jane, Ratty and Izzy corroborated her story, the police drove them back to the village. When they got close, thin wisps of fog drifted over the landscape, but there was no thick bank of fog. As they drove down the lane, they passed an area of dead grass. Chase guessed it was where the buildings should have been and they stopped the car and got out to look. But apart from large square areas of dead foliage and some holes where posts might have been, there was nothing to suggest buildings had been there. The four of them kept to their story and the police drove on with little enthusiasm.

When Paradise came in sight, Chase was struck by how beautiful it still looked. Only now she knew what horror lurked beneath the facade, the beauty was tainted, like biting into an apple to find it was rotten inside.

They drove into the village and parked up outside the village shop. In the distance, the church bell was ringing and pigeons raced around the spire.

Entering the shop, the bell jangled and a slightly balding, middle-aged man appeared from out back.

"Can I help you?" He stared surprised and alarmed at the police cramming the aisles.

The first thing Chase noticed were the tins of food. They were all brand name produce. There were none of the white labelled tins on the shelves.

"Who are you?" Chase asked.

"I'll ask the questions, if you don't mind," the police officer that had driven her said.

"Where's Ms Woods," Chase continued, ignoring the policeman.

"Ms who?" The man behind the counter shook his head.

"The owner, Ms Woods."

The man laughed. "I'm afraid you must have made a mistake. I'm the owner. Bernard Jones the name." He shook his head, looking bemused, and turned to the door to the back room. "Kath, Kath love, come here and listen to this will you."

After a moment, a plain looking woman Bernard introduced as his wife, appeared in the shop, wiping her hands on an apron, her face slightly flushed. She listened to the story wearing a bemused grin like her husband.

Chase looked at Jane, Ratty and Izzy and they all tried to protest, claiming that they were telling the truth. But the police ushered them out of the shop, apologising to the owner for wasting his time.

287

It was the same everywhere they went. The residents of Paradise had been replaced and they all refuted the story Chase and her companions told. An elderly couple that nodded sympathetically and offered a panacea of tea to the weary policemen now inhabited High Top Cottage.

In a final last-ditch effort to find something to corroborate their story, Chase took them to the church. Inside she got quite a shock when she saw a vicar kneeling before the altar. From behind he looked just like the vicar who had been killed - she realised then that she hadn't even known his name - but when he turned, it wasn't him at all. He smiled and nodded in all the right places, produced documents to show how long he'd been there and even offered to give Chase and her companions spiritual guidance.

As they were about to walk out of the church, the vicar said, "Faith can move mountains, have faith in the Lord." As an aside to Chase he whispered, "But Moon can move more."

She knew that it was useless arguing further. Moon had told her that the people involved in the experiment were powerful, but only now did she begin to realise just how powerful. They had no proof - Drake had taken Ratty's tape, and they had nothing else.

They kept to the story about Ratty's granddad, even finding the grave. (It was the first time Ratty had seen it and he was naturally distressed). But it didn't prove anything. He was old. Death was inevitable and they weren't about to exhume him to check for foul play. Chase never did find out, but she wondered whether Albert Rathbone had been killed just so that she could be moved into the village. It was one of many questions that went unanswered.

Chase and the others were tested for psychiatric disorders, and when, with the exception of the Paradise story, they were found to be rational and well adjusted, they were released.

The psychiatrists put the episode down to a form of mass hysteria; Ratty and Izzy were released back into the custody of their respective parents and Chase and Jane were released

288

pending a court hearing on charges of abduction and wasting police time!

When Chase finally left the village and returned to her former home, she was in for another shock as there was a family living in it. They had the necessary deeds to prove their ownership, but Chase caused so much of a fuss that the police were called and she was arrested again!

She had a court order served on her, disallowing her from going within two miles of her previous house, so for a while she moved in with Jane. But after Paradise, their friendship was strained. They had been through too much, and instead of drawing them closer, it pushed them apart and they withdrew into their own little worlds of pain. Also, Jane's partner, Gina had not taken to Chase staying. She wanted Jane all to herself so she could help her recuperate, and Chase was the cuckoo in the nest that had taken her away in the first place.

And so Chase had moved into the bedsit; inhabiting one room in a house full of students that played music till late in the night. The sickly sweet smell of drugs also filled the air, and Chase often had to go for long walks to clear her head.

Even though she had wrapped the blanket around herself, Chase still shivered. Today was one of those days to go for a walk. It was often warmer outside than in as the room she occupied was North facing and cold as the Arctic Circle.

Pulling a coat over her flowery maternity dress, she left the house. She was right, it was warmer outside and she ended up having to take the coat off. She waddled more than walked these days, every movement an effort. She had never bloomed during her pregnancy and the last four months had been miserable; she likened herself to Leonard Rossiter who played Rigsby in Rising Damp as she pushed her stomach out, supporting her lower back with her hands. She suffered stomach cramp, had to use the toilet a lot because of the pressure; she also leaked when she coughed, sneezed, or when she laughed (which wasn't very often), her knees hurt, her back hurt, and although she had suffered from vivid nightmares about the condition of the unborn baby, she had been told time and again that it was healthy and that there were no problems for her to worry about. They said her fears were only natural. Everyone had them. Chase wasn't convinced. Was paranoia part of pregnancy as well? Since leaving the village she was haunted by the feeling of being followed, but there was never anyone there. She looked at everyone with mistrust, not knowing how far the corruption had spread. She was slowly getting over it, and she knew that it would be a while before she was back to her usual self, but that didn't help dispel the hair-prickling notion.

Even though she hadn't been in Paradise for that long, it was strange to see traffic again. And although she now only had a portable black and white television, she wondered how people had coped before John Logie Baird invented the window on the world. It had spawned a planet of voyeurs who peered into the fishbowl lives of other people and communication had died beneath its spell.

She still read the newspapers, often second hand when the students had finished with them, as she couldn't afford to buy one everyday. But there was never any mention of Paradise and the strange circumstances surrounding it, which didn't really surprise her. Also, she now had a deep mistrust of letters and the postman. She had letters lying in her hallway that were three months old, but she daren't even touch them to throw them away. Her one highlight of the day had become her one nightmare.

The only people to come out of this mess stronger were Ratty and Izzy who became inseparable. Although there was a restraining order on her, Chase still kept in contact with them by telephone.

At the end of the road, she suddenly had hunger pangs and she licked her lips. Noticing she was next to the mini-mart, she stepped inside the cool interior, the fluorescent strip lights too bright as she wandered along the aisles of produce. Since Paradise she only ate organic food. It was more expensive, and her Social Security cheque hardly covered the household bills, but she thought it was worth it for peace of mind.

Walking past the tins of beans and spaghetti, she walked into the next aisle where the jars of baby food were stacked. She often gasped at the price of it, wondering how on earth she was going to afford to keep a baby, never mind feed it. Of course she could have had a termination, but then she would have been just as bad as Moon. She had told him that she couldn't take a life, any life, and she'd meant it. She was worrying about nothing. Of course everything was going to be all right. Why shouldn't it be?

The shop had just received a delivery, the assistant tearing open a cardboard box of items to put on the shelves.

As she approached the shelf-stacker, he looked up at her and smiled. He was a teenager with a toothy grin, but it was what he had in his hand that sent a sudden chill down her spine: Baby food in white, nondescript cans and jars. Chase felt dizzy, the supermarket beginning to spin around her, the walls closing in, squeezing so tight that she couldn't breath. She clutched her swollen belly as the unborn baby gave her a painful kick.

"Are you okay?" the young man asked, his face showing concern.

Chase couldn't reply. They were going to start with the babies, with the still developing children - catch them when they were young. That damned idiot, Moon was turning the whole country into a test lab.

She dropped to her knees, screaming as her waters broke, the baby was coming, but it was too early! The pain was almost unbearable.

"Someone, help," the young man shouted, looking alarmed as Chase crouched on the floor.

"It's OK, I'm a doctor."

"Thank God," the young man said, moving aside.

Chase looked up. She recognised the voice straight away. It had haunted her for four long months.

Moon looked down, an anxious smile on his lips. Drake stood behind him, emotionless.

"You didn't think I would just let you go, did you?"

Moon scoffed, crouching down beside her. "Yours shall be the first; it shall not be the last. This is the dawning of a new age of evolution, and I had to know..."

As Chase's progeny clawed its way into the world, it screamed almost as much as its mother.

About the Author

Shaun Jeffrey was born in 1965 and lives in Cheshire, England. He grew up in a house in a cemetery, his playground the graveyard - perfect grounding for writing horror!. He has been writing for a number of years, and has had numerous short stories published in genre magazines. He is a member of The British Fantasy Society and The Horror Writers' Association.

Also Available from The Invisible College Press:

City of Pillars, by Dominic Peloso
Tattoo of a Naked Lady, by Randy Everhard
Weiland, by Charles Brockden Brown
The Third Day, by Mark Graham
Leeward, by D. Edward Bradley
Cold in the Light, by Charles Gramlich
The Practical Surveyor, by Samuel Wyld
UFO Politics and the White House, by Larry W. Bryant
Utopian Reality, by Cathrine Simone
Phase Two, by C. Scott Littleton
Marsface, by R.M. Pala
Treatise on Mathematical Instruments, by John Robertson
The Rosicrucian Manuscripts, by Benedict J. Williamson
Proof of the Illuminati, by Seth Payson
The Phoenix Egg, by Richard Bamberg
Diverse Druids, by Robert Baird

If you liked this novel, pick up some more ICP books online at:

http://www.invispress.com/